BELLINGHAM MYSTERIES

COLLECTION #1

NICOLE KIMBERLING

BELLINGHAM MYSTERIES

COLLECTION #1

NICOLE KIMBERLING

**Bellingham Mysteries
Collection #1
By Nicole Kimberling**

Published by:
ONE BLOCK EMPIRE
an imprint of
Blind Eye Books
1141 Grant Street
Bellingham WA 98225
blindeyebooks.com

All rights reserved. No part of this publication may be reproduced in any manner without written permission of the publisher, except for the purpose of reviews.

Edited by Judith David
Cover Art by Amber Whitney
unicornempire.com

This book is a work of fiction. All characters, situations and places represented are fictional. Any resemblances to actual people or events are coincidental.

First print edition July 2015
Copyright© 2015 Nicole Kimberling

ISBN:978-1-935560-38-8

Printed in the United States

PRIMAL RED

Chapter 1

Peter had his eye on the guy in the leather bomber jacket. Tall. Handsome, but with ugly expressions. The man swaggered down the dark alley with an air of authority. He wore Levis and carried a hockey bag, which was odd since it was summer. He didn't look at Peter, too busy was he muttering down his cell phone in Russian and securing the hockey bag in the back of his big, black SUV.

Peter shifted slightly, careful to make no sound. He didn't think the Russian would be happy to find him here, hiding between the bushes and the dumpster, snapping photos of the comings and goings at the Russian Tea Cafe.

Or maybe he should spell it *cummings* and goings when he wrote the article.

If he had been a writer for the Bellingham Herald, they'd never let him get away with it, but the one benefit to writing for a weekly independent was the freedom to be vulgar.

In his mind, he composed a few lines of his expose.

Who hasn't wandered by the Pierogy Tea Café and wondered how it stayed in business? Perpetually empty yet also perpetually open, the café has been a cipher in the mind of many a college student. The few bold souls who got drunk enough to venture into the dining room are treated with scowls, bad service and the worst pierogys ever made.

And there is no tea.

So what, you might ask, does Pierogy Tea Café really sell? That's what I was crouched in a stinking alley between Pierogy Tea Café and the Vitamilk Building trying to figure out.

A big Russian came by. He had a fine ass. Bubble-style. Meaty...

Peter mentally scratched those last lines out. He didn't want to incline his readers toward sympathy for a guy who was obviously in the mafia and probably a pimp.

After the Russian's taillights had faded, Peter carefully stood up, keeping his eye on the café's back door. The next few seconds would be the scary ones, the ones where someone in the upper floor of the café might see him emerge from hiding and walk back toward his car, which was parked in front of the Vitamilk Building.

The night's silence was unbroken save for the squeals of angry skunks fighting in the vacant lot next to the café.

Not that he could see the skunks in the pre-dawn darkness. But he didn't need to see skunks to know they were there.

The Vitamilk Building got its name from the enormous 1930's advertisement painted on its side. A happy, smiling milk carton, two stories high sauntered across the 1920's brickwork exhorting the fishermen in the marina across the street to *Drink Milk!*, presumably with the idea that they would acquire the same jaunty demeanor.

Vitamilk, as a product and a company, no longer existed. The building had been converted into a gallery with artist studio spaces on the second floor but the building's name had lingered on.

Though it was four-thirty in the morning, several of the studio's lights still burned including the corner studio belonging to John O'Donnell his informant.

His informant…

Just the idea that he had something as romantic as an informant filled Peter with fierce journalistic pride. What did it matter that John was more of a tipster than an informant? He'd led Peter to an actual story to investigate. In Bellingham!

The City of Subdued Excitement was not widely thought of as a breeding ground for Pulitzer (or even Tom Renner) winning journalists. The biggest things to come out of the city in years were Death Cab for Cutie and Baker's Breakfast Cookies.

He could use a cookie right about now. He wondered if he had one in his glove compartment. He'd very briefly dated one of the bakers at the breakfast cookie facility and for a couple of weeks he'd been ankle deep in the things. He still he found stashes of them here and there.

He opened his glove compartment and found a slightly smashed Vegan Peanut Butter Chocolate Chunk.

Vegan?

Yeah, Robert had been a vegan, hadn't he? No wonder it hadn't worked out.

He tore open the wrapper anyway and crammed half a cookie into his mouth, washing it down with the cold coffee sitting in his cup rest.

He was too excited to sleep, but too cautious to risk going back into the alley so close to daybreak. His roommate Evangeline had a studio in the building. Her window was directly above the milk carton. Maybe she was still up. He walked around the side to look. Dark.

The one next to hers was on, though, the one belonging to Nick Olson, painter, recluse, Peter's current crush. Nick was the only artist who didn't open his studio for Gallery Walks and never kept his door open when he was painting. Evangeline claimed to have seen a few of his canvases once, but she'd failed to describe them as anything other than "abstract expressionist landscapes" which communicated nothing to him. He'd only spoken to Nick one time at a reception at the Weydert-Harri gallery.

Nick had looked great, wearing a merino wool sweater, jeans and two days of stubble. His hair was blond-streaked brown and his eyes very light blue. His face closely resembled J.C. Leyendecker's Arrow Shirt Man, if the Arrow Shirt Man had been allowed to get really scruffy and walk around in worn denim and paint-spattered steel-toed boots. From his tan and the muscles, Peter would be willing to guess Nick engaged in some sort of healthy Pacific Northwest pursuit, like kayaking or snow camping.

He had a scar just above his left eyebrow and wore small gold hoop earrings and two other plain gold rings one on his left thumb and the other on his right index finger.

Not that Peter had been drawing Nick's visage in the sketchbook of his heart or anything.

He'd tried to summon the courage to approach, but Nick had been surrounded by a flotilla of middle-aged women in hand-crocheted ponchos who made it difficult to advance.

Then Robert, his date, had told him he was having an allergic reaction from "challenging" wheat gluten (by eating a cracker) and Peter had left to drive Robert home. For the last time, as it turned out.

Nick had asked about him after he'd gone, Evangeline had said. He'd seemed interested, she'd said because she'd asked who the thin brunette with the big brown eyes had been. But Evangeline was prone to exaggerating and embellishing details, so he hadn't gotten his hopes up.

Maybe he should just go inside. Pretend to be looking for Evangeline, knock on Nick's door and see for himself if Nick seemed to like his peepers. Before long he forgot the cookie in his hand and started writing the scene:

I knocked at the door, calling out, "anyone home?" by way of announcing myself.

"Come in," the low voice came from inside. I opened the door and stepped inside the studio. The summer night was hot and muggy and the smell of linseed oil hung thick in the air. But there was another scent, low and woody, the smell of another man. Nick stood before an easel, paintbrush in hand, pale eyes regarding me suspiciously. He wore no shirt.

"Peter, right?" He set his paintbrush aside, picked up his discarded T-shirt and wiped the sweat from his tan, well-muscled chest. "I saw you at the Wyedert-Harri. But you were... with somebody."

"Not anymore," my voice sounded husky. I closed the door behind me. "I just wanted to introduce myself."

"Yeah?" Nick walked toward me, keeping his eyes locked on mine, backing me up against the wall. "I'm pleased to meet you, Peter." His mouth closed over mine, hot and sweet. I parted my lips allowing his tongue to slide inside. He pressed his body to mine and I felt his huge boner press against my own. No more need for words—

Wait... boner?

No.

Erection? Rock hard cock? Peter came back to himself, cookie still in hand, feeling a fool. He was standing outside a building in the middle of the night mentally writing imaginary porn about a man he'd never even had the guts to say hello to. He should just call it a night.

Then, from the Vitamilk Building, a woman screaming.

Long, prolonged screaming with a ragged edge that said, "this is not a joke."

Peter rushed forward and, finding the twin glass doors locked, grabbed a rock and smashed it through the glass then reached in and flipped the latch. And just as abruptly, silence. He heard a man's voice now, yelling for help. He raced up the wide, carpeted staircase.

"Where are you?" Peter yelled back.

"On the left, the open door!"

As Peter rushed down the hall, a door opened to his right. A stocky man with a thick, dark beard poked his head out in confusion. A heavy scent of pot rolled out of his studio.

"What's going on?"

Peter shoved past him and ducked into the open doorway.

He was in a very large but well-kept studio. Huge, partially painted canvases leaned against the walls. In the center of the floor lay a woman. Blood oozed from a gash across her throat. Nick crouched over her, shirtless, as Peter had imagined him, but sprayed with blood. Droplets of gore dribbled from his finely furred chest and forearms. Peter's hand went straight to his phone, dialing immediately. He took a step backward. The woman's eyes were open, darting from side to side.

"Jesus, Nick, did you kill Shelley?" the bearded man Peter had nearly crashed into asked.

"Call fucking 911, you idiot!" Nick bellowed.

"I've got it," Peter said. Nick glanced up at him and for an instant confusion drifted across his face. Then suspicion.

"Who the fuck are you?" he demanded.

"Peter Fontaine," he continued to retreat back while the bearded man stepped forward.

"He's Evangeline's roommate," the bearded man told Nick. "Do you have your fingers in her neck?"

"I had to stop the bleeding," Nick said. Then to Peter, "are they fucking answering or not?"

"Not—" Peter cut off his own answer as the operator came on the line. He reported everything he saw, hearing sirens approaching as an ambulance rolled out of the Indian Street Fire Station only a few blocks away.

From the doorway, Peter saw Shelley's eyes flutter and close.

"I think she's lost consciousness," Peter told the operator. He heard the sound of heavy boots running up the stairs. Three paramedics rushed down the hallway and into the studio. One crouched next to Nick. After a moment, the paramedic instructed Nick to pull his hands away. Nick retreated to the far wall, blood dripping from his hands to the canvas behind him, marking it with diffuse red dots.

He looked like a murderer and the police treated him like one surrounding and questioning him, taking him down the stairs and out of Peter's sight.

Peter got his own pair of policemen who asked a lot of questions about Nick and what he was doing when Peter came on the scene. Officer Clarkson was, wiry, blonde and wore a moustache. Officer Patton was a burly woman with one of the five classic dyke haircuts: the curly she-mulllet. Patton asked him what he was doing walking by the Vitamilk Building so late at night.

The sun was just breaking over the horizon and Peter felt dazed and faded gazing into the soft, gray light. He couldn't tell them about the Pierogy Tea Café. Not yet. He didn't have enough material to write his piece. So he said, "I was trying to get up the courage to ask Nick Olson out on a date."

The two police officers glanced at each other then Officer Clarkson said, "I think you might want to re-evaluate your plans."

Chapter 2

Peter reached his house at just past six in the morning. Only ten blocks away from the Vitamilk Building the sun shone down on a beautiful summer morning such as the Pacific Northwest can sustain for approximately thirty days out of the year. Free from the burden of relentless rain, birds sang. Bees gathered thickly around the hedge of Oregon grape that lined Peter's driveway.

A man wearing club gear staggered down the sidewalk carrying a six-pack of Rainer, three cans gone.

He gave Peter a tired salute, recognizing him as fellow night owl just getting in. Peter returned the wave, half-heartedly.

Peter lived in a typical college rental in the York Neighborhood, a collection of early 1900's two-bedroom bungalows that formed the transitional zone between the pricey wooded lots on Sehome Hill and the freeway. Unlike the adjacent properties, Peter's porch was unencumbered by an outdoor couch. Instead a tangle of mysterious machine parts and scrap metal crowded the edges, partially covered by a blue tarp.

Evangeline's cat, Tripod, sunned on the top step. The cat had only three legs but still ruled the neighborhood with an iron paw, routinely incapacitating tomcats twice his size and fearlessly, or perhaps stupidly, engaging the neighborhood raccoons in mortal combat.

Peter stopped to give Tripod a scratch. While doing so his phone vibrated. It was Evangeline.

"Peter! Are you okay?" her voice blasted out from his earpiece and also drifted through the closed front door.

"I'm fine," he said. He took out his keys and entered. Across the living room, he could glimpse Evangeline in the kitchen wearing her fuzzy pink bathrobe, making coffee. She had her phone to her ear, oblivious to his physical presence. And rather than thinking this funny, he found it deeply alarming. Was this what had happened to Shelley? Had she been too distracted to see her attacker? Too in the zone? And who was this Shelley, anyway? He thought he could remember Eva talking about her, but... He hadn't been paying too close attention. He'd thought, "the petty rivalries of small-town artists... Not worth committing to memory." How wrong he'd been.

"Tommy just called me. He told me about what happened at the studio." She still hadn't seen him. Peter closed his phone and stepped aside to let Tripod into the living room.

"Is he the one with the beard?" Peter asked.

"Yes he—" Evangeline froze, catching sight of him then, recognizing him, rolled her eyes and closed her phone. "You can really sneak around, you know that? You almost made me pee my pants."

"Sorry," Peter said. "What were you going to say about Tommy?"

"He just called me from jail. The cops searched his studio and found his stash," she said. "They booked him for possession."

"I don't think the stash could have been that hard to find," Peter remarked. "He was so stoned that I managed find a way to break into the building before he found his own doorknob. Which, now that I think about it, is odd."

"What's odd?"

"That he didn't open his door until he heard me in the hallway," Peter said.

"Maybe he was just too scared to come out until then." Evangeline poured two mugs of coffee. She handed him one. "It must have been awful."

"Yes, it was," Peter sat down on the green, leatherette sofa. Officially, the sofa was on Evangeline's side of the living room, but she had sacrificed the space so that they could have someplace to sit.

The décor in Peter and Evangeline's living room communicated their lack closet space. The couch was crammed into one corner. A small television with rabbit ears sat opposite it.

Before he'd moved in with Evangeline Peter hadn't known they made those anymore.

Beside the television was a drawing table flanked by an assortment of old cabinets and office furniture all surfaces more or less covered with… things. Thimbles, broken drawer pulls, glass beads, doll parts, red and white striped wire-scraps, books of wallpaper samples. Evangeline was clearly moving in the direction of found objects. Or at least she'd gotten to the point that she'd found some objects. What art she would create from them remained to be seen, though she seemed to be assembling a small shrine inside a gallon olive oil can.

The other side of the living room belonged to Peter. His bicycles hung from a hook embedded in the ceiling. A bookshelf, crammed with style guides and dog eared trades like Kristof & WuDunn's *China Wakes* and Sperber's *Murrow: His Life and Times*. Besides this, the only pieces of furniture were an antique desk and chair set made from solid mahogany. The desk looked like it something Daddy Warbucks would sit behind. On the desk's glass top sat a flat screen monitor and wireless keyboard and nothing else. Peter had acquired the desk from a bachelor uncle who'd had a particular liking for him. Peter forced himself to sit at that desk for three hours everyday, whether he could make himself write or not. No winds favor a ship with no destination, that's what his uncle had said to him and Peter had a destination: journalistic greatness.

Now he had two opportunities in one night the mafia and a murder… If only they could be linked he might actually get that Renner. If only he hadn't stopped paying attention whenever Evangeline started talking about the other artists at the Vitamilk Building, he would be ahead in the game, but he had and he'd stopped and now Peter had to ask who she'd been.

Evangeline gave him a look comprised in equal parts of confusion, betrayal and scorn.

"I talk about her all the time," she said.

"I know but… You talk a lot all the time." Peter shrugged. "Sometimes I might not be listening."

"I can tell you must be tired; you can't be charming." Evangeline sat down beside him. "She's a professor at Western Washington University," Evangeline said. "She's just been featured in New American Painter magazine. It's right here. I showed you before."

She pawed through a slumping stack of papers and magazines that sat on the floor by the couch.

"Is she the one who does the abstract aerial views of swimming pools of their suburban youth?"

"No that that's Tommy. You'd recognize Shelley's stuff. She has a huge painting in the credit union lobby. The one with all that forced perspective." She found the magazine and leafed through to find the piece on Shelley Vine.

"I don't like the idea of having my perspective forced, especially not in a bank," Peter remarked.

"Funny," Evangeline handed him the magazine then stood. "I've got to go down to Angie's Bail Bonds."

"You're not going to bail out beard-o are you?"

"His wife told him she wouldn't come," Evangeline said simply. "You're snippy aren't you?"

"I'm just really tired."

Evangeline lingered reasonlessly, biting her lip and looking out the window at the bright morning light.

"Are *you* okay?" Peter asked.

"Tommy said that Nick did it," she said. "He said the police took him away. I can't believe that Nick would do such a thing."

"When I came in he was trying to save her," Peter said.

"Tommy said Nick had his hands on her throat." Evangeline put her hand to her own neck as if reassuring herself it was in proper working order.

"I'm fairly certain he was applying pressure to the gash in her neck." Peter wondered if his own high school first aid class would have prepared him to be first on the scene of a murder. He remembered something about performing a tracheotomy with a pen but he didn't think Shelley had needed an extra hole in her neck.

Evangeline shook her head. "If Nick didn't do anything why did the police take him into custody?"

"Probably because he was standing over her covered with blood," Peter said. "It looked bad but I still don't think he did it. If he'd been the one to attack her, why call for help?"

"Because she started screaming," Evangeline said. "Plenty of people didn't like Shelley, I guess I never thought it would be him. I thought it would be Luna—not that I really thought anyone would kill her. God, it's so awful. I always thought Nick was the sane one in the building."

"I think he still might be," Peter said. "Who's Luna?"

"One of the Spinnin' Wimmin. They make yarn."

Peter nodded, recalling the weird sight of three women with spinning wheels, brightly dyed wool and lots of body piercings during the last open studio night he'd attended. "And Luna said she would kill Shelley?"

"No, she never said that. She just hated her." Evangeline paused again murmured, "Maybe I'll ask about Nick while I'm at the police station," and padded back toward her bedroom.

Tired, but still too rattled to sleep, Peter engaged the magazine.

The article explained that Shelley, or "Vine" as she was referred to by the magazine article's writer had been born in Iowa and educated at University of Wisconsin at Madison, earning her MFA. She taught at Minnesota State University in Moorhead, winning a McKnight Fellowship during her tenure. She came to Bellingham to accept a full-time position at Western Washington University and had, for the past ten years been slowly making herself known in the larger art world. She had recently gained representation by the Lemmon Gallery.

Peter hadn't ever heard of it, but gathered from the context that this had been good news.

Vine's artist statement read as follows:

This series of paintings explores the boundaries between the past and present and between one artist's abandoned or forgotten work and my own inspirations. They capture art as a continuum, which passed from one medium to another but is never truly lost.

The image of Vine's blood marking the pristine canvas flashed across his mind. Primal red. The last mark she'd ever placed on a canvas.

Peter dropped the magazine, admitting to himself, if not to his roommate that he was feeling slightly darker than usual.

Evangeline left while he was showering afterward, unable to sleep, Peter wrote an account of his morning and emailed it to his editor.

As he hit the send button, tension left him and he fell asleep slumped across his desk.

Chapter 3

The Hamster, (short for Bellinghamster) was housed above the Puget Sound Electric Company's State Street office. One large, cluttered room housed all five members of the staff. In addition to writing articles, Peter was in charge of circulation, which meant that every Thursday morning he drove bundles of the free weekly to various locations in the city and in greater Whatcom County.

A glorified paperboy position, true, but at least it was in his field.

The editor in chief was named Doug Bowles. Stout, and in his mid-fifties, Doug played upright bass in a folk trio called Muddy Shovel on Monday nights at Boundary Bay Brewery. He'd been divorced twice since Peter had known him. Prior to landing in Bellingham, he'd spent a decade in Amsterdam pursuing a career in hydroponic engineering, or so he claimed. Doug's red-rimmed eyes, in combination with his long, conspiracy riddled columns detailing local politics, indicated he remained an avid indoor-gardening enthusiast.

But he had a good eye for prose as well as an extremely flexible attitude towards continuing to pay Peter to cover pretty much whatever news he chose.

"I love this," Doug said. "It makes me really feel like I was there in the room with you."

"Thanks." Peter beamed.

"But I want you to dig a little deeper into this Nick character," Doug tapped the stack of papers. "I've heard a lot of stories about him."

Oh God, here we go.

"Like what?" Peter asked.

"Did you know he inherited Walter De Kamp's house and estate? The one they call The Castle out on Wildcat Cove?"

Walter De Kamp—Whatcom county native son who went to New York City, made it big and came back to live as a heroic recluse on a cliff-face house on the water a few miles south of the city.

How the hell did Doug know this stuff? Then again, Peter thought that maybe if he smoked kind bud with everybody in town, he'd also have acquired a wide range of esoteric gossip as well.

"So Nick's rich?"

"Very rich," Doug agreed.

"Where did you hear this?"

"Interestingly enough, it was from Shelley Vine." Doug reached into his pocket, took out folded packet of Drum tobacco and started rolling himself a cigarette. "She found out from a reporter who interviewed her for *Artforum* when she went to New York last spring. Turns out the same reporter had interviewed De Kamp just before he died five years ago and Nick was there at the house apparently living there."

"How come nobody knew this?"

"I don't know if it's true or not. That's something you might want to find out. But the question is why did De Kamp's wife get paid off and Nick get the house and artistic estate?"

"I can think of at least one easy solution," Peter remarked.

"That they were lovers? It's the strongest current theory, but I think that if you were to look a little harder at Nick Olson you'd find that this isn't the first police investigation he's been involved in." Doug opened the window behind his desk leaned slightly out and lit his cigarette. "If you can get me the rewrite by tomorrow morning we can still get it in this week's edition."

"What if it's irrelevant?"

"Who's had sex with who in this town is never irrelevant. Once you get a little older you'll figure that out."

Peter sought Nick out at his studio in the Vitamilk Building. The summer afternoon was warm and humid. He steeled himself against a feeling of childish unease. Award-winning journalists didn't get creeped out by returning to the scene of a murder.

He hadn't felt unsafe in the alley behind the Pierogy Tea Café and he'd been in greater danger then. But then he'd been playing a little, hadn't he? He'd been pretending to investigate, excited by the prospect of finding something terrible.

Now that he'd actually seen something really awful he felt little excitement about the prospect of running into it again. What he did feel was a sense of purpose. He needed to find out why Shelley had been killed, if only to assure himself that the same thing wasn't likely to happen to himself any time soon.

And besides, award-winning journalists didn't pussy out and leg it back home to mommy. If he had the balls to do this job, he'd find out in the next few days.

Still, walking up the stairs gave him a chill, brought back the sound of that night, screaming and sirens, even though the only sound he could hear was the sound of darkwave music coming out of the open door of the corner studio.

He caught a glimpse of a whirling spinning wheel, bright red thread wrapping around a spindle. A gray haired woman sat behind it, her feet pumping the wheel's treadles, head bobbing in time with the late eighties goth music.

Peter knew, from previous encounters, that the woman wasn't old, just prematurely gray at 32.

Luna: one of the three Spinnin' Wimmin.

Their studio occupied the front right corner of the building, adjacent to the wide stairwell. Beside them was Tomas Allende, or Tommy, who'd been arrested the same night for dating Mary-Jane. Evangeline's closet of a studio came next. Nick's studio occupied the back right corner of the building. Across from Nick, was his Pierogy Tea Café informant, John and next to John the enormous studio of the late Shelley Vine.

Nick's door was closed so he walked back toward Luna, the woman Evangeline thought most likely to have killed her studio mate.

Luna didn't look up as he approached, but she said, "what do you want?" by way of greeting. She had her hair braided with coarse blue yarn and coiled atop her head and wore an elaborate black velvet dirndl. Her feet were bare, the toenails painted black. Frida Khalo by way of the St. Pauli girl… with a little Dracula thrown in for good measure.

"I came by to talk to Nick," Peter said. "Do you know if he's here?"

"I saw him go in a couple of hours ago. I'm pretty sure he's still in there," Luna said. She kept her eyes on the thread, joining fluffy tufts of wool onto the end of it a one tiny bit at a time occasionally glancing at thread winding around the spindle as if she were one of the three Norns measuring out a life. Peter glanced around but didn't see the other two, Guinevere and Max. The studio was orderly, the spinning wheel the centerpiece of the room a wall full of square cubbies held skeins of yarn or masses of raw wool, some of which had been felted into shapes: two hats, rectangular box, and a remarkably accurate M-16 machine gun complete with banana clip.

On a long table sat a postal scale and mailing supplies, along with an assortment of needles of different gauge and design.

"You guys do a pretty good mail-order business, don't you?" he asked.

"Not really, we just use that thing to weigh out coke," Luna said.
"I… see."

"Just kidding." Luna finally looked up at him. "We send out about twenty packages a week. Why? Are you writing us up in *the Hamster*?"

Peter shrugged noncommittally. "I thought since the studio had been in the newspaper so often I'd try to do a piece on the artists who are still alive."

Luna snorted. "That's not the way the art world works, babe. Death is the best thing that can happen for anybody's career. Shelley's trite shit has already tripled in price. Even dead she's going to make more money than all of the rest of us this year… Bitch."

"I take it you didn't care for her too much?"

"If you looked up the word 'sell-out' on wikipedia you'd find a picture of her. And she was a snob. Her opinion was that what we did was craft and not worthy of being considered art." Luna kept joining up tufts of wool, her foot working the treadle evenly, though bitterness hardened her voice. "How can anybody think that is craft? What practical use does it have?"

She jerked her head toward the felt machine gun.

Peter gave a non-committal "Hm."

"Were you here that night?"

Luna shook her head. "I go to sleep with the chickens. But Robert tells me she had another boy in that night."

"A boy?"

"Student assistant," Luna said, rolling her eyes. "She liked to fuck them in her personal studio instead of her office up at the college. She didn't like to shit where she ate. But I don't want to talk about her any more. It just pisses me off. What would you like to know about the Spinnin' Wimmin'?"

Peter spent the next hour learning more about wool than any modern man needed to know. But between the explanations of the various forms of fleece and acid dyes he'd managed to build a pretty good financial picture of The Vitamilk Building. Luna, Guinevere and Maxx definitely occupied the lowest artistic run in the building, having the twin disadvantages of being both women and successful business people.

Their neighbor, Robert, hadn't sold a painting in over two years but had once had two paintings in a student show at the Seattle Art Museum. He worked as a home care attendant for severely mentally disabled adults four nights a week, spent the other three in his studio and according to Luna, was on the brink of divorce.

Apart from working with Luna, as a barista at the Black Drop Coffeehouse, Evangeline did good business selling found-object trivets at the Allied Arts Christmas market, but sold little else.

According to Luna, John used to do a good business in dry-point etchings of famous local buildings, but had given that up to concentrate full time on painting several years before. He'd had moderate success, selling a few paintings a year to the cadre of retired real estate developers who owned the big houses on Chuckanut Drive.

"Big couches need big paintings to go over them," Luna said. "His day job is teaching at Sunrise Alternative High School."

Peter nodded, he'd known most of the information about John already.

"He and Shelly were a item for about a week back when they were both still in school."

That Peter had not known.

"It couldn't have ended too badly though." Luna shrugged as if there was no accounting for amiable breakups. "They stayed friends."

"What about Nick?" Peter asked.

"He's a mystery. I really don't know if he sells anything, but he's here as much as I am, maybe more." Luna leaned forward. "I think he might be living here, which is illegal, so don't print that. I'm a gossip, not a narc."

"I'm not sure much of what you told me is printable," Peter commented.

"Spinnin' Wimmin' is having an pre-winter sale and conducting a mitten making seminar at the end of September. There's a flyer for it right there," Luna grinned up at him. "That's printable, right?"

"You bet."

Peter folded the flyer and put it into his pocket.

So Luna didn't know Nick owned the The Castle on Wildcat Cove. Interesting. But he supposed Doug had heard it from Shelley Vine, who might not have told Luna.

He took a deep breath, walked down the hall, past Shelley's studio, doorframe still criss-crossed by police tape and knocked on Nick's plain plywood door.

Then he waited. Nothing. No acknowledgement at all from inside. Just as he was about to knock again, the door opened and there stood Nick.

Shirtless.

Which wasn't surprising, considering the muggy heat, but still took Peter by surprise, on account of his frequent fantasies about the other man. He'd realized that in his imagination, Nick looked more like a porn star. In reality, he had, for example, chest hair. Fine blonde hair. And a treasure trail. And small tattoo on his upper right arm, some kind shield in blue and silver. Family coat of arms?

"Hi there, I'm Peter Fontaine." He managed to shove his hand forward, while simultaneously forcing his voice out of his mouth. "We met the other night. I don't know if you remember."

"It would be tough to forget," Nick remarked.

"I'm a reporter," Peter continued, "and I—"

Nick cut him off. "I don't do interviews. For anything."

"I'm not asking for an interview," Peter didn't miss a beat. "I've already done my work for today. We're doing a feature on the Spinnin' Wimmin'—*the Hamster*, that is."

"So, what did you need?"

"I was hoping to ask you out on a date," Peter blurted out.

"A date?" Nick's eyebrows rose. His expression conveyed first confusion, then mirth. "Well, come in then. Close the door behind you."

Peter followed Nick inside, closing the door as he'd been instructed. Nick's studio was a nearly perfect square about twelve by twelve feet, judging from the big 72 x 72 canvases propped up against the walls. Wide windows lined one wall. Powerful, color-correct lamps shone on a canvas sitting on an easel to the left. Abstract expressionist certainly described it. Gray and celadon like the Bellingham Bay sky and sea, the view that Nick would see outside of the Vitamilk window (though today this glistened with rays of uncharacteristic sunshine.)

Nick picked up a tube of paint-- Paynes' Gray. The one paint name Peter actually knew, because he liked it so much. Payne's gray was the soft blue-gray color of the Pacific Northwest sky when it was dark with unfallen rain.

"So, you want to ask me out?"

"That's about it, yeah."

"Why?"

"Because you're gorgeous," Peter said. He fell back on his old lie. Well, not really a lie—more like a half-truth. "The reason I was outside the building in the first place was I was trying to get up the guts to ask you out."

"You're saying you're attracted to men who are drenched in blood?" he asked, not looking up from his palatte. He dabbed his brush in white and started to mix it in with the Payne's gray.

Peter flushed scarlet. "I didn't know you were drenched in blood at the time."

"That's comforting," Nick replied. He gave Peter a quick, evaluating glance. "What did you have planned?"

"Planned?"

"For the date you were going to ask me on," Nick's voice remained very soft, almost as though he was talking to himself, or worried about disturbing the painting with excessive volume, "what sort of plans did you have?"

"I thought I'd take you to Nimbus for a drink."

"Fancy," Nick said. "And then?"

"I thought I'd see how it went from there," as Peter spoke, the line between what was actually true and his own deceptions began to blur. Yes, he had fantasized about taking Nick to Nimbus, a dark, expensive bar on the 14th floor of the Bellingham Towers. That fantasy always ended with the two of them getting

27

stuck in the unreliable elevator and having to entertain each other until the help arrived.

Entertainment normally included at least one blowjob. Then, if Peter still hadn't fallen asleep by then, help would appear in the form of burly firemen.

Sometimes the firemen joined in and the entire elevator became a sordid scene of man on man on man on man on still yet one last man action.

All of that seemed ridiculous, now that Nick was within arm's reach. Was the murder an excuse to talk to Nick or Nick the excuse to delve further into the murder? He was no longer sure.

Nick pulled back from the painting, wiped the excess paint off the end of his brush, then swished it though a jar of something that looked like water but wasn't. He set the brush aside.

"I think I could go for a drink or two, but I have some more work to do. How about you come back at 9:30? We can walk over from here." He turned to Peter and smiled and Peter felt the expression as though it was a physical force, pressurizing the air, making the rest of the world recede in importance.

"I'll see you then."

At fourteen stories, Bellingham Towers far outstripped any other building downtown. The restaurant atop it did not rotate, but it did have a good view of the downtown core and the bay.

Dark with rich red walls, Nimbus dreamed it was in a bigger, more sophisticated city. Seattle maybe, or just across the border in Vancouver. And dressed with the natural style possessed by artists, Nick fit in. Even in jeans, a printed T-shirt and a blazer. Even with bed head.

Both men and women looked Nick's way as they passed by, their eyes lingering on his long legs. Nimbus was the place the thirtysomething crowd took their first dates and celebrated their professional achievements. Peter had only ever been here with Evangeline on Industry Night, when the place filled with area cooks, servers and baristas all drinking on a twenty percent discount.

Coming on a Friday night with a handsome man Peter felt a sort of self-conscious pride. They were obviously gay and obviously on a date and obviously the only gay date currently occurring in the building. At the bar two older women whispered and smiled, but kindly.

Nick took a seat in the corner, next to huge plate glass windows. Peter followed. They ordered drinks and entered the dreaded dead time between sitting down and having a beverage.

Peter gazed down at clots of people on the sidewalk far below, standing smoking outside less expensive bars. Beyond them a curve of lights defined the edge of Bellingham Bay.

Nick followed his lead.

"There's Guinivere and Maxx," he said, pointing down at the concrete in front of The Grand Ave. Even from this height the women's yarn-woven dread's were unmistakable. "They haven't spoken to me since Shelley's death."

"Why not?"

Nick shrugged. "Who knows? That's the problem when people aren't speaking to you. They don't explain why not. But I think they think I'm guilty."

"Maybe they just don't know what to say to you," Peter said.

"How do you mean?"

Peter looked out the window again, taking in the dark mass of lightlessness that was the water of Bellingham Bay.

"Sometimes if you think a person has seen something really horrible you don't want to bring it up with them, because you don't want to make them uncomfortable," Peter said.

"And what if you've seen the same horrible thing yourself?" Nick asked. "How do you feel then?"

Peter kept his eyes on the dark water, wishing his dirty martini would arrive. He needed an object to worry and a toothpick full of olives seemed like a good choice.

"You feel like you want to talk about it even more," Peter said.

"Then why don't you talk about it." Nick leaned back against the leather booth like a psychiatrist settling in for a session.

Peter thought of opening his heart then and letting his feelings gush out but he thought they might wash away any kind of seductive mystique he currently commanded. He curled his mouth up into a wicked half-smile.

"Because I don't want to wreck my one chance to get with you for just one night," he replied.

Nick, too, seemed relieved that he hadn't slid into the Maudlin Sea.

"You'd have to go pretty far to wreck that," Nick said, laughing. "But seriously, I did wonder if you were all right after that night. You must have been scared. I know I was. When you came in I didn't know if you were there to help me or the killer coming back to finish the job."

"You didn't look scared," Peter said. "You looked pissed."

"That's just my sexy look," Nick joked.

"Really, I thought this was your sexy look," Peter spoke without thinking, as if he had no game at all.

Nick smiled and Peter smiled back and between them the attraction seemed tangible, like a haze of sunlight narrowing down into a laser. Peter slid his hand across the table and laid his fingers lightly over Nick's wrist.

He said, "I'm glad we met, though, even if it had to be like that."

Nick uncurled his hand, opening his palm to Peter's touch.

"I'm glad too," Nick's voice remained as soft as it had been when he'd been talking to his painting.

Peter said, "I know the girl tending bar tonight."

"Oh?" Slight confusion creased Nick's brow, but not so much that he pulled his hand away.

"Right behind the bar, there's a door that leads out onto the roof." Peter moved his hand more boldly now, confident in

Nick's response. "The staff goes out there to smoke so they don't have to ride the elevator all the way down to the parking lot. Sometimes, if they know you, they'll let customers go out there."

"Sounds dangerous," Nick remarked.

"Are you afraid of heights?"

"Not at all."

When the waitress arrived with their drinks, they'd already slipped away.

The roof outside Nimbus was limited to an L shaped space twenty feet long and ten feet deep. Dim lights studded the walls at five foot intervals, but between these, only darkness. No railing prevented them from falling. Warm wind whipped around Peter as he stepped out onto the pebbled tar roof. He ventured farther, keeping one hand against the brick wall. Glancing back over his shoulder he saw Nick pause in the doorway and survey the blackness in front of him as though it were a vision of a terrible future. Then he gingerly put one foot out the door. Finding solid ground he moved out further keeping a cautious hand on the brick wall.

"Come on," Peter offered his hand. "There's plenty of room."

Their eyes met and they both laughed. Nervous but full of exhilaration. Nick's hand closed around his and they both leaned against the wall, staring out at the bay. The high, white moon cast a long reflection across the dark water.

Stars blazed overhead, neon flashed below.

"I didn't even know this existed," Nick said.

"This city's full of secret places," Peter said. "But I guess every city is."

"Not everybody cares to look for them, though." Nick squeezed Peter's fingers.

"You say the nicest things."

Desire ignited in Peter like a fever, fed on the giddiness of being atop a building in the dark with a near stranger. Peter could find no good reason not to lift Nick's hand to his lips. The faint scent of linseed oil and artist-grade turpentine clung to his skin, along with some warm cologne that smelled almost like whiskey, full of licorice and tobacco notes.

Nick's face was too shadowed for Peter to see his response, but he heard the intake of breath.

The door to Nimbus opened again and a short, swarthy man in checked pants and a stained chef's coat strode out onto the roof, talking on his cell phone and lighting a cigarette simultaneously. The noise jolted them both and their hands separated.

The cook regarded them questioningly, but did not engage them, preferring to continue his conversation, which to Peter seemed to be with his wife.

"I guess our drinks are probably getting warm," Nick said.

They edged their way back inside and had drinks and shared a house-made charcuterie plate, talked about movies they'd seen and books they'd read, careful not to move into deeper conversational waters, then it was 11:30. Last call on weeknights.

He walked Nick back to the Vitamilk Building, where Peter had left his bike. Nick paused on the uneven sidewalk outside the building and turned to study the moon for a long moment. Peter waited through Nick's decision-making process, hoping that he'd make the cut and get invited inside, or better still, back to The Castle.

Nick turned, leaned close and pressed his lips to Peter's cheek, then said, "goodnight."

Temporarily denied, but still feeling good, Peter rolled up his pantleg and pedaled the few short blocks to his house, hoping the exertion would take the edge off his thwarted desire.

It didn't and Peter once again found himself lying in bed alone, an elevator full of firemen in his head and Nick just out of his grasp.

Chapter 4

Back at *the Hamster* office the next morning, article unrevised, Peter stalled.

"I went to the Vitamilk last yesterday, but didn't get a lot out of it. Just common knowledge stuff." He leaned forward, elbows on knees, trying to seem trustworthy and reliable. "And I think that all that information would undermine the immediacy of my first person account anyway. Could you just run the article I already wrote and do a follow-up piece next week?"

"There's no guarantee the story will still be news next week." Doug took a couple more puffs off his cigarette then pinched off the cherry and dropped the butt out of the window into the alley below. "What else have you got for me?"

Peter told him about the mitten workshop and the strange comings and goings at Pierogy Tea Café. Alarm spread through Doug's placid features.

"I don't know if it's all that smart of you to antagonize the Tea Cafe guys in print," Doug said. "And even if you did write the article I'm not sure that I would run it."

"So what you're telling me is that I must harass an innocent artist but can't touch a bunch of pimps?" Peter said.

"First of all, you don't know that Olson is innocent. Second, that bunch of pimps will have no hesitation about using you and me both as crab bait," Doug returned.

"But breaking a story like that could make us," Peter insisted.

"People read *the Hamster* to find out which bands are playing at what bar and what developer is fucking with their island view this week. Get over yourself. This isn't the *Washington Post* and you're not Deep Throat." Doug sighed and stared out the window, out toward the marina and the Tea Café in question.

Peter thought of at least six jokes he could make and abandoned them all. He was too angry.

"Okay, fine. Then how about I write the piece on mitten seminar?"

Doug sighed again, as though depressed by his own assessment of *the Hamster's* importance as a news source. "Write it up in 500 words or less. I'll send the photographer down to the Vitamilk Building. Those Spinnin' Wimmin' are pretty foxy."

"Done." Peter stood.

"I still want a more in-depth piece about the Vitamilk artists, just in case one of them turns out to have done it," Dough said.

"You'll have it in one week." Peter turned to go.

"And stay away from the Russians. They are not to be fucked with," Doug's voice came from behind him.

Google revealed many, many pages wherein Nick's name was linked with De Kamp's. In the oldest references, those from nearly fifteen years prior, twenty-two year old Nick was called a "studio assistant and sometimes model." De Kamp was fifty-three at this time and at the height of his celebrity in the New York gallery scene.

Peter decided to take his search to the Wilson Library magazine archive on the Western Washington University campus, which sat just over the Sehome Hill arboretum from his rental place. He took his road bike up the hill, skirting the edge of the dense trees and then taking Indian Street straight into campus. For the first time, he noticed the youth of the students lounging by the fountain in Red Square. Two shirtless boys threw a Frisbee, trying to attract the attention of a pack of girls. Excited, nervous, talking too loudly or hunching too self-consciously, they seemed like children to him. So much that he had to look away from the stocky brunette kid's effortlessly flat abs as he sent his Frisbee sailing. Where did these teenagers come from? Had they always looked so fresh? How could he feel decades older than them at a mere twenty-eight?

As he chained his bike up he saw a large sandwich board sign reading, "Freshman Orientation A-L, PAC Room 102" and another directing the "M-Z" crowd to Room 104. Alongside these he spotted a Xeroxed photograph of Shelley Vine's face. Threading his way through a stream of tense students and edgy mothers, he drew closer. An open memorial gathering for Vine would take place later in the evening around her favorite sculpture, Tom Otterness' *Feats of Strength*, located in front of Parker Hall.

That smelled like exactly the kind of story Doug would want him to write up for *the Hamster*: human interest. Plus Luna had mentioned that Shelley had brought a student back to the gallery that night. Maybe someone at the gathering would know who that student had been.

With a couple of hours to kill before the memorial, he headed towards his original destination, Wilson Library and his date with reference desk.

Ten years of photographs and articles showed Nick growing more and more prominent in De Kamp's life, so that the last photograph, from *Architectural Digest* showed Nick by De Kamp's side on the balcony of The Castle, a modernist masterpiece whose architecture had been joined so closely to the cliff face that it seemed as if the swirling sandstone had been convinced to rise up and assemble itself into clean and orderly angles.

The Castle also had a lap pool, gray water system, solar panels and a sauna. It was as if the architect had deliberately set out to give Peter a hard on.

And it was all Nick's.

De Kamp had died five years prior after having been diagnosed with pancreatic cancer. Peter had been a senior at Western at that time writing for the college paper, *The Western Front*. He recalled that there had been an investigation of De Kamp's caretaker. Rumors of assisted suicide and a contested will swirled through the town, but on campus the concern had not been about whether the old man got murdered or who got the money. Issue after issue of *The Western Front* had been filled with academic arguments about the Right to Die. Hard facts about Nick Olson, the mysterious caretaker, were nowhere. Not even in the *Bellingham Herald*, where the reporter had at least bothered to learn Nick's full name: Nicholas Zimmer Olson.

He had enough dirt to satisfy Doug, though. Not that that made him happy. He paid for a few photocopies and shoved them into his bag, next to his helmet and cycling gloves and made his way toward Parks Hall.

Already a trio of people gathered on the crescent-shaped concrete benches.

Feats of Strength had also been his own favorite among the many sculptures on the Western campus. It had the distinction of being the only representational piece in the entire sculpture garden collection and as such the most accessible to the wider student population. It consisted of several child-sized bronze figurines who had the same round smoothness and proportions as the Monopoly Man holding enormous boulders two or three times their size. Peter's favorite was a knee-high figure with the prim bun and low breasts of a grandmother who stood on a six-foot rock and held another rock the size of a sumo wrestler high over her head. She'd always looked, to Peter, as though she was about to drop that rock on some clueless undergrad.

He ambled up beside two virtually identical young women in tank tops and shorts. Both had long brown straight hair that had been streaked with blonde highlights and perfectly even tans. They sat directly beneath the grandma, arms around their stomachs, puffy-eyed, fingertips stained red. Four big cardboard boxes sat stacked beside them. On the sidewalk in front of the bench a large line drawing had been traced on the sidewalk in red chalk. From the shape of the nose, it was unmistakably Vine.

Peter sat down on the bench nearby acknowledging them with a smile.

"Is this the memorial for Professor Vine?" he asked.

The two girls looked at each other, then at a young man who stood nearby. Tall but not lanky, he wore khaki Patagonia board shorts and a slim black T-shirt. Something about him said, "rock climber." Maybe his biceps, which were big and bulky as rocks themselves. He couldn't be much past 21, Peter decided, and straight as a Wyoming highway.

Introductions were made. Rock climber's name was Greg and the girls were Sidney and Ceilleigh.

"I'm glad you stopped by, man," the man extended his hand. "How did you know Shelley?"

Although slightly annoyed to be immediately pegged as an outsider on the campus he used to call his own, Peter didn't let it show.

"I took a couple of classes from her," he said. "Back when I went to school here. How about you?"

"She was our advisor," Ceilleigh said, sniffing.

"More like our second mom," Sidney put in. They looked at each other and Peter could see the emotional feedback loop begin. In moments they'd both be crying.

Peter turned his attention quickly to Greg.

"And what about you?"

"I used to be was her studio assistant," Greg said. "Last quarter."

"Greg helped with her latest paintings." Ceilleigh seemed to be pulling it together enough to speak. "They were so beautiful. So creative."

"*She* was so beautiful," Sidney chimed in, miserably. "She took old art that other people had thrown away and gave it a new life. That's special, you know?"

"Peter," a man's voice came from behind him. Turning he saw John approaching, five or six teen-agers in tow.

Peter stood and shook his hand.

"These are a few of my students from the Academy," John waved a hand at the group of youths, whom Greg was currently welcoming. "They worked closely with Shelley over the summer on the mural down by the waterfront."

Greg circled his way back toward them, pulling John into a classic straight guy hand-clasp and man hug. Then he stood up on the bench and held up his hands for quiet. Ceilleigh and Ashley started to unpack the boxes. Plastic tubs of varying size were unlidded, revealing colored sand.

"Thank you all for coming. I know Shelley would have been happy to see us all here honoring her life. Ceilleigh, Sidney and I would like it if you helped us with this piece of collaborative art."

The Academy kids filed over to Greg getting tubs of sand and assignments.

"Looks like they already know the drill," Peter remarked. John nodded.

"Most of them were pretty broken up about Shelley. They wanted to help make a memorial for her," he said. "The first idea was a commando-style graffiti mural on the Marine Drive overpass next to the Vitamilk. I managed to talk them out of that one."

"Probably for the best," Peter agreed.

Greg had finished directing the students and offered Peter a gallon margarine tub full of ultramarine blue sand. "Would you like to help me color in the sky?"

"I'm not much of an artist," Peter demurred. "I don't want to screw it up."

"There are no mistakes in art—that's one of the things Shelley was all about," Greg said. "How about you, John? I've got an awful lot of sky here."

"Sure." John got down on the hot concrete, motioning Peter down beside him. The three of them took handfuls of bright blue sand. Peter followed John's lead, letting the sand fall from his cupped palm in a controlled stream. Greg did the same, but with more motion and flourish so that at times his gestures neared the level of dance.

John emptied his hand and reached into the tub for more.

"I'm surprised to see you here," John said.

"I used to take classes with Professor Vine." No use not sticking to his story.

John laughed gently. "If you had you'd know that nobody ever called Shelley that."

At John's words, Greg looked over sharply, as did Sidney.

"Alright, you got me. I'm doing a story on Professor Vine for *the Hamster*," Peter said.

"Why did you lie to us?" Sidney's voice trembled slightly. She was a powder keg of pent-up emotion waiting for a spark to set her off. Peter held up his hands as though to surrender.

"People get nervous when reporters are around and I didn't want to disrupt your memorial event," Peter said. It was true enough, if not entirely.

"I think you've already done that," Greg said.

"I don't think Shelley would mind if Peter was here," John put in quietly. "Especially when you take into consideration what he's done."

"What's that?" Sidney's entire body trembled. The teenagers had stopped working and openly stared at him with the eerie unselfconsciousness of schoolchildren.

"Well, Peter's the one who called the ambulance," John said. "Isn't that right?"

"That's right."

As if in a classroom, one of the teenagers asked, "you saw Shelley when she was dead?"

"I saw her before she was dead," Peter corrected. "You can read all about it in tomorrow's edition of *the Hamster*. I'd rather not go through all the details again right now though."

Both Greg and Sidney seemed to accept this, since they both started urging the kids back to their work. A few minutes passed and he nearly filled in a square foot of sky. Greg sat beside them again.

"I'm sorry about that," Greg said. "I guess I'm just a little sensitive."

"No worries," Peter said. "I didn't know her like you did, but that doesn't mean I don't care about her. That's the reason I'm writing this article. I watched this woman die. I want to know who she was." Peter hadn't meant to confess this to Greg or anyone else, but it just slipped out. Greg seemed to take it as positive proof that he wasn't heartless. He offered the tub of sand.

Artists, he noted, are fond of ritual and symbolic gesture.

"You were at the studio that night too, weren't you?" John asked Greg.

"Yeah," Greg nodded. "If I hadn't left then maybe this wouldn't have happened." Then, confusion. "How did you know I'd been there?"

"Shelley told me you were coming by the studio to help her get her new show ready." John smiled kindly again. "Plus I heard you and her... working."

"So you were at the Vitamilk too?" Greg asked.

"I left while you were still there," John said.

"Not to be rude, but do the police know you were there that night?" Peter asked Greg.

"You bet. I went to them right away when I heard the news," Greg said. "My father's a policeman here in town. I know they need to get fingerprints from everyone who has been in the room to eliminate them as suspects. Of course, they questioned me for a long time, too."

"Because you were there?" Peter stated more than asked.

"And because we had been, you know, together," Greg lowered his voice. "It's not a secret but I don't like to talk about it in front of the kids. They don't understand women who are free spirits."

Peter nodded and applied himself more diligently to the sky. So, Greg's dad was a Bellingham cop, was he? He wondered how impartial the investigation could really be when you were interrogating your buddy's kid?

Doug would like this angle. Police conspiracy might even trump reclusive homosexual artist in terms of newsworthiness.

And Doug took personal pleasure in fucking with the local cops, whom he referred to as a "fascist mercenary brotherhood."

Peter now knew of five men had been in or around the building that night: Nick, John, Greg, Tommy and himself. One of them, Greg, had been her lover. Conventional wisdom said the odds of the lover also being the killer were high. Greg didn't strike him as a killer, though. None of them gave Peter even the slightest twinge of discomfort.

Not like the Russian had.

"I know this might sound like a strange question," Peter began, "but I was wondering if either of you had ever seen Shelley talking to the Russians next door."

"At the Tea Café?" Greg paused, thinking, "I never saw her talk to them, but she did have a thing with the blonde one."

"What sort of thing?" Peter palmed more sand. How much of a free spirit was this Shelley Vine? "A relationship?"

"Only if you can count fighting over the same parking space a relationship," John said, chuckling. "Since he opened up shop three years ago, Shelley and Dmitri have been engaged in their own private war."

Greg cracked a sad smile and emitted a short laugh.

John continued, "she had this orange traffic cone that she used to put in a certain parking space that she considered to be her own. Everyone just let her get away with it for years. Even the meter maids turned a blind eye. Then the Russians move in and Dmitri moves her traffic cone and parks his SUV in her spot."

"She hated people to park in her parking spot," Greg said. "Especially Dmitri's big black gas-guzzling ozone destroyer."

"Did she pay for the spot or something?" Peter was having a hard time reconciling the woman who rescued art, who was the second mom of Ceilleigh and Sidney, with an apparent parking nazi.

"Shelley believed she had paid her dues and was therefore entitled to certain privileges," John said.

"Like a parking spot?" Peter asked.

"A good parking spot," Greg corrected. "Dmitri liked to yank Shelley's chain because she represents the thing he fears most—a truly powerful, free woman. You know that place is a brothel right? He was constantly trying to dominate her psychically."

"Psychically?" Peter frowned. "You mean… with telepathy?"

"I mean Dmitri is a psychic vampire, feeding off of the negative energy that he creates," Greg said. "He likes to take things away from people—especially women."

Peter wondered at the relevance of this. Surely no one, not even a mafia pimp would kill an innocent woman over a parking spot…

Would they?

The immediate horror of Vine's murder had eclipsed his curiosity about the Tea Café for a time, but now Peter had gained enough mental distance to have his thoughts turn to proximity. If a murder occurs within fifty feet of a barely maintained front for prostitution, could they be related?

Surely the police had already checked out this angle, hadn't they? Impossible for them to not be aware of the business being conducted in the adjacent building, wasn't it? Especially since it was apparently common knowledge among the local student population.

"Did anyone else have any trouble with Dmitri?" Peter asked.

"Only Nick," John said. "Dmitri and he had it out in the alley a couple of weeks ago."

"What was the fight about?" Peter asked.

John shrugged. "You'd have to ask him."

Chapter 5

On the way back home, Peter stopped to pick up a bottle of wine. Pinot Grigio. He needed to tempt Evangeline into giving up some more information on her fellow artists in general and Nick in particular.

He pulled the cork and pressed a glass into Evangeline's hand before he even bothered to take off his bike helmet. Evangeline regarded him suspiciously, as did Tripod.

"What do you want?" she asked.

"Can't a man celebrate?"

"What do you have to celebrate?"

"I took Nick out for a drink last night." He tried to say this with ultimate cool, but he could hear a hint of high-school enthusiasm creeping into his voice.

"And then?" Evangeline leaned forward, immediately engaged.

"And then we both went to our own homes, like perfect gentlemen."

"You're so boring." Evangeline finally took a swig of her wine. "I'm glad you're here though. I was needing a second opinion." She held up a handkerchief-sized square of Astroturf. "How do you think this would look on my pussy?"

"Green," Peter replied. "I'm not sure you want anything green and hairy associated with your snatch."

"It's not hairy, it's blades of grass, which is a natural thing that is controlled anyway being even further controlled by making it plastic and immutable. It just brings to mind all those really groomed porn stars with their clipped landing-strip style pubic hair. Their bodies are as artificial and controlled as this fake grass. And then there are modern ideas of beauty... Many lines of connection exist between Astroturf and porn pubes."

"Including that fact that professional athletes can be found playing on both of them," Peter remarked.

Evangeline ignored him. "The only question is will it stick to my skin long enough to take the picture." Evangeline peered at the back of the Astroturf.

"Is this some new project of yours?"

Evangeline nodded. "I'm making pubic toupees. I'm going to have them photographed on myself and then display the toupees along with the photographs at a group show in December at Jinx Art Space."

"I've never heard of it." Peter fingered the Astroturf. Prickly.

"It's in the basement of Angie's Bail Bonds. I saw the flyer for the group show when I went there to bail out Robert," Evangeline said. "I'm thinking of making about a hundred toupees."

Something about Evangeline's announcement struck him as suspicious, but he couldn't figure out what.

"Sounds like that show's going to be popular with the male undergrads," Peter remarked.

"I hope so. I think it would do them good to see the pussy as a vehicle for art rather than just sexual fantasy," Evangeline said. "Tommy said he'd take the photographs for me."

"I'll bet he did." Peter almost began to tell her that the number of guys likely to be won over to her politics in this fashion was slim to zero, but decided not to. Why burst her bubble? Besides he was sort of curious what materials she'd use for the other 99 toupees. And as for Tommy, even Evangeline wasn't enough of an airhead to see that photographic offer for the come on that it was. If she wanted to accept it, that was her business. After all she'd put a lien on her car to bail Tommy out of jail—she'd already bought that ticket. She should get to ride that ride.

He just hoped it didn't turn out to be a dud. None of his business, though. He watched Evangeline working on the template for her pubic toupees for a couple of minutes then said, "I went to the Vine memorial today. Two of her students were talking about rescuing art. Any idea what they meant by that?"

"They were talking about the new paintings, probably," Evangeline said. "Shelley's new series is done over a series of prints made by another artist. That's one of the things that made it controversial. Luna said she stole them from a student, but Tommy seems to think they had been done by one of her lovers."

"I guess there's no reason it couldn't be both." Peter poured more wine into her glass. Greg fit the bill on both counts there, as well as having a policeman father who could cover up any mistakes that he made covering up his involvement in the crime.

"I suppose not," Evangeline said. "I just can't see Shelley stealing another artist's work, though. She had real integrity."

"She also fought a bitter feud over a parking space," Peter pointed out.

"Nobody's perfect." Evangeline shrugged. "Are you going out tonight?"

"I was thinking of going down to the Vitamilk."

"To see Nick?" Evangeline's eyes lit up.

"And to spy on the Russians," Peter replied. "But I'm going to see if I can get Nick to come along."

Summer sun, in the Pacific Northwest was never a casual, taken for granted affair. Californians, for example, would not have regarded the day as special. But when the sun shone for less than ninety days per year, people greeted its arrival with the wanton abandon of a drunk falling on a bottle of premium vodka.

Poor choices were always made. Mostly involving sunscreen or fashion. Lack of experience made warm weather dressing difficult for the western Washington man. Peter was no exception. He owned a pair of shorts, but they were more accurately described as swim trunks. He settled on a pair of linen pants he'd purchased in Mexico (the only warm country he'd ever visited) and a plain, close-fitting cream silk T shirt.

Then, realizing he'd be riding his bike, he crammed the good shirt into his saddlebag and pulled an old printed shirt over his head. The shirt was from Evangeline's short-lived band, *Sparklejism*. The shirt had been the best thing about the band.

Peter made it down to the Vitamilk around seven, just as the downtown restaurants had filled with the first was of sunburnt early diners.

More carloads of famished weekend sailors emerged from the marina. Peter blasted through the sluggish traffic, easily overtaking vehicles that labored under the weight of powerboats and jet skis. He reached the Vitamilk Building, pulled off his sweaty *Sparklejism* shirt, and replaced it with the nicer one. He checked out his hair in the wing mirror of a powder-blue Westfalia parked curbside. A little sweaty, but it passed for product so that was alright. He turned toward the Vitamilk, whose shattered glass door had been covered with plywood and saw all three of the Spinnin' Wimmin lounging on the steps. Guinivere and Maxx smoked clove cigarettes while Luna applied herself to knitting.

"You look great." As Guinivere spoke the silver ring in her lower lip flashed. Maxx merely gave him a smirk and a thumbs-up.

"Leave him alone," Luna murmured. "He's a friend of Evangeline's."

"But he does look great." Guinevere's tone conveyed the slightest edge of affront. "And I know who he is."

"We know who you are," Maxx told him. Her teased, pink hair stood up in a dramatic bouffant as if she were an extra from some punk version of *Grease*. She had many tattoos.

"Good to know." Peter couldn't tell if they mocked him or just didn't know how normal people acted friendly. He suspected it might be both. Or maybe they really were Norns letting him know they were measuring out the minutes of his life and he should stay on their good side and promote their mitten making seminar like he said he would. He passed them and started up the stairs, a red line of embarrassment creeping up his neck as he went.

Inside, the studio was stifling. All the doors and windows stood open and big box fans whirled at either end of the hallway trying to circulate the stagnant air. Unfamiliar astringent smells lingered with earthy mineral smells and the thick heavy odor of wet wool. Slanting yellow western light illuminated the hallway.

Inside Nick's studio, harsh white color-correct lights cut the warm evening glow. Nick sat on a tall stool in his studio, shirtless again, at work on the same painting as before. Peter briefly wished the heat wave would never end and that Nick, like Michelangelo's *David* would be eternally spared the burden of upper body garments. Nick glanced up and smiled, his pale blue eyes seeming to glow from within.

"I was just going to call you," he said.

"Yeah, you look like it." Peter laughed.

"Really, I was. I've done about as much as I can do to this today. I have to let it dry tonight."

"So it will be dry by tomorrow?"

"Oh, no, no. That will take months, but it will be dry enough that I can move it tomorrow so I can work on something else."

"Do most artists have several paintings going at once?"

"If they work in oils they pretty much have to." Nick swished his brush thoughtfully through a Mason jar full of cloudy liquid.

"Is this one done?"

"Yeah, can't you tell?" Nick's eyes twinkled with amusement.

"Are you making fun of me?"

"A little," Nick admitted. "This one isn't done, but I have to let this layer set before I start working on the next one."

"How long does it take to finish a painting?" Peter asked. "For you?"

"About six months." Nick wiped and then closely examined his brush. Then, frowning, he swished it again. "But after it's done it could take more than a year for it to completely dry. That's why I don't like inviting people into my studio. All they'd have to do is brush against a canvas and six months of my life would be gone."

Peter took a brief inventory of his elbows and knees. He deliberately set his saddlebag down in the hall.

"Then that must mean that the paintings Shelley had finished before she died would have been painted a year ago?"

"Or more." Nick's smile faded a little. "Is that something you're putting in your article?"

Peter nodded. "I want to give a feel of the place and the artists."

"You understand I'd rather not be included in that?"

"Sure," Peter said. "I respect that. I don't quite understand it, but I respect it."

"What is there to understand?" Nick let out a sigh and squeezed a small daub of paint onto his glass palette. Peter's spirits sank. Nick had decided against finishing up and it was his fault. He'd blown it. But he might be able to recover if he talked fast.

"It's just that most artists want publicity," Peter said.

Nick sighed again. Nodded. Peter thought, Note to self: the man can go from interested to taciturn in .05 seconds.

"But you don't," Peter continued. "And that's unusual."

"I guess I've just come to believe that there is such a thing as bad publicity, regardless of what the PR gurus say," Nick said.

"But what makes you say that?" Peter already knew, of course. The legal battle over Walter De Camp's will made him sound like some kind of gold digging hustler. But he wanted to hear how Nick would tell it… Or if Nick would tell him the story at all. They'd only been on one date.

"How long have you lived in this town?"

"Since I came here to go to Western. Ten years next month."

"If you're any kind of nosy reporter you already know that I came here around that time with Walter De Camp and that he left me his house and artistic estate." Nick mixed the paint, blue, with another color… orange?

"I can be naturally nosy, yeah. It makes me good at my job," Peter admitted.

"What wasn't in the paper was that for quite some time I was suspected of murdering Walter, before the coroner ruled his death a suicide," Nick said. "Walter's lawyer managed to stop most of the press, but gossip isn't intimidated by the threat of a lawsuit. The art world is very small and insular. My New York gallery dropped me and I didn't sell a painting for a long time."

"I thought De Camp died of cancer."

"Pancreatic cancer is one of the most painful cancers there is. Walter chose to end his life," Nick said shortly.

"And you helped him," Peter finished, thinking aloud. Nick's mouth tightened slightly.

"Assisted suicide wasn't legal then. But Walter was smart enough to pay his lawyer to represent me in advance. Nonetheless people I thought were my friends witch hunted me and destroyed my career." Nick seemed to just be mixing colors, with no real intention to paint. Peter thought he might be the sort of person who wasn't comfortable simply talking. Then again, who would be completely comfortable talking about something like this? "I just got back into galleries in New York and London. You can see how I wouldn't be excited to find my name in the paper and linked with another murder investigation."

"But you're not a suspect."

"It doesn't matter," Nick replied. "I don't think my reputation would recover. I can barely pay the taxes on Walter's house as it is. Art doesn't exactly make you rich."

Walter's house. Not "my house." Interesting. Also of note: either Doug's wrong about Nick's being rich or Nick's lying.

"You've got a pretty nice car for a poor guy." Peter had admired Nick's Audi on a number of occasions before he'd known it was Nick's.

"It has to be. I think it might be the last one I can ever afford to buy." Nick laughed.

49

Peter wondered if Nick's artistic confidence wouldn't also be destroyed by being savaged by his peers a second time. Let Doug get as mad as he wanted, Peter would not write about Nick's past.

"Can I ask you a question?"

"I might not answer," Nick said.

Peter nodded. "Why did you fight with Dmitri?"

Nick looked up at him as though his question was the most peculiar sentence he'd ever heard uttered.

"How did you know that?"

"I'm not only nosy, but I can also have snoopy tendencies." Peter hoped his smiled looked charmingly sheepish, rather than simply guilty. When Nick didn't immediately answer, Peter explained. "While I was asking around about Vine I came across her parking lot territorial dispute with Dmitri. That led to a mention of the fight between you and him. I happen to have been here the night of the murder because I'm writing a piece on what really goes on at the Tea Café."

"You're a busy guy," Nick remarked. "And I think you might be a little bit of a thrill seeker too."

"Now you're just trying to flatter me," Peter said. He hoped Nick was trying to flatter him, anyway.

"Do you snowboard?"

"I ski," Peter said. "Telmark."

"I'm more of a snowshoe fan myself," Nick said. "If we're talking about playing in the snow."

"I'm not against showshoeing," Peter said. Had he called it or what? Showshoeing led directly to snow camping, which, in his own mind at least, led directly to close cuddling to create warmth and snow cave sex… also to create warmth. "Maybe we could go check out Mount Baker's frozen majesty together sometime."

Nick stretched, rolled his head from side to side, loosening the muscles in his neck.

"I think the only frozen majesty we're likely to find for a while is the shave ice at the Farmer's Market." He laughed and the softness returned to his eyes he gave Peter one of those long, appraising glances then said, "I confronted Dmitri about shooting at things."

"What things?" Peter thought he might be getting the hang of Nick. He had a kind of emotional delay that made him circle around certain subjects—most notably himself.

"Everything and anything. Squirrels, raccoons, opossums, skunks, crows, deer, seals, old bicycles he didn't like the look of. Then man would pull his gun on anything."

"And you were worried that he'd hit somebody?"

Nick nodded. "There are always bums and hookers down beneath the overpass so that worried me, but just the principle of it pissed me off. What kind of dick fires four rounds at an opossum? What could it possibly have been doing to him? Shuffling blindly through the glare of his KC's? He's a dirty, petty bastard."

"He's also a pimp," Peter commented.

Nick nodded. Did everyone in town know? Why didn't someone try and stop it?

Nick said, "I pity those girls he keeps in there, but I don't know if it's safe for you to be poking around the alley as long as Dmitri is so trigger happy."

"I'm through poking around the alley," Peter assured him.

"That's good."

"I'm heading over there for a look inside."

"You're going in there now?" For the first time, Nick stopped mixing his paints. He stopped doing everything but breathing and staring in disbelief.

"Want to come with me?"

"I don't think Dmitri would let me in the door," Nick replied.

"Dmitri's not there. Or his car isn't, at least and he doesn't strike me as the kind of guy who ever walks to work."

"What do you hope to find in there?"

Peter shrugged. "Maybe nothing. Maybe a story about women being kept against their will by international Russian mafiosos."

"I think Dmitri's from Ferndale," Nick said.

"Okay then, maybe I'll find a story about pandering and human trafficking on the part of Ferndale gangsters or maybe I'll find some deeper connection between Dmitri and Vine. Maybe they weren't arguing about a parking spot after all. Maybe the parking spot was just the tip of the iceberg."

"I feel slightly surreal asking this, but are you laboring under the delusion that you're some kind of amateur sleuth who's going to solve Shelley's murder?"

"No, of course not," Peter grinned crookedly. "I'm a low-level investigative reporter who's going to solve Shelley's murder. There's a big difference."

"You're crazy," Nick commented.

"Will you come with me?" Peter asked again. "We're just going in and ordering some pierogies and seeing the inside. That's all."

"Do I have to eat the pierogies?" Nick asked. "Because I think I'd rather eat the freezer-burned rockfish in my fridge."

"You don't have to eat anything you don't want to," Peter assured him.

Chapter 6

Peter pulled the door of the Pierogy Tea Café open and stepped inside. He paused a moment, letting his eyes adjust to the dim interior. When he saw the squalid dining room, he almost wished he'd remained blind. Mentally (and automatically from four years of writing up new restaurants) Peter began to compose:

If you thought the ambiance at Grandma's discount rest home was nice when you visited her last Christmas, you'll feel right at home at Pierogy Tea Café. Each cracked vinyl chair has a story to tell, every peeling linoleum tile, a lifetime of experiences to relate to any crime scene investigator who cares to amble by and spray a little luminol on it.

The waiter is that same thick, ugly man last spotted on the 11 o'clock news wearing a nurse's uniform and being arraigned for elder abuse. The flickering florescent lights give his ruddy skin a greenish cast. His mouth opens and his lips form the words, "we're not open yet."

Peter blinked. He'd expected this guy to have a Russian accent. He sounded like he was from California.

"The sign says you're open," Peter said. Nick stayed within arm's reach of him and also of the door. He looked like he was contemplating throwing Peter over his shoulder and taking off. He could probably do it too, Peter thought. His shoulders were huge.

"The sign is wrong," the employee whom Peter had assigned the term "waiter" to on account of the fact that he was carrying a damp, soiled bar towel lumbered toward them. At the back of the dining room, down a narrow hallway, Peter thought he saw motion, a young woman gazed out from behind a red, beaded curtain.

"We'll come back later." Nick had his hand on the doorknob. "Do you have a take-out menu?"

"A what?" The waiter screwed up his lip.

"I'm Peter Fontaine. I'm a writer for *the Hamster* and we're doing a special piece on inexpensive dining options and someone recommended your place, so I was hoping we could at least get a take-out menu." Peter took a card from his wallet and handed it to the waiter. Then came another rustle, a clattering of beads and the waiter whipped around with a suspicious glare.

"Look you can't stay in here. We're closed. Come back tomorrow and we'll get you some pierogy's okay? We have a plumbing problem today." The waiter (or whatever his job was) muscled them back toward the door and out onto the hot sidewalk.

Peter glared at the now locked Tea Café door, disappointed.

Nick seemed relieved. He stuck his hands in his pockets and said, "I've still got that rockfish in my fridge. Want some?"

After wedging his bike into the back of Nick's silver Audi A6 Allroad, Peter settled into the leather passenger seat.

Nick smiled and with the push of a button opened the moon roof. Or was it a sunroof? The roof opened up, anyway letting the evening in.

Chuckanut Drive hugged the coastline, curving through towering cedars. Water on one side, cliff faces on the other. The sun was just setting behind the islands igniting the sky and the bay in electric shades of cantaloupe and punk girl pink. The smell of sea spray and pine hung in the air.

"What color of paint would you use to make that sky?" Peter asked above the roar sound of the wind.

"What part?"

"Any part."

"Cadmium red medium, naples yellow and just a touch of ultramarine violet. Or maybe dioxazine purple." Nick turned and gave him a quick smile. Inside his fancy new car and wearing designer sunglasses, Nick could have been mistaken for a movie star. Peter felt himself becoming mesmerized by the glamour of Art with a capital A. He wondered if he could enter Nick's world as a "sometimes model." He had a nice enough body, in a thin dark way. Did abstract expressionists even use models? Focused as Peter was on the lure of the naked body, Nick surprised him by saying, "How would you describe the sky for *the Hamster*?"

Truly? Did Nick just ask him about his mind? Peter thought he might faint, but rallied.

"I'd say something like: *the summer sunset in the Pacific Northwest is the best, cheapest spectacle you can find in the month of August. All along the edge of the water parked cars line the road. Some folks sit inside, listening to the radio but most get out and stand facing the amazing warm light finally knowing why they moved here in the first place.*

"And then probably I'd give a list of best places to go to watch the sunset. Most likely it would wind up being a plug for the Boulevard Park Summer Concert series."

Nick nodded, signaled right and slowed way down.

"I'm pretty certain that my patio could give Boulevard Park a run for its money," Nick remarked. He turned onto a private road.

So now that Nick had chosen to brag "Walter's house" had become "my patio." Peter just went with it.

"Does your patio have a hippie jam band and shave ice stand?"

"No, but it does have a wet bar."

Peter held up his hands in surrender. "You've already won."

Nick steered up the steep narrow road and pulled up to the beige and gray concrete façade of The Castle. For such an enormous house, The Castle was fairly well hidden by surrounding cedars. Only from the water could its majesty be appreciated. The interior was just as Peter had seen it in *Architectural Digest*. Open and airy with slabs of rock and wooden beams, designer furniture and large abstract paintings. Some De Kamps, but many Peter didn't recognize.

This room, thought Peter, is so large that my desk would look proportionate. He then pushed that thought from his mind. He had just been invited back to Nick's house for a sunset drink and already he was imagining how his furniture would look in Nick's house. What was he? A lesbian?

"What are you smirking at?" Nick asked.

"Nothing," Peter said. "I'm just making a pact with myself to never bring you back home to my place."

"I've been to your place, actually," Nick said. "I gave Evangeline a ride home a couple of months ago and she had me in for tea."

"You drink tea?"

"Not usually, but I thought she wanted to talk to me about a problem she'd been having with Tommy so I came in. You have a very nice desk."

Peter felt himself reddening.

"It's an heirloom," he said, feeling the need to defend his desk from what was probably an imaginary attack.

"It's more than that. I'm pretty sure it's a partners desk. Probably Georgian. Two men would have both used it sitting across from one another. Does it have drawers on both sides?"

Peter nodded. "You make being a Georgian pencil pusher sound so romantic."

"I think it was just thought of as practical at the time, but it could have been romantic, I suppose. Can I get you that drink now?"

Peter accepted Nick's offer and followed the other man out onto a wide concrete patio. A hundred feet straight down, saltwater slapped against sandstone. Below he could see the last few sailboats heading back for the evening. In front of him, the purple silhouettes of the San Jan Islands stood in contrast to the brilliant orange and pink clouds. Nick built two vodka martinis in glasses that were themselves works of art and the two of them stood, sipping their drinks and admiring the fading light.

"It's so gorgeous here; why do you need a studio?" Peter asked.

"I like the companionship," Nick said.

"Everyone says you always keep your door closed."

"But I know that I can open it, anytime I want and someone will be there," Nick said. "Is that selfish?"

"A little, but I read an interview with Vine where she said the same thing." Peter swirled his martini. "I guess it's the same with any creative person. We all want to have connections without responsibilities. We want grist for the mill without obligations that would interfere with the optimal production."

Nick regarded him, head turned slightly on the side. His hair reflected the firey sky. "You're quite a straight-shooter, aren't you?"

"It's a valuable trait in journalism," Peter said. "Like nosiness."

Nick offered another martini and they drifted inside to see what could be found for dinner. Nick's earlier assessment of his refrigerator's contents was no exaggeration. His refrigerator contained exactly seven items: orange juice, milk, beer, Dijon mustard, hot sauce, a packet of previously frozen rockfish and a take-out container containing remnants of what looked like panang curry. Peter asked for Nick's approval (and street address) and called out for pizza.

They ate on the patio, switched to beer and toasted each other. Peter played his hand close to his chest, keeping his eyes largely to himself… unless Nick was walking away. Then he indulged himself.

On the second beer, Nick suggested Peter might be too drunk to cycle home safely and Peter agreed. Ninety seconds later, he was looking at the bed in the guest room. It was a nice bed, a dark wood platform model sitting atop some kind of fibrous area matt with an intricate woven pattern. The bed was at least queen sized, maybe even king, heaped with beige and cream pillows. A matching plain dresser sat along one wall, it's top slightly dusty. Sheer curtains remained drawn across the south-facing window.

"The bed's pretty comfortable," Nick said. "I've slept here lots of times."

Damn it all, was Nick just playing with him? He was going to have to make the first move or that move would never be made. He took Nick's hand in his and lifted it to his lips. Nick's response was subtle but instantaneous. He stood straighter, leaned just slightly closer, breathed just slightly faster. His attention heightened and narrowed. Just like on the roof of the Bellingham Towers only now the only precipice they stood at the edge of was physical intimacy.

It occurred to him that Nick might be more nervous than him, though how that was possible, he did not know. Nick was gorgeous, tall, out, he had a fantastic house and a rockin' car. What did he have to be afraid of? Whatever held Nick back, Peter decided, wasn't stronger than him. He could break though that line of defense with nothing but a gentle push.

I've got you, Peter thought. Aloud he said, "Want to stay and keep me company?"

"I would."

Chapter 7

Peter took off his shirt. He'd been wanting to anyway, and now he had enough liquor emboldening him that he simply gave in. He knew he would never win the Mr. Universe award, he was simply too thin, but Nick's eyes told him that he appreciated his spare, sinewy body just fine.

Nick held back. Still. And Peter knew everything that happened between them tonight would be because he willed it. That though Nick was bigger, stronger and older than him he was also shy as the quarterhorse Peter's grandmother had kept out on her farm when he was a kid. He'd learned to speak low and coax that big beautiful animal into letting him ride and he realized the very same approach would work just fine with Nick.

The apple and sugar cube had turned into a pizza and beer and Nick wasn't quite big enough to throw him, but the principle was the same. He leaned forward, stretching up slightly to press his lips to Nick's throat and jaw, murmuring compliments as his hands slid down Nick's sides. Nick bent allowing Peter to engage his parted lips.

He slipped his tongue into Nick's hot, soft mouth. Luscious and tasting slightly of malt and hops. Tension still kept Nick's body from meeting his own. His shoulders refused to soften, his arms felt awkward as they surrounded Peter's torso.

Was it possible that Nick hadn't had another man since De Kamp's death? No, Peter refused to believe that. But Peter could believe that he was the first who'd gotten to come home. That's why they weren't in the master room, which he'd shared with his old lover. Inspiration made Peter draw Nick toward the bed, pull back the blankets, like they were already long-time lovers without the need for fiery against the wall sex.

Nick relaxed, allowed himself to be pushed back on the bed, allowed Peter to remove his shirt, revealing the hard, lightly-furred torso he'd already seen but longed to touch. He straddled Nick, running his hands over the heavy curve of Nick's shoulders.

"What is this?" He ran his fingers over the tattoo.

"The insignia for my battalion."

"You were in the army?"

"I was a cryptologic linguist," Nick said. "I read a lot of Soviet newspapers."

"Brainy and brawny." Peter kept his voice quiet, kept himself from grinding his crotch against Nick's abdomen. If he allowed him self that kind of free reign too soon he'd never coax this big beauty into his arms again.

He wondered how long Nick had been a closet case. Had De Camp been his first lover? He shunted thoughts of De Camp aside. It was just the two of them here, now. No dead ex lovers welcome. He returned to lavishing attention on Nick's shoulders. "You have amazing delts."

"Yeah?" Nick smiled, finally sliding his hands up Peter's chest. His expression turned slightly wicked. "How would you describe them?"

Peter's eyes narrowed.

"I don't think I'd ever be required to describe your naked body for *the Hamster*, but if I was writing for a different magazine I guess I'd say something like: Nick's shoulders were exactly the sort of muscles I like to lay my head down on—"

"How sweet."

"After I've ridden his hot, hard cock until he bucked like a wild stallion."

For a moment, Peter thought he miscalculated, then Nick's pupil's widened. He pulled in a sharp breath and pulled Peter down into a dark, sweet kiss.

Clothes of any kind were no longer necessary or welcome and soon they lay in heaps on the floor, banished. No longer held prisoner inside the pants, Peter's aching cock finally made friends with Nick's thick beast. They rubbed against each other while Peter did his best to convince Nick he was the best deep kisser in the world.

When at last they broke for air a sheen of sweat slicked Peter's chest his groin felt tight. He needed his wallet. He needed his wallet now.

Nick made a noise of protest as he moved away but seemed to recognize Peter's motive, rustling through his wallet for a condom and a pillow pack of lube He resettled himself across Nick's thighs, smiled a little and rolled the condom down Nick's shaft while Nick watched, avid and intent. When Peter started to move forward, Nick took the lube from his hand and moved down, guiding Peter up higher so that he could easily slide his finger into Peter's hole. Peter shuddered as pleasure built. His cock bobbed against Nick's chest and he stiffened his arms to keep from collapsing while pressing back against Nick's fingers.

"How does that feel?" Nick asked.

"Like I'm ready for you." Peter heard himself whimper as Nick's fingers withdrew. The sound only made Nick look hungrier. He guided Nick's cock to his opening and pushed Nick into him or himself back onto Nick. Peter took him in inch by inch until he felt the tight curls of Nick's pubic hair against his ass.

"Is that alright?" Nick's hips moved in tight probably involuntary jerks. Peter nodded and started to slide himself upward. He nearly released Nick's cock, but then pushed down once more, impaling himself on Nick's shaft. At first Nick restrained himself then as Peter moved faster, he broke, holding Peter's hips and bucking up into him. Peter smiled so see Nick's reserve so abandoned then suddenly couldn't think of anything but the orgasm building like supernova. Peter's vision blurred and then he came, moaning as his climax burst onto Nick's chest, sticking in his hair.

A moment later he heard Nick suck in his breath and then he felt Nick's release, hot and pulsing, deep within him. Nick's body went turgid and then, instantly, fell back against the sheets.

And then it was over and he collapsed onto Nick, laying his head down on the shoulder, just as he'd described. A chill rippled across his now damp skin as a cool ocean breeze passed over.

The only sounds were their ragged breath and the clang of a far-off buoy bell.

❦

Breakfast was hangtown fry, which surprised Peter because he'd seen neither eggs nor bacon when last he'd investigated in the fridge. Now both seemed to have appeared along with a dozen oysters. The orange juice he recognized from the previous night.

"I went into town to get some coffee and came back with some extras," Nick explained, as he slid the whole delicious smelling mass out onto a plate.

"How did you know I liked oysters?"

"You mentioned the shellfish farm down the road in your sleep last night," Nick said.

"Did I?"

"You did. You mumbled that we should bike down there and get a couple dozen kumamotos since we were so close."

"And why didn't we?"

"Because it was midnight," Nick said. "Also because you were, much like the shellfish farmers, asleep."

Peter shook his head. "Those shellfish farmers go to bed with the chickens." He looked at the clock seven a.m., when had Nick gotten up? Five? Peter suppressed a shudder. If he hadn't smelled bacon he'd still be in slumberland.

"Do you usually eat this much breakfast?" Peter had a hard time imagining anyone cooking like this and looking like Nick.

"No, usually I just have coffee and toast." Nick offered Tabasco and Peter accepted. "But I felt lavish."

"Lucky me."

Peter tucked into the feast, trying to resist the urge to shovel the food in as fast as he could. Nick ate very slowly without handling anything but his toast. He also kept his elbows off the table. He slid Peter the front section of the paper, keeping only the sudoku for himself. And he engaged that with a minimum of brow furrowing. Peter alternately perused and complained about the articles in the Herald. Only once did he borrow Nick's pen to rewrite a headline he felt lacked umph. When he handed the pen back, Nick smiled as though he'd done something unutterably charming, making Peter blush. The morning and the man both stunned; like separate arguments for domesticity and breakfast rolled up into one gorgeous commercial.

Get gay-married! You'll have a majestic house by the sea and a shy stallion of a breakfast-cooking man of your very own!

Peter wondered if he could possibly still be drunk.

The Bellingham Police Department was holding a press conference on the Shelley Vine affair at ten thirty and so Peter finished his breakfast and regretfully informed Nick that he would have to go back into town. Nick helped him shower, which wasn't a huge timesaver, but did assist Peter in reaching some hard to soap areas.

Nick gave him a ride to the Vitamilk Building and he cycled the remaining six blocks to the police station to listen to a five minute statement wherein the police claimed to be pursuing many lines of inquiry. It was over by 10:45.

He considered going back to the Vitamilk Building and convincing Nick that he needed another shower, but decided that duty called. He had to write something for Doug if he hoped to keep his job and his reputation intact.

When he got home he found a beater Subaru of indeterminate age parked in his driveway. Once inside he heard muffled laughter coming from Evangeline's room. And clicking.

She must have completed a pube-toupee.

Peter got a glass of water, sat at his desk and started to type.

The Bellingham Police Department issued a statement today asking for anyone who was in the vicinity of the Vitamilk Building on Tuesday, August 15th who might have any information related to the brutal slaying of Western Washington University professor Shelley Vine to please come forward.

Peter stared at the paragraph. 45 words. Doug would not be pleased with that. Not at all. He copied it into an email and hit send anyway.

He needed to submit some kind of article, preferably before five so the typesetter wouldn't hate him. He pulled out the photocopies he'd made at the library and leafed through them, trying to find any interesting bit of information that might satisfy Doug without betraying Nick. But viewing this stuff through the lens of Nick's disapproval, he couldn't find a single sentence that didn't seem exploitative. He dropped the papers and rubbed his eyes. One night with a guy and already he'd lost his journalistic edge—assuming he'd ever had an edge. Maybe he was in the wrong field.

No—that was just defeatist thinking. Even if he, for completely understandable reasons, had been confused by Nick he still had the guts to be an investigative journalist. So, what did he have? He had a murder and five men who admitted to being in the building, any one of whom could have committed it. Six if he counted Dmitri. He knew he didn't do it and Nick had no motive. He wasn't Shelley's lover, nor did he need her money and he had an artistic career of his own. John also had no motive. That left Greg, the lover and Tommy the man who for some reason had heard Shelley screaming but failed to emerge from his studio to help.

The man currently taking pictures of his best friend's vagina.

A car, probably the world's most ancient Pacer, drove up behind the ratty Subaru. A woman emerged: thin, long, tiered skirt. Long blonde hair. She got out, slammed the door and went to open the hatchback. This took a couple of tries and Peter heard her swear as she wrenched the elderly rear door up. She pulled a laundry basket out of the back of her car and dumped the contents on the lawn. She then returned for another load of clothes, as well as what looked like some CD's and books.

Peter was almost certain he could guess the identity of this lady.

He went and knocked on Evangeline's door. First came silence, then shuffling and Peter had a flashback to his first furtive high school relationship. He and his boyfriend would try to make out, only to be interrupted by his suspicious Mom, who'd knock on the door causing them to spring apart, silent, hearts pounding. Only this time he played the part of Mom.

"Tommy, I think your wife's throwing your stuff on our lawn."

Silence. Some rustling. Then Evangeline's face appeared through a crack in the door. She wore what looked like a hastily applied sheet.

"Is she still out there?"

"I don't know."

"Can you go check?"

Peter dutifully walked back to the living room to observe the progress of Tommy's soon to be ex-wife. A guy walking by on the sidewalk stopped to watch. He held a six-pack of Ranier minus two in one hand and an open beer in the other.

"She's still there," Peter called.

"What's she doing?" Tommy's voice this time.

"She's throwing your electric guitar on top of the pile... And now she's going back to the car for something... Ah, lighter fluid... And that's getting squirted on the pile... And now the whole thing's on fire and the guy on the sidewalk is cheering." Peter glanced over his shoulder. Evangeline's door was closed again. "And now she's driving away. I'm just going to go put that out."

He had just finished emptying their fire extinguisher onto the blaze when Tommy and Evangeline emerged from the house, clothed. Evangeline's face was blotchy and red.

Tommy stood, hands deep in the pockets of his loose, striped, drawstring pants (probably from Ecuador) and frowned.

"I guess I'm going to be staying down at the studio for a while," he said. He didn't seem too broken up about it, just resigned. He stared at the smoldering pile as though it was a sad accident that had occurred to somebody else.

"Speaking of staying at the studio," Peter said before Evangeline could offer use of their house, "there was something I wanted to ask you about the night Shelley Vine died."

"Shoot." Tommy pulled a small glass pipe out of his pocket and started loading the bowl.

"If you heard her screaming why didn't you come out of your studio until I broke in the door?"

"I opened up my door because I heard Nick yelling then the glass breaking." Tommy produced a lighter and took a long toke.

"But not for the screaming?"

"I knew she was in there with that Greg kid so I expected screaming," Tommy remarked mildly.

"Shelley was a screamer." Evangeline sniffed. "That's one of the reasons she always brought her studio assistants back to the Vitamilk Building instead of her apartment. I guess she got the police called on her at a motel once. I'm going to miss her stories of conquest." Evangeline let out a sad little laugh and wiped her eyes, Tommy put his arm around her shoulders.

"So what you're saying is that because you thought Shelley was having sex you didn't come out when you heard her screaming?" Peter wanted to be absolutely sure about this.

"That's right," Tommy said. "I didn't want to spoil her party."

"Just out of curiosity, have you ever done any printmaking?"

"Only one class in college. I took a woodblock class. You can see one of the blocks right there." Tommy pointed down at the pile.

"Where?"

"Right here." Tommy grabbed a stick and nudged a pair of singed Evergreen University sweats aside to reveal a partially burnt rectangle of wood. Evangeline rushed into the house, returning with a set of oven mitts. She pulled the three woodblocks out of the fire as well as a half-burnt sketchbook.

"Just leave it, Evie," Tommy said.

Evie? Just how long had they been sleeping together? And how had he not noticed until now?

"It's your art," Evangeline said simply. "You're going to want it again someday."

"Not those," Tommy pointed at the woodblocks, "it's a picture of her. That's why she set it on fire."

"All three of them?" Peter asked.

"It was a three-color print."

Peter picked up the block, looking down at the negative image of a woman carved into the wood. It would have taken weeks to carve the tiny details. Then to replicate the image two other times to get the other colors. It could represent six months of a person's life, easily. Or, if you were Tommy's wife, several years. He let Evangeline take the block from his hands.

"You want to know who I think killed Shelley? I think it was Greg." Tommy produced the pipe and lighter again.

"Why's that?"

Tommy blew out a long plume of pungent smoke and replied, "Isn't it always lovers who murder each other?"

Chapter 8

The management of *the Hamster* didn't gaze kindly upon reporters who turned in only 45 words. Doug phoned him to say as much, but Peter had wisely decided to screen his calls and thus was spared the necessity of formulating an instant excuse for his tardiness.

Evangeline and Tommy had cleaned up the charred and powder-covered remnants of the bonfire and had decided to go out to dinner. Much as he liked his roommate, he was glad to see them go. He needed some silence and some space to get some work done.

He'd started working on the piece shortly after putting out the bonfire and had become instantly absorbed.

For some, Shelley Vine's death might be the first time they've heard of the Vitamilk Building or the artists who work there. Others might have gone through the building on a Gallery Walk, eaten a couple of crackers and gone home feeling happy to have touched base with the local art scene but simply gazing at finished art is not the same as watching artists at work. That's what I've been doing for the last week.

I started hanging around the studio space with the idea that I could make sense of the experience I had one week ago—the experience of watching a woman who I did not know—die in a man's arms. Since then I've come to know—

Come to know what? How hot Nick's skin felt? How much he wanted Nick? He could simply imagine it:

Since then I've come to know that I want to suck Nick Olson's cock. I want to slide my tongue over the head of it, teasing. I want to hear him moan with pleasure as I pull it to the back of my throat. I want to nuzzle my face into the base of his shaft, feeling his stomach tighten. I want to watch him come just like I did last night... and again this morning. Is that so wrong? So greedy to want more of what I've already had?

More than that I want to fuck Nick—to make him want me...

And now the blood went rushing down to his cock. He had to stop thinking of fucking. It did his writing no good. But images collided hot and close in his mind and he found himself simply sitting, staring, imagining. His stiff cock poked up inside his loose pants as if independently seeking the way out. It would never be able to undo the drawstring by itself, so he felt relatively safe from total shame should Evangeline suddenly arrive home. But it definitely had to be dealt with.

Shaking himself from his reverie he had two options: a trip to the bedroom visit his old boyfriend, Roddy Palmer or booty-calling Nick.

He chose the booty call.

Nick arrived minutes later, flushed and seemingly just as ready as he was. Peter opened the door and Nick kissed him right there on the porch in front of God and everyone, including the three children playing across the street and the ever-present Rainier guy, who hooted from his own front porch three doors down.

"I'm glad you called," Nick said. "I've been thinking about you."

"What have you been thinking?"

"It's more a series of images than anything else," Nick said, smiling. "Can I come in?"

Peter stepped aside and allowed Nick to cross the threshold. He glanced at Evangeline's side of the room and shook his head then glanced to Peter's sparsely furnished side.

"Your desk might be huge but it doesn't take up as much space as a million thimbles," he said. Then, seeing the tenting front of Peter's pants, Nick smiled, glanced around.

"There's nobody here," Peter said. He unbuttoned the top button of Nick's shirt, placing a kiss on each collarbone. Nick smelled faintly of cologne that Peter was sure cost more than his bicycle had. (He'd seen the bottle then Googled the price.)

"Why don't you try out my chair?" Placing just his fingertips on Nick's chest he pushed him back into his office chair. He finished unbuttoning Nick's shirt, ending on his knees. He unbuckled Nick's belt and kissed the skin hidden beneath. Less cologne here—just the smell of Nick.

"What if your roommate comes home?" Nick's voice was husky.

Peter smiled wickedly, shrugged and pulled Nick's jeans open.

To have a fantasy of this very act then to actually realize it right here in the living room nearly brought Peter off right there. He eyed the waistband of Nick's boxers like Genghis Khan must have eyed the walls of Yanjing and breeched them just as quickly.

Nick watched him intently with hungry eyes. A flush colored his cheeks. He ran his fingers through Peter's hair tentatively, as if almost nervous about urging Peter forward.

Peter took the initiative for him. He pulled Nick's cock into his mouth, tightening his lips against the hard shaft. The feel of Nick's cock actually made his mouth tingle.

He sucked hard reveling in the intensity of the sensation. His mouth watered. His hand went to his own crotch, his prick twitching in his hand.

The sound of a car driving down the quiet street and coming to park close by increased his urgency. Nick's hands twined in his hair now.

"You like it dirty don't you?" Nick murmured. "You want to get caught."

Peter didn't answer, only blushed, swiping his tongue over the head of Nick's cock.

From outside: voices on the sidewalk outside. Evangeline? Jehova's Witnesses? Anyone coming to the door and looking through the tall, narrow window would see him like this, on his knees, between Nick's spread legs, mouth full of Nick's cock.

One more stroke and he came, shuddering, covering his hand in sticky warmth. The voices faded and he made getting Nick off his sole mission. He placed one hand on Nick's shaft, the other gently squeezed his balls. Nick's stomach tightened. Peter withdrew slightly working Nick and watching. Nick's semen spurted on the skin of his cheek and throat.

Nick leaned back, chest heaving goofy grin on his face that Peter found himself mirroring. Suddenly Nick leaned forward drew him up into a forceful, grateful kiss.

"You are a bad man," Nick said.

"Not at all. I'm a small town reporter," Peter countered.

"Yeah, you're a real Brenda Starr. I get the very strong impression that if I keep dating you, I will end up in the Mile High Club."

Peter laughed. "That has always been a goal of mine."

"How did I guess?" Nick leaned back in the chair again, let out a satisfied sigh and then by sheerest chance, glanced over at Peter's desktop. Then he frowned.

"Why do you have a picture of Walter on your desk?"

Damn it! How fucking stupid was he to leave that out, knowing Nick would be here. Peter pulled back and stood, sweaty. He brushed his hair back and his hand came away sticky with Nick's cum.

"I was researching the Bellingham art scene," Peter said. Nick pulled away from him, muscles tense and breathing hard. All sensuality fled him. He yanked his pants up and his belt closed.

"You were researching me," Nick stated flatly.

"I was—"

"I asked you not to." Nick grabbed the papers and leafed through them. "These are all about me."

"I wasn't going to write—"

"Bullshit!" Nick threw the papers at him, passion changing to anger so quickly, using the same endorphins to reach raging inferno levels. "You two-faced little bitch."

"Bitch? Did you just call me a BITCH?" All desire to explain himself fled. "Get the fuck out of my house!"

"Gladly." Nick yanked open the door, turned and said, "if you print even one word about me you'll be hearing from my lawyer."

"Unless you want to hock your fancy car, you don't have enough money to pay a lawyer," Peter spat. "So don't make empty threats."

Nick took a step toward him and for a moment, Peter thought the other man would slap his teeth right down his throat. Instead, he turned and slammed the door with window-rattling force.

Peter stood, fists clenched, eyes closed, listening to the Audi's nearly silent, supercharged V6 spark-ignition engine drive away. What the hell had just happened? Nick had shown his true colors, that's what had happened.

Peter slumped into the chair and laid his head on the desk. The long evening light turned quickly to darkness and he no longer heard to the children playing outside. Even Ranier guy had probably gone in. A light scratching came at the door. Tripod, probably.

Puffing, trying not to shed the angry tears welling up in his eyes he went to open the door.

Tripod galloped in with one ear bloody and reeking of skunk. The cat yowled and glared at Peter as though it was his fault.

Peter pressed his palms to his face and let out a rough little laugh. What a shitty, shitty night this had turned out to be.

Chapter 9

A restless night did nothing to help Peter's mood. Cleaning up Tripod had taken his mind off Nick for a while, but the rest of the night had been spent in a tumultuous half-sleep where he woke hourly from dreams of a better comeback.

At three he gave up and decided to do something useful. He dressed in the straightest clothes he could find (some old Carharts he still had from the summer he'd spent framing houses) and decided to make another attempt to summit of the Pierogy Tea Café.

Whatever secrets that place held, he felt pretty sure they were on the second floor. The question was: how to get there? Surely, if the place truly was a brothel, he should be able to simply buy a girl and get in. What would he do with her then? Interview? Probably not. But he could get some information. He was sure of it.

Fired with determination, he jumped on his bike and rode down. Downtown was quiet at three, as most of the rowdier drunks had found their way to taxis or the back seats of friend's cars by then. The neon sign if Pierogy Tea Café still blinked open, though, as if did all night every night.

Peter slowed as he approached. He'd almost put his foot down when from a door flung outward from an SUV parked half-on half-off the sidewalk. He slammed into the door, his bike and himself falling sideways. Pain exploded from his shoulder as he hit the concrete. Lying on the ground, he looked up into the hard face of Dmitri.

"I'm sorry. I have done this not on purpose." Dmitri shugged in the exaggerated manner of a circus clown. "Are you hurt?"

"I'm fine." Peter tried to stand up but Dmitri shoved him back down. Over Dmitri's shoulder, he saw Luna rush into the Vitamilk Building. Fucking coward. Artists were cowards.

"No, you should sit for a while, let me look at your bicycle." Dmitri reached into the cab of his car and pulled out a toolbox and opened it up. Inside among the pile of ratchets lay a number of tools Peter could not identify. Many of them were sharp or pointy. Some even seemed to be caked with rust... or was that dried blood?

"I don't think there's anything wrong with my bicycle." Peter tried to get up and Dmitri shoved him back down again, with greater force that painfully jarred his shoulder.

"A reporter like you needs transportation." He hefted a wrench. "Jerry tells me that you gave him your card."

"Yes we're doing restaurant reviews," Peter watched the wrench. No other soul walked the darkened street. He thought of calling for help, but the only person he knew was close had already fled.

"I hope we get a nice review." Dmitri brought his wrench down hard on the bicycle's rear derailer, slamming the entire housing into the gears. Peter thought the frame might be bent. Neither he nor anyone else would ride that bike again.

"I'm sure you will." Peter smiled as hard as he could.

Dmitri brought the wrench down again in a massive clang that resonated through Peter's already swimmy brain, he pressed his eyes closed.

"I think that bike is fixed now." Undisguised mirth Dmitri's at smashing Peter's bike filled his voice. Then a long string of what sounded like swearing. In Russian.

He opened his eyes to see Nick grappling with Dmitri. Nick twisted Dmitri's wrist and the wrench fell to the sidewalk with a clang. At the same time Luna's face close to his, "come on!" She grabbed his arm urging him up.

Irrationally, he grabbed his bike, dragging it with him to the Vitamilk steps while Nick and Dmitri pounded each other. Nick swept Dmitri's legs out from under him and they both went down together, clawing and grunting. Dmitri spewing what must be epithets because they infuriated Nick who pounded Dmitri's head agianst the cement.

Luna left his side to pry Nick off Dmitri.

Nick stood, allowing the other man to scramble away to his SUV. He threw his toolbox into the seat, turned and jabbed a finger at Nick.

"You are dead, you filthy fucking faggot," he hissed.

Nick took a step forward and Dmitri retreated into the driver's seat, fired up the engine and roared off into the night. Nick watched him go before walking up the stairs to him. He crouched down and peering into Peter's eyes.

"Are you okay?" Nick asked. "Did he hit you?"

"Only with his car," Peter said. It felt good to have Nick leaning over him, to see the concern in his face. "I'm fine."

Nick nodded. He drew himself up and glared archy down at Peter.

"See?" said Nick "I'm not the only person who doesn't like reporters writing stories about them."

Peter drew breath for an earth shattering comeback but before could answer Nick had gone back inside. Coming up alongside, Luna let out a low whistle and said, "I had no idea he could be that much of a prick."

"You must not know him well."

"I guess not," Luna cocked her head giving him the once-over. "Come on, I think you should go to the doctor about that shoulder."

At nine in the morning, Peter entered the office of *the Hamster* with a sling, a split lip and nothing else. Doug's face screwed up in pain. "Tell me you fell off your bike."

"I fell off my bike."

"Good."

"After a Russian gangster deliberately doored me." Peter threw himself down in the chair opposite him.

75

"Did you fall into a dead skunk?"

"No, I smell like that because of Evangeline's cat."

"You are not supposed to be going after Russian gangsters. You are supposed to be writing me an article about how our art community came together after Shelley Vine's tragic death. Or at least an expose on Nick Olson. What have you turned in? Forty-five goddamned words that I strongly suspect you copied directly from the police handout. Did you even go to the police press conference?"

"Yes, I went to the police conference," Peter said. "The forty-five words are mostly not copied, but it's pretty hard to put my own special panache on a police statement."

"Well it's a good thing that you didn't manage to get the piece on Olson in anyway. I've just been contacted by Leonhardt & Liu, attorneys at law, regarding your story about Mr. Olson."

"I didn't write a story," Peter said glumly.

"And they're very adamant that it stays that way," Doug said.

"Looks like the Russians were a better bet after all," Peter remarked. "Oh, wait, except for the dooring."

"How did that happen, exactly?"

Doug rolled a cigarette while Peter told the story. At the end, he licked the gummed strip on his rolling paper and asked, "This Nick who saved your ass, is that the same Nick Olson who sicked Leonhardt & Liu us?"

"Yes."

"Why would he do that?"

Peter considered taking the gentleman's path—saying that Nick simply had a very strong sense of fair play. But it was Doug he was talking to. His editor.

"He fought Dmitri because I slept with him," he said.

"Dmitri?"

"No, you jerk, Nick." Peter sighed. "I slept with Nick."

Doug's facial expression did not change for an entire second, then the grinned like an old man at the beach and said, "see, I told you."

"Told me what?" Peter slumped more heavily on his good arm.

"In a town like Bellingham, it always matters who's fucking whom." Doug pushed open the window and lit up, as was his custom. After a couple of puffs he continued, "Have you seen that there's going to be a benefit?"

Peter pressed closed his eyes. He hoped it wasn't for the hospital or Boys & Girls Club. He could not handle going from mafia and murder to charity bingo in twenty-four hours.

"Is it for the Bellingham chapter of Amnesty International?"

"No, it's for some kind of fruity organization that feels it can heal the world through modern dance. They're collecting money for it at the Vitamilk Building during Friday's art walk. Apparently it was Shelley Vine's favorite charity." Doug paused to drag on his cigarette. "In order to help the public experience their experience of Shelley Vine's death, they're going to have her studio open as an exhibit. They've hired security."

"They're charging admission to a crime scene?"

"Not exactly. They're taking donations to peer through the police tape at a crime scene. Vine's sister has apparently signed off on it. She said that she thought Shelley would be happy that people could have this one last unique experience because of her."

"Does the sister inherit the artistic estate?"

"How did you guess? The place is going to be swarming with reporters. I've heard that some guys are coming from New York to check out the scene."

"Leonhardt & Liu is going to be busy," Peter said ruefully. "Why are you telling me this?"

"Because you're going to be there covering it for the good ol' *Hamster*," Doug said. "Just don't write about Olson. I can't take the lawsuit."

Chapter 10

The Vitamilk Building buzzed with activity. Gallery Walks were always popular but Vine's murder had cast a dark glamour on the building so citizens not normally inclined toward art packed the narrow halls and staircase hoping for a chance to see the scene of the crime without seeming like gawkers.

Peter shouldered his way up the wide staircase, through a thick clot of soccer jocks who smelled of vodka. Well, he would have shouldered his way up if his shoulder had not been tender and still in a sling. As it was, he wove through the crowd, protecting his arm, but not letting it get in the way of quick progress.

The Spinnin' Wimmin seemed to be having their best night ever. Two skeins of hand-spun yarn protruded from the tiny, Louis Vitton handbag of the woman directly in front of Peter. And another bunch of multicolored strands protruded from the jacket pocket of a middle-aged man wearing a pink polo shirt. For some reason he doubted that either of these individuals knitted or even crocheted, but he supposed that at least they'd had the good grace to pay a price for admission to the scene of the crime.

At the top of the stairs the resident artists had set up a card table that held a framed photograph of Vine and a gallon jar asking for donations for Vine's favorite charity, the Prism Foundation. Pamphlets were also provided. They detailed Prism's theory that the world could be healed through art and dance and similar expressions of individual spirit. Peter tried not to roll his eyes, since he thought it would be tacky to be disrespectful to the flaky ideas of dead. He wondered if the guys down at the Pierogy Tea Café had that same idea only they were healing the world through lap dance one customer at a time. Still he dug in his pocket for some change and plunked it into the jar, already half-full of other people's impromptu guilt donations. He folded the pamphlet into his pocket.

He wondered how the Russians were doing. It couldn't have been good for business to have the block swarming with cops during the days following the crime. But he also thought demand for the oldest profession couldn't have been completely quashed by their presence. Maybe the Tea Café's usual clientele just started ordering "take out" instead.

The window of John's studio offered a great view of the back of the Tea Café. He should go take a look.

As Peter threaded his way though the crowd toward John's smaller, more cramped room, he crossed in front of Nick's open studio door. He told himself that he would not look inside. Eyes front. No sidelong glance. Not even a blink in Nick's direction. He did not want to even see Nick's face after what he'd said, but as he passed by his eyes turned toward Nick anyway as if of their own volition.

His eyes apparently not only wanted to see Nick they wanted to linger on him, staring.

He wore gray slacks and a blue wool sweater. Probably both from the consignment store, but they looked like they'd been made for him. His rings and watch glinted in the bright studio lights. He'd recently shaved and gelled his hair. Peter was too far away to tell but he suspected that Nick was probably wearing that cologne that he liked so much as well, damn him.

And damn him for choosing that moment to survey the studio and see Peter lingering in the doorway. Caught, Peter found he couldn't move. They observed each other as people walked between them, jostling past Peter to get inside. They faded in significance seeming almost to be nothing but blurred shapes of people moving around Nick while Nick's pale eyes watched him, seeming for a moment to forgive him.

If he holds out his hand to me, Peter thought, I'll go to him. I'll tell him I didn't mean what I said. I'll swallow my pride and tell him he was right.

But Nick's expression turned hard and he moved deliberately away from Peter to address the man at his left.

Peter's surroundings abruptly came back, the loud laughter and hushed whispers and most of all the sycophantic praise of the fashion-conscious undergrad dominating Nick's attention. Peter walked on down the hall. Nick was just a man. He'd had plenty of them and he could get plenty more. His cold shoulder didn't matter. The story mattered.

John also had his studio open but few people wandered inside. Even John appeared to have stepped out, leaving behind two lines of display easels and barely any room to walk around them. This was not because John was a bad artist. He wasn't. But he was a worse pack rat than Evangeline. Floor to ceiling shelves lined all the walls of his studio and each of these shelves was packed with items: paper scraps, paintbrushes, broken canvases tiny sample tubes of paint. Then there were jars of acid and caustic lime and row after row of tools that made Nick's collection of brushes and palate knives seem minimalist. There was also the faint smell of skunk. Peter knew it wasn't him and followed his nose to a set of paint-spattered Converse in the corner.

Maybe Dmitri had been right to take out a few skunks. They seemed to have gone on the warpath in the last week, spraying everything that dared move at night.

Everything was neat but the sheer multitude of tiny items gave a feeling of orderly claustrophobia. John's studio was in the corner and had two windows. One facing the bay and the other the alley of Pierogy Tea Café. Dusky orange sunset light poured through the studio imbuing the whole room with a magical, children's-movie feeling, like all those little items on the shelves were going to suddenly grow arms and legs and faces and start singing and then break into a big dance number that taught him about color theory or composition.

He wondered if living with Evangeline was having too great an effect on his imagination.

Since John had vacated the premesis, Peter went immediately to the window overlooking the alley. As before, he had a clear view of not only the back of Pierogy Tea House but he could see, through a narrow window, the upstairs hallway with it's four unmistakably hotel-like doors and tacky, flocked wallpaper.

No activity in there.

Peter was about to turn away when he caught sight of a motion down in the alley. The slanting orange light made it hard to see them, but Dmitri was down there talking to a man who looked a lot like John.

In fact, he looked exactly like John.

And it looked exactly like John was handing the Russian a wad of money. The Russian shook his head. John shrugged helplessly. The Russian smacked him in the side of the head and John cowered.

What. The. Hell?

John's pantomine clearly conveyed that he was pleading with the Russian and after a few more seconds, Dmitri relented, shoving him aside. John headed toward the back entrance of the Vitamilk Building.

From directly behind him, a woman's voice in his ear.

"Why are you always checking out garbage cans?" The words floated toward him with the scent of bubblegum and patchouli. Evangeline.

Turning, he saw his roommate in yet another completely new outfit. This one seemed to be Bo Peep meets Bob Marley. Long yellow and green ribbons were woven into her braids. Her skirt belled out around her like it was stolen from the wardrobe department of The Scarlet Pimpernel and seemed to be made entirely of surplus Jamaican flags.

"I'm checking out the alley," Peter said.

"Anything interesting?"

"Maybe."

"Nick's here," she remarked.

"Isn't he always?" Peter asked sourly.

"No, he doesn't usually open his studio for Gallery Walks. He doesn't like to talk to people about his art," Evangeline said. "It's weird that he would do it now when he knew there would be so many people."

"Maybe he thought it would make him seem less guilty if he acted like a normal person."

Peter kept an eye on the door, waiting for John, wondering how he was going to eject Evangeline when John arrived.

Evangeline scanned the shelves as if taking a mental inventory of things she might want to collect.

"First of all, Nick's not even a suspect and second, how can you be such a cynic? He's obviously here because he thought you'd be here." She crouched down to look at a small copper plate leaning against the wall. "He even shaved."

"He's not here for me," Peter said.

"Have you gone into his studio?"

"Is there a huge canvas that's just a painting of me naked with godlike light streaming in all around me?"

"Yeah," she said. "It's seven feet tall. You look hot."

"Really?"

Evangeline rolled her eyes. "No. But you should go in anyway."

"I stopped at the door. He gave me the cold shoulder so I kept on walking."

Evangeline sighed and tossed a beribboned braid over her shoulder. "You're such a baby."

"Hey, I'm not the one giving the cold shoulder. He—" Peter's next sentence died on his lips as John came through the studio door. When he saw Peter by the window, a flash of naked fear crossed his face before being subsumed by a hard and enthusiastic smile. Like Nick he'd cleaned up for the event. He wore his best khakis, a left-leaning T-shirt and Birkenstocks. He'd pulled his silvering hair into a ponytail and even trimmed his beard.

"Hey there, how are you two tonight?"

"I was having a few cramps because of my period but I took this remedy at the co-op that has crampbark and squaw vine in it and so now I feel great," Evangeline said.

Peter winced, but saw that John took it in stride. Of course he did, he was used to artists and their weird inability to edit their interior monologue. Then, a stroke of genius: he could use Evangeline's weapon against her.

"I'm a little sad because I had a fight with Nick," he said. "But I'm hoping Evangeline goes over and tells him how shitty I feel so I don't have to."

"Using me for your dirty work, are you?" she asked archly, but he could see the excitement light in her face. Meddling in his romantic life was an honor she'd always aspired to. She gave a dramatic sigh. "Well, somebody has to help you boys."

She turned and bounced out, looking like a little girl who'd discovered her first bag of weed under the mattress in her big brother's room.

Knowing he didn't have a lot of time, Peter cut to the chase.

"So what was that all about in the alley?" he asked.

"What?"

"You, the Russian and the money. What's it all about, John? Why did you have me out in that alley in the first place?"

John took a quick step back and closed studio door. Peter took his own step back. Though the window was open and big enough to get through easily, but it was a long drop to the pavement below. But the back of the building was covered with ivy. Only a couple of feet away, the fire escape. He could try for it.

If it came to that.

If John came at him. John didn't, though.

Instead his face contorted with remorse and he said, "they're blackmailing me."

"The Russians?"

"Yes, I… used their services a few times when Liz and I were going through some tough times. I was drinking a lot and I wasn't really myself. I stopped going and they started shaking me down. First it was only twenty dollars here and there but then I think he realized that I would pay him what he asked for and started asking for more." John ran his hand along the top of a canvas. "I don't have the guts to go to the police about it because I know they'll find a way to tell Liz and it would break her heart."

"So you tried to get me to expose them?" Peter asked.

"You were talking about how there was no big story to break in Bellingham. I thought we could both benefit." John walked to the window, staring down into the alley. "This whole year has been so hard. Shelley was a good friend of mine."

"I wish you had told me straight out," Peter said.

"I'm sorry."

"How much have you given them?"

"About six thousand dollars now."

"Is there anything else you've neglected to tell me?" Peter felt very tired, but also excited by this new layer of information. Maybe the Russians weren't related to Vine's death, but they weren't completely unrelated to the artist at the Vitamilk either.

"That's everything," John said.

Peter nodded. He did not for a second believe that John had told him everything. John had a twenty-first century artist's marriage. He could not possibly be so afraid of his wife Liz knowing that he'd had a drunken affair that he would let Russian gangsters extort six grand from him. What had he done, then? Or what was it that he liked to do that he wouldn't want anyone to know about? Just how spicy did he like those pierogys?

Suddenly he didn't like being alone in the room with John anymore.

"I should go say something to Nick," he said.

"Are you still going to write your article about the Tea Café?" John asked.

"I doubt that Doug would publish it even if I did." Peter shrugged. "I think you need to speak to your wife and then call the police."

"Fuck." John ran his hands through his hair. "God, I'm tired of being stolen from and pushed around."

Peter wasn't sure of what to say. He'd known John for a few years but just as an acquaintance. He wasn't sure if John was the type to go off the rails or just have a little blow out and then pull himself together. Either way Peter was pretty sure he wanted out of the studio.

John gave him a rueful look. "I shouldn't have gotten you involved. I was just looking for an easy out but you're right. I'm just going to have to deal with what I did and what Dmitri has on me."

A knock at the door startled both John and Peter. John seemed to suddenly remember that his studio was supposed to be open to an awaiting public. He quickly opened his door. Curious art patrons wandered in and Peter slipped out, only to be immediately collared by Nick.

Chapter 11

Nick had a hand around Peter's upper arm, and leaned forward to be heard above the roar of conversation. "We need to talk."

Peter shrugged off Nick's hand. "What about?"

"Can we go someplace quiet?"

Peter nodded and they went back to Nick's studio, which he'd apparently cleared just for this conversation. Peter found almost touching until Nick closed and locked the door behind him. Then he found it slightly creepy. Why did all men suddenly want to lock him in their studios with them?

Nick cast his eyes down and said, "I'm sorry I called you... I'm sorry I swore at you the other day."

"Are you sorry you gloated after I got doored?"

"I wasn't gloating," Nick said. "I was trying to tell you that you should be more careful."

"You were gloating because I got doored because I wasn't careful enough, which made you right." Peter waved it aside.

"I know I over-reacted and I'm sorry, but it's just very important to me to not be dragged down again," Nick seemed to want to apologize without giving Peter permission to write the article, which just came across as awkward. Peter took pity on him. He might have overreacted too. Maybe.

"Look, just because I had information about your life doesn't mean I was going to write about you. I have information about everyone involved in this thing. It's called research. Just because I do the research doesn't mean everything's going in the article. I know how much you all make and where you went to school—" Peter broke off.

Where they went to school...

The pieces fell into place. John and Shelley had gone to college together. They had been lovers way back in the day. And John had been a printmaker. He'd just said it: he was tired of being stolen from and pushed around.

But Dmitri hadn't stolen anything from him, per se.

"Nick, what if the prints Shelley had painted over were John's?" he asked.

The anger in Nick's face turned to confusion.

"Shelley didn't paint over prints she added elements to dry point plates, printed them and painted over that," Nick said.

"So she in effect, defaced the plates," Peter said. "And in doing so took away part of his life."

He wondered if the time John had spent etching those plates had been during their life together. What memories had been corrupted? Was that really enough to kill over?

"You could say that," Nick remained confused, but now curiosity crept into his expression as well. His voice dropped to a whisper. "Are you telling me that John killed Shelley?"

"Do you have any idea what kind of tool might make a triangular puncture like the one we saw in Shelley's throat that night?" Peter found himself whispering as well. "Is there something like that?"

"A three-sided hollow scraper," Nick said immediately. "I already told the police that, and they confiscated ever scraper in this building. None of them have any trace of blood."

"They told you that?"

"No, but if one of them did I think one of us would have been arrested by now."

"Nick, I think I know where that scraper is."

Nick shook his head. "John's studio has already been searched."

"It's in Dmitri's car. In his toolbox."

"So it was Dmitri after all?"

"No, it was John," Peter said. "John killed Shelley because she had defaced his original print plates then used the prints she made in her most recent paintings without telling him."

"But if that's true, why wait all that time to kill her?" Nick finished.

"Shelley was killed the day after the magazine featuring her paintings hit the newsstands. I think that John didn't see the paintings until that night and in a fit of rage he killed her," Peter said. "And as he was fleeing the scene, he dropped the scraper he'd used to kill her in the alley. But he was seen."

"By Dmitri," Nick finished.

"Right. But being the criminally minded guy that he is, he didn't turn the scraper into the police, he used it to blackmail John," Peter said. Briefly he'd explained the scene in the alley only minutes before.

"But you don't know any of this for sure," Nick said. "What if John's telling the truth about Dmitri blackmailing him over seeing a couple of hookers?"

"Skunks," Peter said, simple.

"Come again?"

"John or at least John's converse were recently sprayed by a skunk. On that night, I smelled skunks in the area. I would be willing to bet that those shoes in his studio were the ones he was wearing when he killed her."

"So what now?" Nick asked. "Call the police and tip them off about searching Dmitri's vehicle and questioning the area skunks to see if there's an eyewitness?"

"I think it would be faster if we just got the scraper and turned it in ourselves," Peter said. "I know where I can find a pointy rock."

"Not necessary, I've got a slim jim in my car."

"Why do you have that?" Peter eyed Nick quizzically. Was he supplementing his income by stealing car stereos? He really needed to put his crushes through a better vetting process before he started dating them.

"I used to be a rent-a-cop back in New York," Nick replied. "I find that having one of these things around always comes in handy. That and jumper cables."

"Really?"

"That's how I met Walter. I was in charge of parking lot security at his building," Nick said. "He was always locking his keys in his car and having me get them out."

"I thought you were a model," Peter said.

"I became an artists model after I started seeing Walter, before that I was a security guard. It was an easy job to get right out of the army." Nick glanced out his window. "But you know I don't think we're going to need my military car breaking expertise. I think John may have figured out where that scraper is too." Nick pointed down toward a figure creeping along the side of the building.

"Crap!" Peter took off down the stairs, not waiting to see whether or not Nick followed. If John got to the murder weapon before they did there would be no evidence. He shoved his way through the crowd, wincing every time some bystander jostled against his shoulder.

He made it to the back stairwell, sidestepping Tommy and a couple of other guys smoking themselves out on the landing.

"Where's the fire?" Tommy asked as Peter raced past. Then a moment later, "Oh, hey Nick."

Peter burst out the back door into the alley in time to see John pulling Dmitri's toolbox out of the big black SUV. Shattered glass sparkled on the asphalt.

Strange... He would have thought Dmitri would have had a car alarm. The door fell closed behind him and John's head came sharply up.

"Oh, it's you," John said. Relief spread across his face and his voice dropped to a stage whisper. "I think he may have put my money in here. We need to get out of here before he comes back."

"John—" Nick's voice came from behind him.

"Okay, I know it's not alright to break into a car, but I need this money back."

"We know what's in the toolbox, John," Peter said. "Give it up."

For a moment, John almost denied it, then his shoulders sagged and he held out the toolbox. Peter took it and immediately handed it off to Nick. The thing weighed a ton.

"It was just a moment of rage," he said. "No jury of artists would convict me."

"You killed her because she destroyed one of your printing plates," Peter said. "A human life is worth more than a little sheet of copper."

"No, I killed her because she profited from the destruction of one little sheet of copper." The fire lit in John's eyes again, consuming what remorse had been there. "She traded on our friendship and made a lot of money off it. I made that plate for her. It was a long time ago, but it was still a gift and she destroyed it. She destroyed me."

"If it was a gift, then she had the right to do whatever she wanted with it." Nick spoke this time. "Including destroy it."

"How could you even say that?" Anger and pain surged through John's voice.

Nick shrugged, "a gift is a gift. You shouldn't have given away anything you couldn't stand to lose."

John's expression crumpled.

"I think we'd better call the police," Peter reached into this pocket for his phone.

"Police is not necessary," an accented voice from the shadows coalesced into the shape of Dmitri. And he had his gun. Of course. Peter's hands went automatically into the air. "You will give me back my tools, please."

How could he have ever considered this guy sexy?

"Why are you waving a gun?" Peter asked. "What are you going to do? Shoot all three of us?"

"I have more than three bullets." Dmitri shrugged. "And I'm allowed to shoot at men who are stealing from me."

Peter wondered, abstractly, if that were true. Did Washington State have a Make My Day law? It seemed like he should have taken the trouble to discover this before he started playing in the mobster leagues.

"There are at least two hundred people in the gallery behind us. You'll never get away with shooting three of us," Nick commented. "At best you'll hit one of us."

"Da. I've already made my choice. Get on the ground you fucking faggot and beg me for your filthy life." Dmitri leveled the gun at Nick.

"I don't think so." Nick hurled the toolbox into Dmitri. A gunshot boomed through the air as the toolbox slammed into Dmitri's chest knocking him off balance.

Two more shots cracked the air. Brick exploded next to Peter spattering his side with shattered mortar. Nick lunged onto Dmitri and both of them hit the ground. As they fought two more shot rang out. Then Nick wrenched the gun out of Dmitri's hand and jammed the muzzle in the other man's mouth.

"Don't even blink," Nick growled.

Attracted by the noise, people spilled out the Vitamilk Building's back stairwell into the alley, ringing them. Just standing and watching.

Peter rushed to Nick.

"Are you alright?" he scanned Nick's sweater for blood, but it was so dark he couldn't tell. "Did he hit you?"

"No," Nick kept his eyes on Dmitri, "he's not that good a shot."

"Nick, I think you should take the gun out of his mouth," Peter whispered. "What if it goes off? People are staring."

After a moment's pause wherein he seemed to be considering the validity of Peter's reasoning, Nick complied, sliding the barrel from between Dmitri's lips.

"Don't you even fucking move," he said, then augmented his statement with a string of Russian words that Peter couldn't understand. Nick glanced behind him and said, "where's John?"

Peter spun, saw John retreating through the yielding and passive crowd. He rushed after and tackled John who went down, kicking and struggling. To his left he heard someone say, "I don't get it. Is this supposed to relate to the installation piece upstairs?"

Peter whipped his head toward the speaker and found himself staring at none other than his neighbor, Ranier guy. This time his six pack was four cans gone, but it was the same damn guy.

"This isn't a piece of performance art!" Peter bellowed. "Call the fucking police!"

"They're already on their way." Luna stepped through the crowd, followed by Gunivere and Maxx. She held a skein of red yarn, which she offered to Peter. He wound the thread around John's hands and tied them and still had half a skein left. The blue strobes of the Bellingham Police Department began to flash across the alley and John ceased his struggle.

"Allow me," Luna said. She bent, peered into John's eyes and said, "I'm sorry."

Then, with a pair of scissors shaped like a small crane, she cut the thread.

Epilogue

"This very day last year, the city of Bellingham was rocked by the news that a popular high school teacher had been arrested for murder. It led many to ask, could it happen again? Who are the teachers responsible for educating our children and what secrets might they be keeping? This week begins a six part series focusing on that most important of role models, beginning with perhaps the most influential of all, the football coach."

Peter took his hands from his laptop and rolled his eyes. Sometimes he hated himself for being so good at his job.

The laptop had been a gift to himself. He'd purchased it with his IRE award money (he'd won in the local circulation weekly category for his story, *The Art of Murder*.) He needed a more portable solution to his computing needs now that he was spending a lot of time at The Castle on Wildcat Cove.

He snickered. Just the name sent him into a Hardy Boys-style fantasy where he and Nick solved crimes together Lived and loved together. Engineered the freedom of East European sex slaves together…

On the pretense of searching for further withheld evidence, the police raided Pierogy Tea Café and liberated twelve women between the ages of 16 and 41. Dmitri was originally arrested for obstructing justice, but now the judge just kept tacking on charges. Extortion. Human trafficking. He was being held without bail. Peter expected him to turn State's evidence.

In the aftermath of John's arrest, the artists of the Vitamilk Building went through a period of estrangement. The Spinnin' Wimmin' rented a storefront and started a regular retail business. The three empty studios went unrented for months until finally Nick moved over to Shelley's old space. Then new artists took advantage of the reduced rents. Peter hadn't met them yet, but Evangeline seemed to like them.

Then again, Evangeline liked everybody. And everybody liked her now too. Her pubic toupee show had been the surprise hit of the winter. It sold out entirely and then was ripped off by a big time photographer. At Luna's urging, Evangeline filed suit and used her settlement to buy her own Westfalia and take herself to Florence for half a year.

Tommy had moved in to catsit Tripod and never left. While Peter welcomed the reduction in rent, he sometimes found living with a pothead difficult.

But his room was nice and he spent most of his time here at Nick's anyway. So he contented himself with sitting on the patio of The Castle watching Nick do pushups.

He was up to twenty.

Nick glanced over his shoulder and said, "I was thinking your desk would look pretty good in the living room. It's got the right proportions."

"You think?" Peter opened up his laptop again, focusing on the screen to keep from being caught grinning like an idiot.

"Don't you?" Nick went back to doing pushups, channeling his uncertainty into physical motion.

"I do."

EVERGREEN

Chapter 1

Dying in an avalanche was one fear that had never plagued Peter Fontaine. But glancing up at the walls of snow rising on either side of Nick's Audi, Peter thought that might have been an oversight. Nick's expression remained unconcerned as they wound their way through a narrow canyon of snow. Peter's chest tightened. The snowy walls seemed to be leaning toward him. A chunk of white fell to the wet black ribbon of road. His heart hammered as he envisioned himself being buried beneath the building-sized blocks of snow. Sweat beaded his brow. He glanced at himself in the mirror on the back of the passenger-side visor.

A gray-faced ghoul stared back at him.

From the driver's side, Nick asked, "Are you all right?"

Nick, of course, looked absolutely handsome. Through a vigorous regimen of snowshoeing, he'd retained his summer tan all the way till Christmas and beyond. His brown hair was streaked with straw-colored highlights. He wore a trim beard and mustache. It kept his face warm in the winter, he claimed. His pale blue eyes seemed like they could have been made from winter sky.

"I think I might be feeling a little confined," Peter admitted. "How stable do you think these walls are anyway? Have any DOT snowplows gone missing in the last few weeks?"

Nick gave him a level glance. "We're almost there."

"Seriously, this is like driving down a Manhattan alley," Peter heard himself say, heard the note of hysteria in his voice, and yet was unable to stop himself talking. "Have I mentioned how much I hate Manhattan alleys?"

"Maybe you should try to think of something else."

"Like what?"

"Tell me about the article you're going to write."

"What article?"

"You always write an article for *the Hamster* about every place we ever go." Nick smiled easily, carelessly, as if he had no fear whatsoever that he would be imminently crushed under tons of snow, which was probably the case.

Peter took a deep breath.

"I think it will go something like, *Anyone who stays in Bellingham for very long will become familiar with the number 542. You see it on bumper stickers, T-shirts, and even occasionally on "scenic highway" road signs. Highway 542 goes fifty-five miles east and five thousand feet up from Bellingham Bay to the Mount Baker Ski Area. If you're lucky enough to not be suffocated in a freak highway avalanche, you will reach Artist Point—*"

"We're not going that far," Nick said. "The sno-park is just past Glacier."

"Hooray," Peter weakly rejoined.

"Once we turn off the highway it will be more open. I promise," Nick said. "I didn't realize you were so claustrophobic."

"I don't think it's claustrophobia so much as fear of being buried alive."

"If you want me to take you back to Bellingham, I can do that and still make it back up in time for the festival."

Peter shook his head. "I really want to be there. I can tough it out. I promise."

Nick nodded but seemed worried.

"It's just that I don't ever remember you saying you liked snow camping."

"I like the *idea* of snow camping," Peter offered. "And I want to be with you for New Year's Eve, and this is where you're going to be, so…"

Nick broke out in the sort of smile that had once made him the darling of the Manhattan gallery scene.

"I really think that after you get used to the cold you're going to like it. The Freezing Man festival is a lot like Burning

Man, only colder and with fewer hippies on acid—and with more snow sculpting."

"But there will be *some* hippies on acid, right?"

"Only if you invited your friends."

When Nick had first proposed the idea of spending New Year's Eve huddled together in a recently erected igloo, Peter had been torn.

Because their families lived in different states, they had decided to spend Christmas apart. Nick had entertained his cousin Kjell's family at the Castle, the enormous, cliff-face domicile that Nick had inherited from his first partner. Meanwhile Peter flew to Austin to visit his folks, who had moved to Texas once Peter graduated from college.

One guest at the Fontaine Christmas barbecue, Larry Polk, happened to be a newspaperman. He happened to offer Peter an interview at the *Austin Chronicle*. Peter happened to accept.

He'd been drunk at the time, but he'd agreed to the interview again, sober, three days later.

"*The Hamster* is too small a venue for an award-winning journalist," Larry had told him in his flat, east Texas drawl. "You need to come on down here. We'll treat you right."

Peter loved *the Hamster*, loved the city of Bellingham, loved his friends here, but he also had a little something called ambition. And to satisfy that he would have to trade up. He needed a bigger city with a bigger paper and bigger circulation.

He hadn't told Nick about either the job or the fact that he'd agreed to an interview; he couldn't. He, constantly talking, constantly writing copy in his head, could not find the words to say that he was thinking of leaving Bellingham. Not even now.

Peter found himself staring out the window and made himself look at Nick instead. He filled up his eye with the image of his lover...felt himself relaxing enough to stare hard at that beard Nick been wearing since November.

Peter didn't know if he liked it, but thought maybe he might. He wondered if he should grow a beard himself, before remembering that he couldn't. Mustaches barely managed to take hold on the outcropping of his upper lip. An entire beard would never grow on the thin, barren planes of his face.

And he could probably count on never having too much hair on his chest, unlike Nick, whose hairy Viking ancestors probably had never needed to wear shirts at all.

Though not born a true Pacific Northwesterner, Nick had nonetheless adapted to local ways and therefore ran the air conditioner in his car anytime the thermometer went over sixty.

Peter preferred to engage the car's heated seats rather than the air conditioner, but then, that followed. An old boyfriend of his had once remarked that he was "as cold as a woman," and that was just about right. He didn't have a lot to keep him warm. He had what some kindly referred to as a "runner's physique" and others, such as his grandmother, called "skinny little string bean."

He had no idea how he was going to survive the weekend in the wilderness and even less idea how he would bring up the job in Austin.

Because he didn't want to leave, really. He didn't want to leave the Pacific Northwest, and he didn't want to leave Nick. But he wanted to level up—go out into the larger world and prove what he could do. Comfort, even affection, couldn't satisfy that desire to compete, to go further. It stayed in Peter's chest, a hard, gnawing anxiety.

The anxiety apparently showed on his face, because Nick said, "You know, there's a lodge on the property about half a mile from the campsite. If it's too miserable, we can always go there."

"That wouldn't impress your outdoorsy friends much."

Nick snorted. "Once they let me out of the army, I no longer had any desire to exercise my machismo."

"That's because you have a natural rugged manliness that makes machismo completely unnecessary," Peter said. In spite of his claim of imperviousness to the opinions of others, Nick beamed smugly at Peter's comment. "I, on the other hand, wouldn't call myself rugged."

"No," Nick agreed, "you're more like a greyhound. Sleek, skinny, and always on the scent of a good story."

"And exactly like a greyhound, I think I'm going to be shivering in this snow."

"You can always curl up on my lap for warmth." Nick grinned.

Peter rolled his eyes. "There is no way I'm going to cuddle up to you in front of all those burly, sporty dudes."

"You will, once you're cold enough. Or drunk enough."

"There isn't enough vodka in the world. And you would die of embarrassment if I did."

"So you think."

"So I know, Mr. I-Don't-Even-Hold-Hands-During-the-Pride-Parade." Peter laughed. "You're shy. Just admit it."

"I admit nothing."

Nick turned right and started up a narrow, slippery side road that seemed more like twin ruts in the snow than a paved surface. Though it was more treacherous, Peter felt better about this road than he had about the snow canyon that was 542. Sliding into an icy ravine seemed preferable to being crushed beneath tons of snow, though he couldn't generate any logical reason why. After ten minutes of slow, careful driving, he saw a handwritten sign ahead:

FREEZING MAN PARKING.
AVALANCHE WARNING IN EFFECT.
HAPPY FUCKING NEW YEAR!

Chapter 2

Like many of the trails systems in Whatcom County, Salmon Ridge Sno-Park had been built by a team of dedicated snowshoeing enthusiasts, including Nick's second cousin, Kjell Van Beek.

Kjell had taken up plein air painting as a way to express his feelings during a personal crisis he'd experienced in his midthirties, and five years later he'd become not only quite good but a well-known fixture in Bellingham parks and on Whatcom County's many scenic byways. Like Nick, Kjell had a near-superhuman tolerance for cold. Peter had once seen him standing at his easel in the middle of Boulevard Park in a prosaically beautiful snowfall wearing a parka, snow boots, and cargo shorts.

Peter had met Kjell before, briefly, when Nick had had a show up at Mindport Gallery. He'd talked mostly about his recent conversion from painting with oils to painting with acrylics.

More than the sign, it was sighting Kjell standing alongside the road in that very same outfit which told Peter they had arrived at their destination. The fresh, powdery snow stirred up by Nick's car stuck to the dark, curly hair on Kjell's meaty thighs, but he didn't seem to notice, being deeply engaged in scumbling a thin layer of white paint over the painting on his canvas, giving the thing the same hazy, misty look as the surrounding scenery.

"Shouldn't we stop and say hi?"

Nick shook his head. "He wouldn't talk to us if we did. He's in the flow."

"Do you ever do that?"

"Get in the flow? All the time."

"No, I mean stand around painting exactly what happens to be in front of you at the moment."

"Not really. Sometimes I'll sketch something I've just seen, but I've never been much of a plein air guy. They really love to capture the light and energy and immediacy of their environment. The gestalt of the moment. Including whatever random bugs and twigs fall into their paint. Kjell once painted over a whole cloud of gnats that slapped into his painting during a windstorm. That certainly lent the piece a unique texture as only encountered outdoors."

"Bumpy?"

"But uniquely, organically bumpy." Nick pulled the car alongside a string of around thirty similarly snow-worthy vehicles.

Peter hadn't expected the Hilton, but he had expected at least one building to be visible. The promised lodge, for example. Nothing, not even an outhouse, marred the expanse of snow and trees. He zipped up his coat, summoned his manly sense of adventure, and opened the car door. The air was chilly but not bitterly cold. Huge white snowflakes drifted down through the still air to alight on the cedars, the car, Nick's woolen toque.

A few yards down a gentle slope a few people in brightly colored winter gear tromped through the snow, erecting poles and packing snow into blocks. The puffiness of their parkas changed their proportions, giving the scene the impression of extremely industrious children busy making the world's greatest snow fort.

"I came up Wednesday and scoped out our site and started our structure." Nick hauled rucksacks of equipment out of the back of the car. "It's right down there. See the red flag?"

The red flag was really more of a banner such as one might see a costumed knave carrying in a renaissance fair. Two golden letters adorned the red field: *N* and *P*. It hung alongside a little mound of snow that seemed to be getting gently covered with a blanket of cotton ball-sized snowflakes.

Was getting buried in the snow his theme for today?

Without really thinking, he started to internally write his own obituary: *Peter Fontaine, winner of the Investigative Reporter's and Editor's Award, died Saturday after being suffocated inside an artistic igloo. Fontaine's lover, prominent Bellingham painter Nick Olson, escaped the igloo with only a mild chill. Fontaine's blue, frozen body will be on display at the Freezing Man Snow Sculpture Festival until the North Cascades experience a significant summer snowmelt.*

Perhaps sensing Peter's uneasiness, Nick said, "You know, I didn't realize you had this claustrophobia problem when I built the shelter. It's pretty tight in there." Nick paused, seeming about to reiterate his offer to take Peter back to Bellingham.

"I'll be fine as long as there's enough room for you to warm me with your body." Peter forced a lewd smile.

Nick smiled back—a smile of relief and gratitude. "There's sufficient space inside to generate heat-producing friction."

"Then let's go down so I can see the accommodations."

Nick led the way, dragging their gear behind him on a pulka that he'd made from a plastic sled he'd bought at Canadian Tire and some half-inch PVC pipe. Peter watched Nick—bearded, dressed in well-worn GORE-TEX, polarized shades, and dragging a sledful of cargo—and he didn't think that Nick could have appeared more rugged if he'd planned it. And he fit right in with the other men there, though it was sometimes hard to tell the men from the women beneath all the protective gear. The only sure indicators of gender were the colors pink and purple for women and beards for men. Otherwise everyone looked the same in snow pants.

They all seemed to be engaged in various stages of building snow shelters. Nick greeted them, introducing Peter as he went.

The igloo closest to the road was inhabited by a chef named Henry Swank and his wife, Janelle. Both seemed to be in their late thirties, and they had obviously been interrupted in the middle of an argument. They owned a catering business in Bellingham. Peter knew them from their *Hamster* ad, which highlighted their organic produce and membership in Sustainable Connections, one of Bellingham's many left-leaning business associations.

Janelle smiled warmly and shook Peter's hand, while Henry only gave them a cursory wave. Peter couldn't decide who had been winning that argument. Henry probably, since Janelle had been happy to be interrupted.

Next came a Martin Wells, who seemed to be in his midtwenties. He and two friends, Rick and Shane, seemed to be bent on creating an entire mansion. Three domed humps stood clustered together. Peter wondered if they somehow had to make three different rooms to avoid sleeping close to each other. They seemed to be the type of guys who would be worried about being perceived to be fags.

"Martin's got an engineering degree but no job offer. He and two buddies apparently spend all their time on the mountain perfecting their snow- and ice-building techniques. I cannot compete with them." Nick indicated his own snow mound. "It's only one room."

"Igloo sweet igloo," Peter remarked.

"Technically this is a quinzhee." Nick crouched down and opened the tiny, cupboard-sized door. "You make it by mounding up the snow, letting it set, and then digging out the middle. We'll be cozy in here, that's for sure. Just about the only thing that can bring it down is rain."

"What if it rains?" Peter thought it was a fair question, rain being quite common, even in January.

"Then we run back to the car and drive back to Glacier and get a hotel."

"Can the hotel room have a hot tub?"

"Absolutely." Nick opened the little door. "After you."

Peter crawled through the entry and found himself in a surprisingly bright domed room. Though there was not quite enough height to stand up straight, the top of the ceiling was about five feet high. A raised platform took up half the floor space. A red votive candle stood in a nook carved into the wall. There was a small hole in the top of the dome that Peter imagined must be for ventilation.

Nick sat down on the platform, beaming.

"How do you like it?"

"It's pretty cool," Peter said. "No pun intended."

"Funny."

"This is our bed." Nick indicated the raised platform. "The rest of it is our living room. Except the foyer, of course." Nick pointed at the little tunnel leading to the cupboard door.

"Where is our bathroom?"

"You always think of the most romantic things," Nick said. "We set up a couple of tents of portable toilets, and I've got WAG BAGs on the sled. We have to pack everything out, per Washington State regulations, and that includes toilet paper."

"That puts an amazing image in my mind."

"You can always go without. Kjell never uses it. He claims that a snowball does the trick, and you can just bury it afterward. The snowball, I mean. Everything else goes in the bag."

"You know, Kjell is exactly the kind of person I would expect to wipe his ass with a snowball," Peter remarked. "I think I'll go with the standard-issue TP."

"I tried the snowball method once."

"I bet you did. How was it?"

"Chilly. Very, very chilly." Nick gave an involuntary shudder as he brushed the snow off his mittens. "Let's get our stuff inside so we can join the fun."

After they moved their gear and set up their sleeping pads, Peter reluctantly acquainted himself with the toilet tent, which turned out to be not that bad.

It was two in the afternoon, two hours and twenty-nine minutes until sunset. Nick suggested they spend the time snowshoeing around the campsite so Peter could get the lay of the area.

In spite of only having worn snowshoes on one previous occasion, Peter got along fairly easily on his rentals. He followed Nick down a trail leading between snow-draped stands of western hemlock and fir. Overhead, the sky was deep blue. Weak winter sun shone from the south. Nick took him down to the trail's terminus at the edge of the North Fork of the Nooksack River. Even in deep winter, water still flowed quickly and freely at the center. He pointed out the line of the riverbank and the treacherous ice that grew in a thin, deceptive sheet across the surface.

"And if you look up there"—Nick pointed up at a field of snow—"you can see how there are fissures in the surface of the snowfield?"

Peter squinted up. "Yes, I think so."

"That slope is highly unstable and likely to come down. I'd stay away from it."

Peter couldn't help but smile at the seriousness of Nick's tone. He sounded like a troop leader addressing an errant and death-prone Boy Scout. Or maybe this was just his army survival training kicking in. It was insufferable in any case.

Peter said, "I don't know why you think I'm going to be traipsing around out here by myself. I don't even have a map."

"You never know," Nick said. "People get separated for a lot of reasons. And then they end up dying. And you should keep an eye out for tree wells too. If you fall in one of those, you could break both your legs."

"I really don't think I'm going to be straying farther than the toilet tent." Peter stopped, planted his ski poles firmly in the snow.

Nick stopped and turned to face him fully. "I'm only telling you this because you're naturally curious and inquisitive and also secretive. You're the kind of person who'll sneak off to check something out without telling anyone. I just want you to know that there are a lot of ways to get hurt out here, so you shouldn't go out alone."

"I promise that if I decide to go poking around, I will take an equally nosy buddy. But seriously, I plan on spending most of my time here either looking at snow sculptures, snoozing in the igloo, or drinking vodka in full view of everyone, including you. Now please stop treating me like a girl."

"Quinzhee."

"What?"

"It's a quinzhee, not an igloo."

"I'll make a note of it for my story."

Nick nodded, apparently satisfied. He stared up at the trees for a few moments, then said, "I'm trying to make sure you're safe."

Peter thought: *Nick Olson, king of communication, stated the obvious today on a snowy trail in the Mount Baker National Forest. Bystanders described his remark as "sincere but also easily observable by anybody."*

Then he stopped his internal rant. Nick should be given credit for saying anything at all. Plus he was right. Peter was nosy and secretive. He was withholding quite a whopper right that very second. He was just mad at Nick for knowing him well. He felt his ire leaving him.

Peter said, "But you know, drinking vodka is not the only activity I had planned for tonight."

"Oh yes?"

"Well, night's going to last for a long time. My only concern is that if I expose any flesh, I might catch a chill."

Nick gave him a long, silent look and then smirked. "I think I can find a way to protect any flesh you may choose to expose."

"We should probably get back and make some dinner and get right to bed, then."

Getting right to bed, when the bedroom was basically a hollowed-out snowball, required a little more planning than Peter had initially expected, but anticipation made them both giddy. By the light of a single flickering candle, they arranged what Nick referred to as their nest.

Nick could not stop smirking as he inflated their Therm-a-Rests and arranged them on additional pads. Peter tried to take mental notes on this process, feeling an informative article coming on, as he always did when Nick dispensed wisdom, but he absolutely could not focus on the benefits of closed-cell camping technology. The cold, the sounds of people walking, laughing, talking just outside the snow walls, propelled Peter into a heady, giggly, almost-childlike state of excitement.

And more than that, he had no idea how they were going to have sex. The air was cold. Cold! He didn't think he'd be able to take off his clothes and get sweaty without freezing. Nick seemed to have a plan about how they would proceed, but was keeping it to himself. Every few seconds, though, he shot Peter a look, as if he'd just had some new, lascivious idea that he couldn't wait to try out.

When he had the sleeping bags rolled out, Nick said, "Time to get your boots off, camper."

Camper?

"So you're the hot camp counselor and I'm the homesick kid who wants to sleep in your tent with you?" Peter drawled.

Nick looked genuinely surprised for a moment; then his expression changed back to the strangely wicked smirk he'd been wearing for the last forty-five minutes.

"If that's the way you want to play it, sure." He leaned close and whispered, "Do you miss your mom and dad?"

"I just don't want the rest of the guys to see me crying." Peter swooned melodramatically against Nick's chest. "I just miss home so much."

Nick laughed out loud. "I cannot imagine you ever crying about missing home."

"I thought we were fantasy role-playing," Peter said.

"We're already in the snow; how much more fantasy do you need?" He knelt down in front of Peter and pulled off one boot and the other, and then Peter's snow pants, and pulled back the flap of Peter's mummy bag. Then, seeming to remember something, he blew out the candle. "No use giving everybody else a show."

The light extinguished, he pulled Peter's long johns down and off, leaving only his socks in place.

"You don't want to get these damp," he whispered. "They'll freeze."

The cold assaulted Peter's skin, and he felt his scrotum sucking up into his body. Not exactly sexy, and yet the scrape of Nick's GORE-TEX and leather gloves against his thighs left his skin tingling, tightening. And they hadn't even kissed yet. Usually Nick kissed. He kissed a lot. But today locking lips didn't seem to figure in with his approach.

If Peter were perfectly honest with himself, he had to admit that he hardly ever gave Nick the opportunity to take the lead in sex. Though he often found a way to get Nick's cock inside his body, Peter's own aggressive sexual hunger meant that he called the shots.

Maybe it was the unfamiliar environment making him unsure of what to do, but he felt strangely passive. Or maybe it was that he was naked from the waist down, being very gently felt up by a fully dressed man. The gloves reached his genitals, and the shock of the cold battled against the delight of being held at all.

Delight won.

He arched against Nick's palm.

Nick gave him a little squeeze and said, "You should get covered up."

Peter wriggled his naked lower half quickly into the sleeping bag.

Nick moved in, situating a towel underneath him. "Wouldn't want to get your sleeping bag damp either."

"What about my jacket?"

"Maybe leave that on for right now."

"Even my mittens?"

Nick gave out a low chuckle. "Especially your mittens."

"So it's a mitten job you want, then? I should have known you had some weird perversion like that. You just like shopping for snow gear too much." Why did the words *mitten job* suddenly sound sexy?

"You have no idea."

Just that sound sent a twitch through Peter's groin. What, really, was Nick going to do? Have him on his hands and knees in the snow? He didn't think he could relax enough for that.

Then again, in a few minutes he might not be as chilly as he was now. Peter let Nick push him back into a semirecumbent pose, propped up on his elbows with the lower half of his body in the sleeping bag. Nick pulled off his own gloves and slid his fingers under Peter's jacket. His chilly fingers traveled up to tease Peter's nipple. A moan slipped from Peter's lips, and finally Nick kissed him, muffling the sound beneath his own warm and giving mouth. Nick's whiskers, like every other part of him, were cold, and they tickled Peter's jaw, then his throat, when Nick's mouth moved there.

Nick's hands had apparently decided to visit the world inside the mummy bag, now visibly tented, despite the dimness and the loft of the down.

Peter bit back his moans as Nick worked him. Which he liked, but he wanted more. As always.

"If you're planning on fucking me, you'd better get going with that."

"Not part of my game plan, actually," Nick said. "No lube."

"There's sunscreen."

Nick's laughter rumbled through his chest, shaking both of them. "You've got it all worked out, don't you?" He moved his fingers down, maddeningly circling Peter's opening.

"I just like to come when you're fucking me," Peter said. "And you haven't used a condom for months."

"What about what I want?" Nick nipped the side of Peter's neck. Not hard, but with a hint of rebuke.

"What do you want?" Peter got the sudden weird impression that they weren't talking about sex anymore.

"I want you to shut up and let me finish what I started," Nick said. Though his words were hard, his tone stayed playful, his fingers light on Peter's delicate skin. "Or don't you trust me?"

"I trust you."

"That's good, because wilderness survival is all about trust." Nick pressed the tip of his finger, and Peter wriggled to get it farther. Nick withdrew, guided Peter onto his stomach. Peter heard zippers unzipping, Velcro ripping open, then the snap of a cap popping open. Looking over his shoulder, he could see the shadow of Nick, hulking in winter gear, coat hanging open, working his own stiff cock. Peter pushed himself up on his hands and knees, excitement zinging through him, hardly feeling the cold anymore.

Nick pushed a slick thumb into Peter's hole and, after only working him for a moment, pushed his cock inside.

Peter yelped with pain, and Nick held still, letting the heat of his thighs warm and relax him, stroking Peter's exposed lower back while he adjusted.

"You didn't really think I'd hold out on you, did you?" He pushed slowly, incrementally, in.

"No, you wouldn't." Peter's voice was a ragged whisper. And suddenly he felt vulnerable saying it, so he looked back over his shoulder and added, "Not if you know what's good for you."

"That's my newshound. I was worried that you'd gone all soft for a second."

"Soft doesn't describe any part of me right now." Peter humped back against Nick, urging him to motion. Nick finally complied, pumping him hard and fast like he liked it. Peter met him every stroke, chasing that blinding sensation of orgasm, feeling no cold, no pain, just the hot, white moment of pleasure, that burst of physical joy, shooting out in jumpy strings. Nick's fingers clenched around his hips, and Peter felt the slippery warmth as Nick emptied himself inside him, and like a chain reaction, Peter tensed in a shaking paroxysm of ecstasy.

Nick kissed him one last time, breath shaky and heavy, then handed him his long johns.

"You don't want to catch a chill."

Chapter 3

The Freezing Man Snow Sculpture Festival is essentially a snowman-building jamboree. Since there is no judging, winner, or prize, it can't strictly be called a competition. But human beings are by nature competitive, and the Freezing Man celebration is no exception. The only rule is that you start building your snowman at daybreak on New Year's Eve and finish by midnight, so the snowpeople will be able to ring in the New Year. Dozens of intrepid visitors come to see the sculptures on New Year's Day, mostly after going on the Polar Bear Swim in Birch Bay.

Peter put his stubby pencil and Moleskine notebook back into his pocket. Outside, he could hear Nick cooking and talking to Kjell. The smell of frying sausages lured him out into the cold, bright morning.

Nick poured and handed him a cup of coffee in a thermal aluminum mug. It was true. Coffee did taste amazing after spending the night in a hollowed-out snowball.

This forest, this country, truly was full of natural wonders.

Guilt moved within him again, and he realized he had to tell Nick about the interview. They'd been living together for a year and seeing each other for two. Because if he got the job, then what?

What was he so afraid of? That Nick would be angry that he was contemplating a decision like moving to Austin, surely. But honestly, Peter knew what really frightened him—that Nick would refuse to move away from his beloved Castle on Wildcat Cove and that Peter would be, himself, unable to leave.

Seeming to notice Peter's deep distraction, Nick said, "Formulating an article about camp-stove cooking? My secret is Jimmy Dean."

"Yes. I'm going to start it off with the statement: *My boyfriend is the best camp-stove cook in the Pacific Northwest, but the rest of you losers can still try to acquire a little of his prowess by following these simple instructions.*"

Kjell chomped a sausage, chewed it thoughtfully, then said to Nick, "Good night last night?"

Peter reddened as Nick said, "Yeah, it was snug in there."

Kjell nodded. "I always want some company about four o'clock in the morning, but it's nice to get away from the kids every now and then."

"How many kids do you have?" Peter couldn't recall ever having seen Kjell with any, but he mostly saw the man at non-child-friendly events like art openings.

"Three. They're nine, seven, and three. Having them up here would just be a nightmare. One of them would be down a tree well in thirty seconds. Probably the oldest one. She'd climb down there on purpose, and then the youngest would try to follow her, get caught up in the branches, fall, and break himself somehow. Then I'd have to go get him."

The specificity of Kjell's theoretical example indicated a wealth of experience to Peter. And the high, drifting snow in the area did mean that a variety of tree wells existed. Kjell's daughter could have her pick of conifers. Peter thought he might climb down one himself later. But that was only two children dispatched by the environment.

Peter said, "What about the middle one?"

"He wouldn't be any trouble. He'd just hang around with the women, drawing. The only danger would be him getting into the flow and freezing to death accidentally." Kjell grinned. "He's a lot like Nick was when he was a kid."

"I was plenty adventurous," Nick said, affronted. "I just liked to draw. So did you."

"Not like you, though. There's a reason I'm a hobbyist and you're a pro." Kjell wiped his greasy fingers on his pant leg and said, "I think I'm going to try to get in another painting this morning before I start building my snowman."

"Seems risky. You only have seven hours of daylight," Nick warned. "Your snowman might end up being severely substandard."

"I'll paint for an hour, tops. I'll set my watch alarm. I just don't want to waste this amazing light."

Kjell moved off, marching through the snow with the casual ease that other people walked down a sidewalk, without a single misstep or hint of awkwardness. This is what the old pioneer mountain men must have looked like, Peter thought, only with a lot more high-tech fabric and reflective jacket piping.

"He's a lot more sensitive than he looks," Peter observed.

"He's a lot better artist than he claims to be. That's just our family, though. Lutherans."

"What does that mean?"

"None of us have an easy time taking too much pride in our achievements. Especially not something as insubstantial as art." Nick laughed. "I'm just lucky my father was an atheist. It gave me a fighting chance at personal success."

Peter nodded again. He'd never met Nick's parents, though he'd spoken to Nick's mother on the phone a few times. His father was a retired career army officer, and his mother was a nurse, also retired. They lived in Arizona but spent most of their time crisscrossing the country in their RV, visiting their friends. The one time the RV had brought them north, Peter had found a reason to be gone. Not that he thought they were bad people. He was just a coward about meeting fathers—especially army fathers.

Or maybe cowardice was his new mode of interaction these days. Fathers, moves, career stagnation. The list kept growing.

Nick used a handful of snow to clean the grease out of the skillet and stowed the stove. Then he said, "Should we go look at our patch?"

Informal the competition might be, but it was still a competition and, as such, was taken very seriously by the competitors present. Though the sun had barely risen, apart from Kjell, Nick and Peter were last to start building their snowman, at the staggeringly late hour of five past eight a.m. To their left, Martin had already laid out a series of snow blocks, and to their right stood a waist-high column. The builder was nowhere in sight. Presumably he'd gone to get more material.

And there was already a controversy. Someone had obviously built their snowman early.

How this was possible, Peter didn't know, since they would have had to start molding snow in the frigid dead of night. But a snowman—or more accurately, a snow sculpture—already stood, or rather, lay—in the field.

Nick shook his head. "I get the idea of a recumbent snowman, and this one is pretty good, but I still think it's a cheat."

Martin looked up from his building and said, "I think it's Rick's. I told him he couldn't start till sunrise, but of course he didn't listen." Martin bent over his project again. He'd clearly laid out an elaborate schematic complete with measurements and some sort of timetable.

Nick shrugged equanimously. "It's not like we're competing for money. We should put a whiskey bottle in its hand, though. It sort of looks like a party casualty."

Martin snorted. "Rick's the party casualty. He went down to Glacier last night and never came back."

Peter did the math, and it didn't balance.

"If he went to Glacier and didn't come back yet, how did he make this snowman?"

Nick cocked his head slightly. Gave Peter that "you're being really nosy" look. Martin stopped working, seeming to also belatedly be doing the math.

"He must have done it before he left, 'cause he knew he was too big a pussy to spend the night in the snow and wouldn't be back until this morning. I mean, it's obviously a really shitty job, and Rick's the only guy here with no pride whatsoever."

Evergreen

Martin kicked the side of the snowman, and a chunk fell off. "All I can say is that he better be bringing a lot of whiskey back with him."

"That's just what you guys need. More whiskey." Janelle was walking toward them, a square pink bucket held in each of her gloved hands. She looked fresh, walked with a spring in her step. She unmolded the buckets, adding a couple of bricks to her monolith. Her husband was nowhere to be seen.

When Martin saw Janelle, he smiled, drew himself up, and brandished his plan. "I'm gonna kick your ass this year, Janelle."

"Not possible." Janelle smoothed the seams in her sculpture. "This year I am unstoppable."

"I thought you said these weren't judged." Peter found himself suddenly feeling very competitive.

"They aren't, but you know how it goes. There's usually somebody whose sculpture is clearly better." Nick cast a glance back. "Or clearly worse."

"Do we have a plan?"

"I had the idea of trying to build a block, then carve bas-relief people out of it." Nick produced a piece of paper with the sketch of what he planned to build.

"It looks...difficult." Peter chewed his lip. It looked exactly like the kind of thing he'd screw up. Sensing Peter's hesitation, Nick pocketed the design.

"That's just an idea, though. What were you thinking?"

"I was thinking of two snowmen holding hands," Peter admitted sheepishly. "You know, with the stick arms. But that would be incredibly gay, wouldn't it?"

Nick nodded. "It would be incredibly gay, but we could do it anyway. Freezing Man could use a little gaying up." He took out his pencil and drew the new idea. Twin Frostys in love. "So these guys are so easy that we can do it the old-fashioned way by rolling up three big snowballs and still have enough time to go on a hike before it gets dark."

"*Easy* more accurately describes my artistic skill level," Peter said, relieved.

117

While at first their gay Frostys design drew some scorn from the more ambitious snow sculptors, their quick, done-by-lunchtime execution—and the subsequent free time that gave them—produced at least one jealous stare. This was from Martin, who seemed to be weighing his ambition to destroy Janelle against the pleasure of showshoeing on a perfect afternoon. Janelle looked blissfully blank, content in the way artists in the thrall of their work often could be.

Building the snowmen hadn't presented any opportunity for an intimate conversation, but the hike would. They'd be away from people. Peter took a deep breath, preparing himself. It would be okay.

Chapter 4

All Nick said was, "Please tell me you're joking."

Peter gulped, staring up at the beautiful snowflakes falling from a gray sky. Finally he managed, "I'm not joking."

The muscles in Nick's jaw clenched and flexed. Although Peter could not actually see this through the beard, he could see Nick's whiskers moving, which amounted to the same thing.

"You realize that if you get this job, you're going to have to move to Austin, right?"

"It's not like I wouldn't want you to come with me," Peter said. "I would. I do. I want you to come with me to Texas. I'll admit it's not that romantic, but they have good steak there. And I'm pretty sure eating out is tax deductible if you're writing a restaurant review."

"I can't move to Texas," Nick said. "I don't have any connections there."

"You'll make new friends."

"I don't mean friends. I mean other artists, gallery connections. You really have no idea how I make money, do you?"

Stung, Peter's patience began to thin. "You're an artist. You can do art anywhere, but there are only so many newspaper jobs available. There are only so many newspapers left."

"Painting is not a job that you can do just anywhere." Nick pulled off his polarized sunglasses and rubbed his eyes. "Painting is a deeply regional profession, and it takes years to build up contacts with local galleries. Even palates are considered to be regional. In essence, I would have to start from scratch."

"But that doesn't make sense. You show in Germany and Prague."

"I show as a Pacific Northwest artist," Nick said.

"Listen, I don't think *the Hamster* is ever going to pay me enough to even buy my own car, let alone fund my retirement."

"Fund your what?" Nick stared at him as though he'd suddenly begun speaking in tongues. "You're only twenty-nine. Wait a minute… That's what this is about, isn't it? You're panicking because you're going to be thirty."

"No, I am not. I'm trying to make a reasonable upward move in a very difficult business with increasingly dwindling openings."

"But the reason you're trying to make the upward move is that you're scared about being thirty."

Peter's temper flared. He could feel his face reddening. "Why is it that whenever I talk about having ambition, you always think I'm trying to compensate for something? I am ambitious. There's a difference. For the record, I'd like to get this clear. I do not think I'm inadequate. If anything, I think this town is inadequate to my needs in that it lacks any kind of major newspaper, free or otherwise."

"And I think Texas is inadequate because it doesn't contain this town," Nick replied.

A silence settled between them, and they only went a few more yards before Nick said, "We should turn around and go back."

It took about forty minutes to walk back, and neither spoke the entire time. Peter cursed his stupidity at bringing up a touchy subject while in an environment where they couldn't get away from each other and where yelling could trigger a deadly avalanche. Frankly he didn't know if he could find his way back to camp without Nick, and worse, Nick knew this. They walked together out of Peter's dependence and Nick's sense of obligation. And suddenly Peter wondered if this walk mirrored their relationship—if he stayed with Nick because Nick was the best he could do in a small town, and Nick stayed by him because…

Honestly he didn't know why Nick was with him. The beauty of the snow and cedars faded, and all Peter felt was the cold.

⛄⛄ Evergreen ⛄⛄

Once at the edge of the camp, Peter finally felt like he could speak again. He said, "So it's my career or yours?"

"I guess so." Nick squinted at the sky. "I think I might go borrow Kjell's paints while there's still some light."

Peter nodded. "I need to jot down some notes and get some action shots of people enjoying themselves at the festival."

He forced himself to get out his Moleskine and stubby pencil just so that he would think about something other than Nick.

With only an hour of daylight left, the pace picks up at the Freezing Man. Some sculptors put the finishing touches on masterpieces of snow, while others scramble to repair cracks or even catastrophic structural collapse.

Speaking of that, one of their snowmen's tree-branch arms had fallen off. He rose and started pushing it back in, careful not to wreck the image of super gay happiness that they had created. Above all, he didn't want the straight people to see him weep.

He had to stop being so maudlin. All around him, people were having a great time. He just had to catch a little of that enthusiasm.

Peter got out his camera and wandered from sculpture to sculpture snapping shots of smiling faces and truly awesome snowmen. He cheered a little. Their nearest neighbors, Martin the engineer and his somewhat-less-intelligent buddy, Shane, approached their art sculpture as if it were a military campaign. Diagrams abounded. Shane did as he was told, clearly taking little joy in the act of creation but eager to please Martin.

Janelle was just the opposite, smiling and humming to herself as she stacked blocks of snow atop each other. Her husband, Henry, had apparently opted to sit out this part of the sculpture-building activity. Peter wondered if he'd gone down to Glacier for snacks.

Just as he was finishing, Nick's boots walked up beside him. Peter leaned back so that he could see the rest of Nick, keeping his expression calm. Janelle and Martin were right there, so he didn't expect Nick to say anything meaningful. Just small talk. What Nick said was, "I can't find Kjell."

"Maybe he went into town," Peter said.

Nick shook his head. "His car is still here, but no one has seen him since this morning."

Janelle stopped working and drifted nearer. "That's a long time, even for him."

"I know. I'm going to go look for him," Nick said.

"Alone?" Alarm prickled at Peter's skin. "Isn't this how whole parties freeze to death on the mountainside? By going one by one to search for each other, getting separated, and dying?"

"He's right. You have to have your transponder set to receive if you're going to try and home in on Kjell's signal," Martin commented.

"See?"

"Or you can take mine if you want, and switch. Then you'll have one to search with and one that will transmit a signal in case you get knocked out."

Peter glared at Martin. His problem-solving skills were beginning to test Peter's patience. Or rather with his insistence on only solving the problem of how to make ridiculously dangerous activities seem safe.

"It's still not smart to go alone," Peter said. "I could—"

"You're not a good-enough snowshoer to go with me," Nick said flatly. "It's close to dark, and you don't know the terrain."

Peter's temper flared at the high-handed truth of Nick's statement. Their eyes locked as a torrent of profanity began to swirl up Peter's throat.

"I'll go," Janelle broke in. "We'll both have our transponders on, and we'll take Martin's to search."

"Right. If we don't come back in an hour, drive into Glacier and call search and rescue."

Nick tossed Peter his keys. Then, almost as an afterthought, he leaned forward and gave Peter a quick kiss. He murmured, "I'm not going far. Really. I just have to see."

"Don't fall in a tree well and break yourself," Peter mumbled back.

As he watched him walk into the dark forest, Peter realized that he loved Nick. Truly and deeply now. But loving a man didn't erase Peter's desire to take his career to the next level. It only eroded his determination and screwed up his priorities so that he had actually had, for the first time, to contemplate that he might not be willing to sacrifice everything to the gods of journalism. He might just end up sacrificing journalistic advancement to the god of love.

And that shook him. It didn't sit right alongside his Investigative Reporter's and Editor's Award. It made him feel…weak.

He stared again at the rough snowman laying next to him. The heat kicked off by Martin's portable campfire was starting to melt away the details, and so he moved it farther away.

A chunk fell off the snowman.

Peter could plainly see that there, buried in the snow, was a human hand.

Chapter 5

For exactly one second Peter wondered if the hand was part of the art.

He carefully reached out and touched the hand. Ice-cold. Unresponsive. This hand, if it was attached to anything, was attached to a corpse. The wind whipped up, swirling heavy snowflakes around his face, momentarily blinding him.

"Martin?" he said. He didn't know why he called Martin, except that he knew his name.

"Don't worry about it. Nick and Janelle won't stay out if this wind keeps up." Martin didn't glance up from his snowman to say this.

The hand was not only cold, it was frozen. For a horrible moment, he thought it was Kjell, but no, the snowman had already been here this morning when he and Kjell had been eating breakfast. So who?

"Martin, I think you should come look at this."

"I'm running out of light."

"I don't think your snowman matters so much right now. I think I might have found Rick." Peter began gingerly to unbury the arm. He felt for a pulse that he knew wouldn't be there, but he felt for it anyway. Nothing.

Martin straightened. "Look, I know nobody but me cares about beating Janelle this year, but I—Holy shit!" He dropped his trowel and rushed forward. Martin dropped to his knees, clawing at the snow.

"Martin—"

"We've got to get him out of there."

"Martin, he's dead."

"He might just be in a deep state of hypothermia." Chunks of snow fell away, revealing snow pants, the side of a Patagonia jacket. "Fuck! It *is* Rick."

Peter said, "This snowman has been here all day."

Martin kept digging. His frantic action attracted Shane and Henry.

"Martin, wait!" Peter grabbed Martin's arm and was instantly shoved aside. He fell back into the snow.

"Don't fucking touch me!"

Peter fought to maintain his calm. "Don't you get it? He didn't fall inside a snowman by accident. Somebody put him there. He was killed. You're disrupting the crime scene."

"What the fuck are you talking about?" Martin stood, chest heaving, but controlling himself. Attracted by the noise, Janelle's husband, appeared, looking pale and ill.

Peter tried his phone. No coverage. Of course. "I'm saying that this snowman is part of a crime scene."

"What are you saying, man?" Shane, stepped up. "What crime?"

"Rick has obviously been killed."

"How do you know he didn't do it to himself?"

"How do I know he didn't *bury* himself?" Was Shane really that stupid? Or was this some kind of clever diversion? Peter studied Shane's face. He did not seem clever.

"It would be like Rick to bury himself as a joke and then end up freezing to death. He really liked practical jokes like that." Martin sniffed, dragged an arm across his nose. "He was such an asshole."

Peter could not quell his skepticism at this theory. "I just can't believe he buried his own face with snow, then buried his own hand."

"Maybe someone helped him," Shane offered.

"Did you help him?" Peter asked. Shane shook his head.

"We don't even know for sure that it's Rick." Shane's cheeks reddened, and Peter started to feel sorry for him. Clearly he was the sort of person who dealt with stress by denying the obvious.

Martin balled his mittened hands into fists. "It's Rick, okay? That's his jacket."

"But we don't know for sure."

"For fuck's sake, Shane! Here—" Martin clawed at the snow covering the body's face, uncovering Rick's frozen profile. He still wore his goggles. At the back of his head, a vibrant, red mass of frozen blood glittered. Martin recoiled, flicking the sanguine crystals off his hands.

Shane staggered behind a quinzhee and vomited.

"I think we can rule out death by misadventure now," Peter said drily. He retrieved his camera and took a few more photographs. When Shane gave him the stink eye, he said, "I'm a reporter," by way of explanation.

Martin had slumped over, hands on his knees, breathing hard. His hands were bare, his mittens lying in the snow a few feet away.

Peter said, "Someone needs to drive into town and get the police."

Henry seemed to have the same idea. Or some idea that required complete expedience, because he beelined for the parking lot, leaped into his car, and tore out, tires spinning in the snow.

Only Peter watched him. The other two were still staring, aghast, at Rick's frozen corpse. Peter gained his feet and followed Henry. Was he running to get help or running from the scene of the crime? Wind gusted again, encasing him and them all in a wall of dim, cold white. When it quieted, he started forward again, running clumsily through the unevenly trampled snow.

Henry's car weaved, fishtailed, and then as Peter watched, slammed directly into a tree. His car perfectly perpendicular, blocked the narrow road.

Peter ran in earnest then, pulling frigid air into his lungs, sprinting toward the still-running car.

Henry lay slumped across the steering wheel, unconscious.

Peter tried the door and found it open. He carefully reached around and turned off the car, then undid Henry's seat belt. The man stirred, and Peter jumped back, still unsure. Martin and Shane had made it to the car and pushed their way forward, shaking Henry by the shoulder, rousing him.

Henry shifted groggily. "I've got to get to town."

"It's no use," Peter said. "The guy is already dead."

"We've got to get the police. Where are my car keys?"

"I have them." Peter held them up.

"Give them back to me."

"I'd rather not. I don't think you should drive." Peter stepped farther away, out of reach.

Henry put his face into his hands. "My head hurts. Am I bleeding?"

"There's a little cut."

Henry took stock of his situation and said, "Help me dig this car out. I've got to get to town."

"I don't think anyone is going into town tonight."

Turning, Peter saw Kjell moving toward them, coming out of the darkness of the road and storm. Something about the way he moved seemed suddenly sinister. Or maybe it was his statement that seemed sinister. If Peter were honest with himself, he had to admit that Kjell could easily have buried Rick into that snowman. He was up there alone and wouldn't have to corroborate his story with anyone.

But then, what the hell was he thinking? Kjell was Nick's friend. More than a friend—family. On the other hand, if being a reporter had taught him anything, it was that anyone could do anything at any time, given opportunity and motive.

Kjell continued. "We should probably take Henry up to the lodge. This snow's getting heavy, and I don't think he should be outside. I think he's got a concussion."

Kjell coaxed Henry out of his car and then supported him while he staggered back toward the rest of the camp. The sun dipped dangerously low on the horizon.

Kjell came alongside Peter. "Nick has a sled, doesn't he?"

"Yeah, up by the quinzhee." Peter fought the urge to move out of easy grabbing distance. He would not make Nick's cousin the primary suspect in Rick's murder, not when he had a whole camp full of total strangers to be suspicious of first. Not when he had a man apparently fleeing when the corpse was discovered.

Still, he couldn't help but ask a couple of questions.

"Where have you been all day?"

Kjell gave him that same level look that Nick often did. "Are you my wife too now?"

"Nick went out looking for you because no one had seen you since morning."

"I've been painting like I said, just over that ridge."

"You stood in the same spot all day long?" The guy truly was insane.

"I had to, to get the series right."

"How are your toes?"

"Cold," Kjell said. "Did I hear someone say that a guy was dead?"

On the way back to the camp, Peter explained about Rick. It was a short story, really, so it only took about a minute to tell, even with dramatic embellishments.

"So I, a man who frequently disappears for hours, was assumed to be dead in a crevasse, but the actual guy who went missing wasn't noticed until he was dead? That's a little sad."

"I don't think it's sad. At least you have people who like you enough to go after you. Even Rick's friends just thought he was being a douche bag." Peter stuck his hands in his pockets. "That is a little sad, actually, now that you mention it."

Kjell nodded. "Is that Nick's pulka? It looks like he made it out of a kid's sled."

"I think he did."

"Well, let's get Henry on it. It will be easier to get to the lodge while there's still some light left."

"I want to wait here for Nick."

"That kid Martin can tell Nick where we've gone. I could really use a hand with this, and Nick can get to the lodge blindfolded. We'll have the fire going for him when he gets back."

Peter weighed seriously the possibility that Kjell was the murderer. If he was, the last place in the world Peter wanted to go with him was a deserted lodge in the winter. What if the reason Henry had tried to escape was because he was a witness—because he'd known who killed Rick?

What if Kjell wanted to get both Henry and himself, the nosy reporter, out of the picture?

A brief *The Shining* scenario ran itself through Peter's mind before he talked himself down.

First, Salmon Ridge Sno-Park was not haunted.

Next, he hadn't even started nosing around asking questions yet, so Kjell would have no reason to want to lure him to a remote location to whack him.

Kjell was merely administering the first aid that any responsible adult would give in this situation. Thus Peter trusted Kjell enough to draw close and say, "But what if Henry is the killer? He tried to get away pretty fast when we found the body. What if we take him to that lodge and he goes nuts and makes us into snowmen? What if he's trying to create his own demented snowman army?"

Kjell grinned. "You know, you really are funny. Nick always says so, but I never noticed it until now."

"You can always pull that pulka by yourself," Peter said, unamused.

"If Henry's the killer, he's rattled his brains well enough that he's not much of a threat to us tonight. And if he's not the killer, we could kill him by keeping him out in this cold. Do you want that on your conscience?"

Pulling the deadweight of an injured man on a pulka is hard. Your legs ache, your shoulders ache, and although the guy in the pulka may not have what would be called a life-threatening wound, your mind still goes straight to the worst-case scenarios. What if the weather gets worse? What if you, too, fall? What if your boyfriend, Nick, never makes it to this lodge, and you have to spend the night with two men, one of whom might be a murderer?

One of whom…

Really, there was nothing to say that they couldn't both be murderers, working together.

God, he wished Nick would arrive. He could finally feel safe and actually think about what had happened. He closed his Moleskine and ambled to where Kjell crouched, feeding split logs into the large stone fireplace.

The lodge was surprisingly spacious. It had a great room and two bedrooms on the main floor and a ladder that led to a third bedroom upstairs. It was the standard northwest A-frame cabin architecture. Two-story windows faced south from an interior made primarily of stone and unstained blond wood. There was electricity for baseboard heaters but no indoor toilet. The kitchen nook included a tiny, apartment-sized stove and unplugged refrigerator.

Confused but docile, Henry had happily gone to lie in one of the ground-floor bedrooms. He remained there, resting, clearly visible through the open door.

The sky outside was dark, an ethereal lavender. Snow fell as if it were down drifting from a torn ski jacket. Fear crept in again, and Peter used that energy, turning it around.

He said, "How do you and Nick know about this lodge?"

"My friends own it. They rent it out to skiers during the winter but always make sure it's vacant during Freezing Man, just in case we need to use it." Kjell cast a glance to the bedroom door. "I guess we finally did."

Peter dropped his voice to a whisper. "Do you think he's really hurt?"

"He's got a pretty big goose egg on his skull."

"How well do you know him?"

"Are you asking me this as a reporter?"

"I'm asking as a person who saw him very blatantly flee from the scene of a crime." Peter unzipped his coat. The fire and heaters had begun to work their magic, and although it was probably only forty-five degrees in the cabin, that was at least twenty degrees warmer than he had been in over twenty-four hours. Kjell, of course, was already shoeless and shirtless.

"I met him at the first Freezing Man about five years ago. We meet sometimes at gallery openings or at events that he and his wife are catering, but we don't go over to each other's houses."

"So you don't really know that much about him," Peter concluded.

"I know that he's a great cook and his wife is an excellent ice sculptor."

"Do you know if he had any connection to Rick?"

Kjell shook his head. "I've never seen Rick until Wednesday when we all came up."

Well, that took care of Peter's next line of questioning. He was beginning to regret coming up to the lodge when so many unknown and uninterviewed people remained behind at the campground.

He stared at the snow outside, then saw a star, low on the horizon. A very blue star, bouncing along through the trees. Not a star, a headlamp.

Chapter 6

He rushed to the door and stood on the wooden steps, shivering as the figure approached. Nick led three other people along the track Kjell and Peter had left. Snow clung to Nick's beard. Peter's restraint failed. He ran forward through the deep snow and threw his arms around Nick like an actor in a one of those "there's no place like home" airline commercials.

Nick did not hesitate to wrap his arms around Peter, returning his hard embrace, nuzzling his frigid nose into Peter's warm neck.

"I'm sorry too," he whispered. "When we came back and saw that body in the snow, I thought for a second—"

"That I'd managed to get myself killed after all?" Peter finished; he felt Nick shrug.

"I wish *my* girlfriend was here," Shane murmured.

"He's not my girlfriend," Nick said flatly.

"Don't mind him. He just wishes he had a girlfriend at all." Martin tromped past them.

"Is Henry inside?" Janelle's worried voice jolted Peter out of his Hallmark Holiday Moment. Sensing his sudden tension, Nick released him.

Peter suddenly felt the cold through his thin sweatshirt. "Henry is lying down in the back bedroom. We should go in."

Janelle nodded and made for the stairs. "Martin said he tried to drive into town, and hit a tree?"

"That's right." Peter reached into his pants pocket. "Here are his car keys, by the way. Kjell thinks he has a mild concussion."

Peter waited for her to go ahead of them. This might be the last chance for them to talk alone.

Nick seemed to sense this. "Where did Henry think he was going?"

"He said he needed to get the police. I think he may have panicked when he saw Rick's body. Sometimes people get that way when they see a corpse, but I don't know. He had a certain look on his face."

"What sort of look?"

"Horrified but not shocked. Does that make sense?"

"Perfect." Nick dropped his voice lower. "You think he's the guy, don't you?"

"Not necessarily, but his actions are not what I'd call lacking in suspiciousness." Peter shuddered and rubbed his arms. "And Kjell's got no alibi either, incidentally."

"You don't seriously think my cousin killed Rick, do you?"

"No, but that doesn't change the fact that he's got no alibi. I'm just giving you the facts as far as I know them. How did Janelle react to the body?"

"Both shock and horror. I think you'd better go in now."

Nick laid a proprietary hand on Peter's back, steering him toward the lodge door, where Martin and Shane stood stomping the snow off their boots and stripping off their heavy gear. Peter slid by them and ducked inside. Kjell and Henry were where he had left them. Janelle leaned over Henry's bed, holding his hand, talking too quietly for Peter to hear.

Martin and Shane stayed outside for a few minutes more, smoking a spliff and passing a bottle of vodka between them. Peter couldn't tell if Martin had actually liked his friend Rick or not. He'd certainly never had anything good to say about him. Martin also seemed like the kind of guy who covered up his sensitivity with extra doses of machismo.

And when machismo didn't work, apparently weed and vodka did.

Nick greeted Kjell with a bear hug and a huge smile. "I see you built a fire for me."

"It was the least I could do after you rallied the unnecessary search party."

"What else could I do? You're my favorite cousin." Nick sat on the sofa next to Peter, their knees casually touching. "God, what a hell of a New Year's Eve."

"It's not over yet. Want to see what I got done?"

"Sure thing."

Kjell went to get his paint box, a wooden case with spacers in it that enabled a painter to slide wet paintings in and store them without having them touch each other. "Look out for the edges. They're still wet."

"I thought you said you were through with oils," Nick said.

"In the summer, sure, but in the winter it's too damn cold to use the acrylics. I have to drag out the oils, but then I keep forgetting how long they stay wet." Kjell held up his paint-smeared hands. "I think I've managed to stain everything I own this time out."

Nick eased the paintings out, laying them side by side on the coffee table. They were quick gesture sketches with little detail but exquisite color and light. Cycling through all eight of them was like an animatic of how the sunlight moved over a particular ridge throughout the course of the day. Nick paused over one. "Did you run out of cad orange?"

Kjell chuckled. "Yeah, I used it all on this sunset I painted last night. I had to switch to the pyrrole today."

Peter studied the paintings as well. He couldn't see the difference that Nick had mentioned, and said so. Painting shoptalk still eluded him to some extent.

"If you look at the orange in this painting, you'll see it's more muted, more natural than this one. Only mineral colors like the cadmiums gray down like that. Right here you can see where he ran out of cad orange and switched to a brighter, modern pigment."

"You can't get anything by Nick." Kjell said, shaking his head.

At last Martin entered, Shane in tow, red-rimmed eyes excusable because of drunkenness.

He flopped down on the sofa opposite the one where Nick and Peter sat.

"Thanks for letting us come up here," Martin said. "I don't think I could stand to stay down there tonight. I owe you one. Seriously."

"It's no problem." Kjell threw another stick on the fire. "If you really feel like you owe me, you could share a little of that bottle with the rest of us."

Martin silently passed the bottle over, and Kjell took a swig. He offered it to Nick, who found a shot glass, poured himself one, and slid both the bottle and glass along to Peter, who poured but chose to sip. He wanted to keep his mind sharp. The question was how to interview Martin without seeming unbelievably crass.

Martin saved him the trouble of asking.

"I don't know who would do it," he said. "Nobody up here had even met him before today."

"What about people who weren't up here?" Peter asked.

"Rick had plenty of ex-girlfriends who hated him," Shane said. "But none of them were planning to come."

"I don't want to talk about this." Martin suddenly stood. "I want to have a fucking awesome New Year's Eve. That's what Rick would have wanted."

Peter thought of pointing out that Rick would have most likely wanted his killer found and brought to justice, but then maybe Martin did know what Rick would have wanted.

But what Rick was, was dead. What Peter wanted was to find out what Henry knew about the murder. And he wanted a story. There. He admitted it. He wanted a story that he could sell to somebody outside this town. He wanted to believe that his desire sprang from some humanitarian sense of justice, but really he just wanted the story. The chagrin must have showed on his face, because Nick said, "Want to help me make some cocoa?"

Once they were sort of alone by the small stove, Nick cast a long glance sideways at Peter. "I can sense you sleuthing from here."

"I don't deny it." Peter tore open four envelopes of Swiss Miss.

Nick filled the kettle. "I think you need to be careful about what you say, especially to Martin."

"I think that now that you're here, I don't have much more to say to Martin right now. I think I want to talk to Henry."

"Now that I'm here?"

"To back me up."

"Back you up how?"

"In case he comes after me when I ask him questions."

"So you just want me around to be the muscle?"

"No, I want you around to be *my* muscle." Peter pulled what he felt to be a brazen smile, under the circumstances. "I like having you around."

"Then why even consider leaving?" Nick spoke so quietly, Peter could barely hear him.

"I wasn't considering leaving you. If I go, I want to take you with me," Peter said. "I didn't realize it would be so complicated."

"My job?"

"Your job, our relationship, life… I thought it got easier as you got older, not more complicated," Peter said. "I guess this is just a tiny bit related to turning thirty."

Midway through trying to sink his tiny, freeze-dried marshmallows, he suddenly felt Nick's whiskers, then soft lips as he pressed a kiss against Peter's cheek and whispered, "Thank you."

"For what?"

"At least being honest."

🌲🌲🌲🌲🌲🌲🌲🌲

In any relationship, trust is key. But honesty? Is complete honesty completely necessary?

Peter tapped his pen against his notebook. He couldn't really run with this subject. He thought maybe you had to be some sort of relationship expert to write articles about how to live your love life.

Relationship expert... Yes, he could consult several experts or at least paraphrase them.

What was that, honestly—a relationship expert? Somebody who'd been married a lot? That seemed more like a failed-relationship expert than an expert on how to handle being in love or even being married.

He cast a glance to Janelle and Henry. She was sitting by his bedside, rubbing his back and watching him sleep. He couldn't imagine watching Nick sleep. Okay, maybe if Nick had a concussion and it was medically necessary to watch him sleep, Peter could probably manage to keep up with Janelle's level of devotion, but only until qualified professional help arrived. Peter had a restless body and a restless mind.

So why did his heart, which had heretofore been prone to sailing the seas of love, suddenly feel like it had dropped anchor for good?

After downing their cocoa, Martin and Shane had gone up to the loft to stow their gear, while Kjell and Nick had pulled out the checkerboard.

In the other bedroom, Henry mumbled something in his sleep, and Janelle quieted him. Then, apparently noticing how they all started every time Henry made a noise, Janelle closed the door.

"You know, I've been thinking"—Kjell paused while he jumped one of Nick's checkers—"about what happened to Rick."

"What about it?" Nick asked.

Kjell dropped his voice to a nearly inaudible hum. "I think Janelle might have a motive."

"A motive?" Peter scooted closer on the couch.

Kjell said, "I might be wrong about this, but I'm pretty sure that Rick was the same guy who was riding with Nanette when she was killed."

"I thought that guy lived down in Snohomish County." Nick stopped playing checkers.

"People move sometimes." Kjell tapped the checkerboard. "Are you going to take your turn or just forfeit?"

Nick scowled and took a turn. Peter couldn't believe Kjell could care equally about checkers and murder. "Who is Nanette?"

"Janelle's younger sister. About five years ago she was killed in an avalanche while out riding on snow machines with a couple of boys. She was fourteen at the time, and Janelle took it pretty hard."

Skepticism welled up in Peter. "Janelle doesn't seem like the kind of woman who would murder a man for an accident."

"Even if the boy she was riding with was not only five years older than her little sister but so drunk that he went to his car and passed out without ever alerting search and rescue?" Kjell hopped another of Nick's checkers.

Peter had to concede. "That does change things a little bit. Are you sure that Rick is the same guy?"

"Not really," Kjell admitted. "It's hard to remember faces you saw once in the newspaper half a decade ago."

"I'm sure it's him," Nick said.

"Why?"

"Janelle and I talked about it when we were looking for Kjell."

"Why didn't you tell me this?"

"Because I didn't want you to start cross-examining her. We all have to stay here tonight, and being grilled for details by a veritable stranger does not make for a comfortable and screaming-free evening."

Copy flashed before Peter's mind's eye: *Local artist Nick Olson was cross-examined today during the trial of Bellingham's infamous Snowman Murderer. When asked why he failed to identify the murderer's motive to this reporter, he said that it didn't seem polite.*

Aloud, he said, "It didn't occur to you that spending the night locked in a cabin with a killer might be dangerous?"

Kjell emitted a short laugh. "Janelle weighs a hundred and sixteen pounds soaking wet. Nick and I could definitely take her if it came to a fight."

"If she's the killer, she's already managed to whack a healthy young man to death," Peter pointed out.

"If she's the killer, she has no reason to kill anybody but Rick, so we're in the clear." Kjell dealt Nick a crushing quadruple jump. "King me."

"If PBS has taught me anything, it's that a killer will kill again to cover up the first murder," Peter said.

"That's only if a snoopy reporter starts digging," Nick countered. "You can see why I didn't want to tell you about Janelle. I was afraid for your life."

Kjell snorted, and Peter's cheeks burned. "How can you think this is funny?"

"I don't. I really did think preventing you from investigating was the best way to guarantee your well-being." At first Peter thought Nick had suddenly become a master of deadpan; then he realized that Nick was just dead serious.

"Of all the high-handed, arrogant—"

"What he's saying, in his dumb way, is that you're really good at finding out the truth. I think I'd take that as a compliment," Kjell muttered.

Nick nodded in agreement. "What he said."

Peter let it go...for now. "Okay, then, what if it isn't Janelle? We still have Henry's weird behavior. What if it's him?"

"Head-Wound Henry doesn't scare me," Nick said.

"What if it's a husband-wife team?" Peter pressed on.

"What if it's you?" Kjell asked with what Peter had now characterized as a familial bluntness.

"Me? What reason would I have to kill Rick? I've never met him before."

"That's what you say, but how do we really know that?" Kjell asked. "Nick's my cousin, so I trust him when he says he didn't do it, but you…"

"I—" Peter spluttered.

"Ease up, Kjell." Nick put his arm around Peter's shoulders.

"I'm just trying to make a point. I like you, Peter, but you're being really insensitive. People don't like to be accused of murder or questioned or second-guessed."

"I know, but ease up. Peter's got a valid point." Nick made a series of moves that finished mopping up the rest of the board.

Kjell sighed. "Dammit, how do you always do that?"

"I wait until you get distracted doing something like chewing out my boyfriend, and then I make my move." Nick gathered up the checkers and folded the board away into a battered, old cardboard box. He leveled his gaze on Kjell. "I do want to know one thing, though. If you're so worried about upsetting people with questions, then why bring up Nanette in the first place?"

Kjell moved back to the fireplace and sat, back to them, feeding the fire. Finally he said, "I just think that if she did it, she had a pretty good reason, that's all. I thought since you're obviously going to be writing a story about this, you should consider what might have made her do it."

"Murder is still murder, whether you've got a good reason or not." Though the temperature in the room did not change, Peter felt as though ice crystals had suddenly formed in the air between him and Nick's cousin. "But I appreciate what you're trying to do. I think I'll go lay out the sleeping bags."

As he was going, he heard Kjell say, "Your boyfriend's a real prick, Nick."

And Nick replied, "No, he's just a reporter."

Chapter 7

Alone in the small bedroom, Peter fumed. He yanked the sleeping bags out of their stuff sacks with unnecessary force and hurled them onto the double bed. It didn't take long for Nick to appear. He closed the door behind him and leaned against it, arms crossed, keeping his distance.

"This is not the New Year's celebration I envisioned."

Peter cracked a tiny smile. "Me neither."

"The first night was good, though."

"It sure was." Peter sat on the bed, patted the space next to him. "You can come sit down."

Nick did. His thigh pressed against Peter's; his arm draped around Peter's shoulder.

He said, "If we were in a movie, this would be the scene where we have makeup sex. Do you want to make up?"

"I didn't think we were still in a fight."

"We're not, but..." He rubbed his hand along Peter's thigh.

He caught Nick's hand and held it. "I'm a little bit worried that we're in the sort of movie where having sex results in being immediately killed."

Nick laughed. "No, if Kjell's right, we're in a story of tragedy and personal revenge. People who have sex manage to make it through those kinds of movies okay. Sometimes they're even healed."

"What if Kjell's not right, though? What if we're in a slasher flick? The second I get your cock in my mouth, there's going to be some psycho breathing at the window, drawing up plans, about to make us into his snow sculpture."

Peter couldn't keep his eyes from going to the frosty windowpane. No killer lurked outside.

At least none that he could see.

Nick also appeared to be searching for the bogeyman. Their eyes met, and they shared an embarrassed laugh. They kissed, but not a smoldering kiss. A brief, reassuring transaction. Peter's eyes flicked up to the window again.

This time there was a face. Through the frost-smudged glass, he could definitely see the shape of two dark eyes peering in. He leaped back from Nick, pointing.

"It's him!"

The face vanished before Nick could turn.

"Who?"

"There was a face at the window." Peter backed toward the door. Nick went forward, cautiously but not timidly. He pushed the pane up.

"Don't stick your head out, for God's sake," Peter blurted out.

Nick ignored him, leaned slightly out the window, and said, "The outhouse is over by the woodpile."

A softly slurred voice outside replied, "Sorry, man. Hey, have you seen my phone? I think I dropped it someplace."

"Did you check your gear?"

"Yeah, it's not there. I guess I can't call anybody anyway, but it was a nice phone."

"I'll let you know if I see it." Nick closed the window and drew the thin red-and-white-checked curtain. "Martin's taking a leak out there."

Peter sagged in relief, took two steps, and flopped face-first onto the bed. "That scared the crap out of me."

He heard Nick approach, felt the bed dip as he climbed on, then felt Nick's big hands on his back.

"Baby, you're tense. That's to be expected. You found a dead body." Nick gently massaged his shoulders. "Relax a little."

"I found a murdered corpse," Peter clarified. "I am now having a difficult time relaxing."

"But if you manage it, then you'll stop scaring yourself with imaginary psychos and maybe be able to think rationally."

Nick's hands moved down to the small of his back.

"Aren't you afraid at all?" Peter murmured into the pillow.

"Not really. The chance of there actually being some serial killer lurking in the snowdrifts is really slim. For one thing I'd have seen tracks, and the only footprints I saw in the snow led directly to Martin's fine entry into the yellow-snow-making contest."

"But what if the killer has snowshoes with branches on the back of them that brushed out his tracks so that he could move like a phantom through the dark night? You have to keep in mind that this is Bellingham. We've already hosted Ted Bundy, Kenneth Bianchi, and John Allen Muhammad in our town. We're obviously a lightning rod for homicidal lunatics."

"While it's true that they all lived here, they mostly did their killing outside of Whatcom County," Nick countered.

"And then there's Gary Ridgway in Seattle and Robert Pickton right across the border."

"All incarcerated or executed." Nick kept up his gentle ministrations, and Peter found the tension in his muscles slipping away.

"Okay, if an unknown person who is sexually obsessed with snowmen did not kill Rick, then that means one of the other five people in this cabin most likely did. How is that better?"

"It's better because they have no reason at all to hurt you, as long as you don't antagonize them." Nick rolled him over and comfortably settled his body beside Peter's. The pleasant, warm weight of Nick's thigh fell across his own. "If we can just all get through tonight, then you can start asking questions again once we're not all confined together. I'm not asking you to stop being you. I'm just asking you to rein it in for one night. You can ask questions after the police get here."

There was a certain intelligence to Nick's line of reasoning. Peter said, "Does that door lock?"

Nick rose and demonstrated that it did, then, without being asked, locked the window as well.

"Can you get the lights?"

"Does this mean that you think we can make it without getting killed?"

"It means I want to make it without having Martin peeking through the curtains."

Nick smirked. "And here I was thinking you liked the danger of almost getting caught."

"Not by grieving, drunken bro brahs."

"Agreed."

Nick killed the lights, and Peter felt the bed dip as he climbed on and resettled himself against Peter. Again he took the lead, his soft mouth finding Peter's, teasing it open, going deeper.

After the previous night's semiclothed and frigid engagement, it was nice to let Nick undress him, to feel his hot skin, the tight curls of chest hair scraping against his nipples. Peter's cock moved against Nick's as they leveled up from sweet and comforting to hot and hard.

The world beyond the bedroom door receded into a universe made up of him and Nick and the friction between them. Then, in a blind and shuddering moment, it was over, and Peter was once again in a little lodge in the big woods.

But at least he had someone by his side.

Chapter 8

A knock on the door roused them from a mutual doze.

"Are you guys going to stay in there all night?" Martin sounded slightly less drunk than before and slightly desperate. Peter supposed that Kjell and Head-Wound Henry weren't the New Year's Eve companions he'd been hoping for.

"We'll be out in a minute," Peter called.

"What time is it?" Nick rubbed his face.

"Seven fifteen p.m." Peter gave Nick's chest a last friendly scratch before rising to retrieve his clothes. As he did, he remembered the camera in his pocket.

He switched it on and clicked through the pictures he'd taken. The quinzhee. Sculptures. His and Nick's gay Frostys.

Then came Rick. He'd shot at least twenty images, figuring one of them would be good.

Nick finished zipping up his pants and glanced over Peter's shoulder. "Oh sweet Christ, I thought you agreed to give it a rest for now."

"This is not questioning. This is reviewing my photos. And for the record, I agreed to nothing."

Nick gave him a withering scowl—the kind of narrow-eyed, daggers-through-the-skull glare that gave even Peter, who was normally impervious to evil looks, pause.

He backpedaled immediately. "But I am, right now, agreeing that I will give the interviewing a rest."

"Good." Nick leaned closer, drawn, against his will, by the images. Once a visual artist, always obsessed by visuals. Peter angled the camera so that he could see it better. Nick watched impassively as Peter pressed Next, Next, Next. Then, "Wait. Go back one."

Peter complied, wondering what had caught Nick's attention in the previous frame. It seemed virtually identical to the ones directly before and after it, just closer up. After Nick stared for a full minute, Peter was forced to ask, "What are you looking at?"

Nick pointed to a smudge on Rick's jacket. "That looks like paint."

"Yeah?" The significance of this eluded Peter momentarily.

"It looks like cad orange. It's an artist's color. I didn't realize Rick was a painter; that's all." Nick straightened up.

"Maybe he isn't. Isn't that the paint Kjell was—"

Nick cut him off with a silencing hand. "You said you wouldn't."

"But you brought it up."

"I know. I shouldn't have."

Nick started to open the door, and Peter rushed forward to stop him. "Please, can I ask just one more question? That's all I'll ask, I swear. I just want to ask Martin if Rick was a painter too."

"No, you can't."

Peter leaned in, whispering. "Will you ask, then?"

Nick shook his head. "I'm your muscle, not your legman."

"But what if Kjell truly did kill Rick? He seemed really sympathetic toward the idea of Janelle killing him for revenge. Maybe Kjell has a reason we don't know about yet. Maybe the girl was his secret, illegitimate daughter."

"No, that is not possible."

"But you yourself admit that it's exactly the same color Kjell used in the painting he was doing when we saw him the day we arrived."

Nick pushed the camera aside. "You can't even be sure that that's paint. It could be anything."

"It could be, but we could solve that question right now. We could go back down and look at the body again."

"You want to hike back down there in the dark? No. It's way too cold to do that. And it's stupid to go outside when we don't have to."

"I think we have to be sure. If only to know that we can rule Kjell out completely." Peter kept his voice reasonable, calm, hoping that his tone alone would inspire reciprocal reasonability. It didn't.

"First of all, Kjell's right about one thing: it's not up to you to rule anybody out. I don't know who you think you fucking are sometimes."

"I'm an investigative reporter. I investigate. It's my job."

"Investigative reporters investigate things like political scandals and corporate corruption. They read and decipher fine print. You are just a curious motherfucker who thinks he's Miss Marple and can't stop taking pictures of dead bodies."

"I do not think I'm Miss Marple, asshole. I think I'm Jim Rockford."

Nick gave him a long, perplexed look, as though he couldn't decide whether he wanted to laugh or punch Peter in the face. Finally he said, "Yeah, well, you're not. If you fall anywhere on the continuum of fictional detectives, you fall within the nosy-old-woman category. And as a reporter, you're sort of an ambulance chaser."

"They're one and the same," Peter replied archly. "And I'd like to point out that I am an award-winning ambulance chaser, so fuck you. But you are not going to derail my inquiry by insulting me. If you want me to believe that your cousin is innocent, take me back down to Rick's body and prove to me that what I saw wasn't paint. It's only seven thirty, for God's sake. We can make it there and back before prime time is over."

"You realize that even if we do this, it won't eliminate Kjell from our pool of suspects. It won't tell us anything except that the spot is or is not paint."

"But I still think it's important to know."

"And if I do that? If I go along with your absurd demand, what will you do for me?" Nick remained stoic.

A glimmer of optimism sparked up in Peter's chest. Nick was softening; he knew it. "I would think that clearing your cousin's name would be enough of a reward, but what do you want?"

"First, I'd like to reiterate that proving something to you doesn't clear Kjell's name, because you have no legal authority whatsoever. But yes, I do want you to believe me when I say that he wouldn't knock out a complete stranger's brains."

"Maybe he wasn't a complete stranger," Peter put in quickly.

"Are you going to listen to my terms or not?"

"Please, go ahead."

"After dinner, I will take you back down to the camp. If we go down there and find out that you're wrong and that it's not paint, you have to reconsider going to the interview in Austin."

"So if this one lead turns out to be wrong, I have to give up my chance at a better job? That is incredibly fucked-up, Nick."

Nick shrugged. "I'm desperate. What did you expect? If you're right, and it is artist-grade paint, then I'll move to Texas."

Without question, it was the dumbest proposition he'd ever heard. What did the identity of Rick's killer have to do with their relationship? Nothing. And yet before Peter opened up his mouth to say so, he was struck by the fact that they were arguing about where they would live together. Not *if* they would live together, but where. By default that meant that they would stay with each other—that Nick would follow him if he needed to go.

Great tenderness welled up, dissolving most of his anger—though not his sense of irony that Nick would arrange the challenge in a way that linked staying in Bellingham with intellectual failure. But that was an artist for you. Much emotion, minimal analysis.

"You've got a deal."

Chapter 9

Peter lagged behind, not eager to face Kjell again, and not just because of the problem of the paint on Rick's jacket. He'd been called a prick by plenty of people. Men, women—probably some cats and rabbits thought he was a prick as well but had merely been unable to communicate their disdain. But Kjell's special status as Nick's favorite cousin made him want to make it right between them—elevate himself out of the doghouse.

That desire warred with his internal reporter.

Building a timeline of events came to Peter as naturally as breathing. The smear of cad orange on Rick's jacket meant that Kjell had put a hand on him the night he died. More than that, no one could verify where he'd been or what he'd been doing all that night and most of the following day.

But was that smear of color even paint? To be sure they'd have to go back down to the camp, and making that trek would be impossible for him without Nick. He just wasn't that good at orienteering in the dead of night through a snowy forest.

So Janelle had a motive, and the man who could back up her alibi not only had a concussion, but being her husband, Henry would be naturally inclined to support her, even if that meant he had to lie.

And Henry had attempted to flee the scene. Why?

Peter's eye fell on Shane, who stood in the kitchenette helping Kjell rehydrate freeze-dried camp fare. What was his story? Could he have killed Rick? He didn't seem intelligent enough to have tried to hide the body in plain sight in a snowman. Then again, that plan clearly had flaws, as had been demonstrated when the snowman fell apart.

Martin beckoned them over to the sofa, pouring out more vodka shots.

"This one's for Rick." Martin lifted his glass. Peter politely sipped, and to his surprise, Nick resisted the temptation to slug the liquor back. Peter took this as proof positive that Nick did feel at least a marginal amount of tension regarding their unsolved-murder problem.

Nick said, "I didn't get that much of a chance to know him."

"He was just the average shredder prick, but he was my friend." Martin sniffed. "This shouldn't have happened."

Peter almost asked if Rick had any hobbies, say, painting, then forcibly bit his tongue. To his shock he heard Nick say, "He must have been a little bit of an artist, though, right? Otherwise why would he have been up here?"

Martin laughed sadly. "He was up here because he knew Shane's sister was supposed to be coming up tomorrow. He's been following her around for a couple of months."

Ah, perhaps Shane did have a motive after all.

"How do you mean he was following her?" The words were out of Peter's mouth before he realized he was going to be speaking. Nick didn't seem to mind, though.

"Not in a creepy way. Just going to parties he knew she'd be going to, like guys do when they want to score with a girl." Martin suddenly seemed nervous. "I mean guys like us. I don't know what you guys do."

"Pretty much the same thing," Nick said. "Only it doesn't take months to get to bed."

Silent until this point, Shane said, "That must be so cool."

"You're welcome to join our team at any time, but there are some hefty dues that I don't know you want to pay," Peter called back.

Shane pinkened, laughed nervously. "That's okay. I'm pretty good where I am."

Silent until this point, Kjell said, "I'm going to go see if Janelle and Henry want some dinner." He gave Martin a short, severe look. "Maybe we should stop talking fondly about Rick for a while."

Martin nodded, though surliness edged his apparent compliance. "I get it. She doesn't want to have to think about him like he was a human after what he did."

Kjell coaxed Janelle and Henry out of the bedroom with the promise of reconstituted food. They sat close to each other, Janelle rubbing Henry's back intermittently.

Shane found a pack of cards and dealt out hands for gin rummy. The game provided a good distraction for all of them, except Henry, who was still too disoriented to play. He talked about the food, musing over various gourmet dishes that could be freeze-dried.

"Sushi would be funniest, don't you think?"

Peter gave him a smile. "Steak tartare would be pretty hilarious too."

Henry cracked a grin and laughed, then held both his hands to his head. "God, what a headache."

"That sucks that your car got wrecked," Shane said.

"Yeah, man, why were you driving away so fast?" Martin laid down three jacks.

Peter did not allow himself a smug look at Nick. He merely listened intensely.

"I guess I panicked." Henry prodded his food with his spoon. "I've never seen a dead body before. I just thought that I had to get help. I guess I screwed up."

"It's okay, baby." Janelle squeezed his hand. She laid down her cards and leaned back against the couch. "He asked me to forgive him, you know. Rick, I mean. He said he'd gone into treatment, and he had come up here to speak with me personally."

Absolute silence settled across the room. Peter didn't dare meet Nick's eyes as he asked, "What did you say?"

"I told him there was nothing to forgive. I said I hated him, and I always would. And I still do." She stood and brushed herself off. "I think I need to use the restroom."

"It's out back about twenty feet," Kjell said. "There's some paper by the door."

After she went, Martin began to cry. Tears leaked down his cheeks, and he brushed them away, glaring viciously at his cards.

"It's my fault," Henry announced into the dismal atmosphere.

"What's your fault?" Peter asked.

"Rick came to me beforehand and told me he was going to do it." Henry rubbed his face. "I told him that if he sincerely asked to be forgiven that Janelle might do it. He did feel remorse, I think. I believe that. But I didn't think he'd confront her here."

Martin threw down his cards. "He was a dumbass if he thought that would work. Nobody forgives anybody, really."

Shane said, "Sometimes it works."

Martin shook his head. "Only if people believe in God."

Nick shocked Peter by saying, "Then what do you think happened, Henry? Do you think Janelle…"

"No, no. Janelle wouldn't ever hurt anybody. Not even Rick. I think I know her well enough to say that. Besides, she was with me all night."

A gust of cold wind announced Janelle's return. She stomped the snow off her boots and announced that she'd called the sheriff's department.

A ring of puzzled faces greeted her. Finally Martin said, "How? By smoke signal?"

"No, for some weird reason the phone works in the outhouse. I only know because my phone rang while I was in there. They're a little bit behind because so many people are stuck on the roads, but they're sending two guys up on snowmobiles." She shrugged off her coat. "They said they could be up here around midnight."

"Did you tell them there had been a murder?" Peter said. He would have thought a murder would have ranked higher than stranded motorists.

"I said there had been an accident. I figure he's already gone, and we're all safe. There was no use taking up their time on a guy who's beyond their help, right?"

Peter did not like the sound of Janelle's reasoning at all, but liked it even less when Kjell, Martin, and everyone but Nick agreed. He began to formulate the idea that maybe they were all in on it somehow. That the entire Freezing Man festival had been a setup to kill Rick, *Murder on the Orient Express*-style.

He began to feel distinctly unsafe. Turning to Nick, he said, "Didn't you promise me a stroll after dinner?"

Nick nodded. "I did."

"That's not too smart," Janelle remarked.

Nick waved her concern aside. "We won't go too far."

Kjell said, "You better not. We don't want to have to mount two search parties in one day."

Chapter 10

In the darkness of the forest, the abandoned Freezing Man camp seemed like a ruin of some ancient snow kingdom. When they got to Rick's body, Peter found that someone had covered it with a blue tarp. Drifting snow had nearly reburied him.

Happy that no one was around to see them tampering with the crime scene, Peter peeled away the tarp to reveal Rick. He carefully brushed the snow away from the mark on the sleeve. Up close, Peter could see that he had been absolutely right. The mark could be nothing but paint.

"See, it's right there." He pointed.

Nick leaned in close, not touching the fabric but examining the smear of cantaloupe-colored paint for a long time. Finally he straightened up. "I guess I'm moving to Texas."

And suddenly Peter wanted to be wrong, not because he didn't want a new and better job, but because of the naked pain visible on Nick's face.

Shakily he said, "Don't pack your bags yet. Just because it's paint doesn't mean Kjell's the killer."

"No, but it does mean that he knows something he's not telling us. I could see him not telling you, but holding out on me..." Nick gazed up at the wild night sky. "Maybe we should move. This town is screwed up."

"It's no more screwed up than any other place. It's just that other places don't have good reporters in them, so you never find out how screwed up they really are."

Nick appeared to take no comfort in this thought at all. "When we get back to the lodge, I'll talk to Kjell. But I want it to be me, alone."

Evergreen

Peter agreed, and together they carefully drew the tarp back over Rick's frozen body, tucking in the edges. It was as Peter was doing this that he found Martin's cell phone. He must have dropped it when he was trying to dig Rick out, when he still illogically thought Rick could be saved.

At least that was one mystery solved.

They made their way back up to the lodge, Peter following in Nick's footsteps, unspeaking. He wondered what was going on behind that beard but left it alone. More than Peter, even, Nick disliked being questioned about his feelings.

Peter left Nick at the cabin door, his heart once more warring with his professional pride.

He had absolutely wanted to have his theory validated—to have caught a break in the story, and yet he absolutely did not want Kjell to have had anything at all to do with Rick's murder.

He stared up at the fat snowflakes, still falling out of the pink winter sky, wondering if Edward R. Murrow ever had this problem. He couldn't imagine it. Whatever his personal feelings on the matter, he still had to write a story for *the Hamster*. Human-interest feature turned into a weird murder wasn't too bad an idea to pitch to his editor. He decided to phone it in.

He tromped through the snow toward the back of the lodge and the outhouse where Janelle had reported actually getting bars. Sure enough, somehow the exact geographical conditions in the frozen shitter were perfect for cellular reception. Just as he was about to dial, he remembered Martin's phone.

In fact, he remembered it with a kind of burning curiosity that made it impossible to keep from drawing it out of his pocket. Once the thing had come out, snoopiness won the day. He very casually checked for missed calls. There were thirty-four. Peter momentarily marveled at Martin's popularity.

The first five names appeared on the small screen. No one Peter recognized. He scrolled down and saw that the seventh name to appear was Rick's.

Nothing special about that; they'd been going to meet each other.

The call had been placed on Tuesday night at nine eighteen, after Rick was supposed to have left to go back to Glacier. The call itself was evidence that Rick had indeed left, or at least gone far enough toward town to pick up a signal. Why, then, had he come back?

Peter faced a quandary. If he listened, then Martin would almost certainly find out that he'd played his phone messages, an infraction on par with drinking your roommate's last beer while also wearing the guy's socks and underwear. But then, he didn't have to tell Martin that he'd found his phone yet. If he listened to the message from Rick, he could wait until they were about to depart to return the phone, and he'd still have the inside scoop on what was probably Rick's last phone call.

Ethical quandary solved.

He started to listen to the messages. The first two contained references to paying Martin back, and the next four contained oblique references to pot and whether the caller could score some. None of them mentioned the drug specifically, but four consecutive phone messages that requested Martin provide poinsettias for people's New Year's Eve parties formed a distinct absent reference that took the shape of a five-fingered leaf. Martin was, without question, a dealer, probably of marijuana.

So what, though? In Bellingham, half the city sold pot. His best friend, Evangeline, had supported herself for an entire year selling "pot holders."

Last came Rick's message. Hearing the voice of a recently deceased person always gave Peter the chills, but static and distortion made Rick's voice that much more ghostly.

"I'm sorry, but I just can't take it anymore. I don't deserve it. I'm going to tell Janelle the truth when I get up there, and then you can fucking deal with her hating on you for a change. I don't care anymore. I have more than paid you back. I just want her and her fucking husband to leave me alone."

Oh my.

After pausing only long enough to locate his pen, Peter jotted down Rick's exact message, including the time; then he pocketed Martin's phone.

He needed to find Nick. He'd been going at the story all wrong. If Rick was going to tell Janelle a specific truth that would make her hate Martin and leave Rick alone, that could only mean one thing. Martin had been the other snowmobiler who had been with Janelle's sister and Rick on the day that she died.

He shoved open the heavy wooden door and immediately got shoved back inside. He fell back onto the wooden seat; Martin's hand clamped around his neck.

"Give me back my phone." An edge of hysteria tinged Martin's voice. Tears streamed down his face.

Peter clawed at Martin's sinewy arm, but the other man's grip was too strong. He kicked hard at Martin's legs. The man gave out a grunt and slammed his fist into the side of Peter's head.

"Why do you have to be so fucking nosy? I didn't want to do this. I don't even know you, man. Why did you have to make me do this?"

Peter hissed out two words: "fuck off." He got his hand down, found Martin's cock, and twisted as hard as he could. Martin crumpled with a yelp, and Peter broke the choke hold long enough to take a breath. Then Martin's body slammed into him, pinning him into the deep snow. Against the side of his neck, he felt the unmistakable press of a gun barrel.

Chapter 11

"When I get off you, you're going to stand up and not make a fucking sound. Got that?"

"Yeah, I got that." Peter coughed, barely able to get a word out. Not making a fucking sound was going to be pretty easy, he figured. Martin shifted off him, and Peter pushed himself to his feet. He kept his hands in plain sight. Only twenty feet away, the windows at the back of the lodge leaked warm yellow light onto the snow.

He stared at the window, willing anyone to look outside, to see the tableau, to help him, but no face appeared in the window. They were all in the front room by the fireplace. He wondered when Nick would come looking for him. How many minutes it would take for him to start thinking that Peter had fallen or gotten lost. It depended on how the conversation with Kjell was going, he supposed. One thing was certain—it would take less than a second for Martin to blow his head off.

"Walk." Martin ordered. Peter obeyed, his feet sinking into the deep snow. Past his knee on some steps. Slow going. Martin marched him through a stand of trees, directing him on a course that he seemed to know well. Gradually the trees obscured the light from the lodge.

Nick would come for him; that was sure. And he'd be able to follow their tracks in the snow. The important thing was to buy himself a little more time.

"It must have been hard for you," Peter said.

"Shut up." Martin shoved him hard, and he went down in the snow. His gloves were still in the outhouse, and his hands numbed almost instantly. Peter struggled back up to his feet.

"I figure you're going to kill me now." Peter continued reasonably. "I just wanted to say I think I can understand why you did it; that's all."

"Why I did what?"

"Killed Rick."

"Oh yeah, why did I kill Rick?" Martin's voice had a strange quaver, like he would start to cry again. Did he really feel remorse? Maybe.

And maybe Peter could parlay that into a few more minutes.

"I think you were really the person on that snowmobile with Janelle's sister. I think that you convinced Rick to take the fall for you."

"I didn't convince him. He offered. He owed me."

"Owed you?"

"Money. A lot of money. I don't even know why I'm talking to you."

Because you're drunk and you're scared and you feel bad for what you've done, Peter thought. Aloud, he said, "Rick offered to take the blame for the snowmobile accident, and then he changed his mind five years later?"

"I know. It doesn't make any fucking sense, but Rick didn't make any sense. He paid the restitution, went to jail for manslaughter. All that without saying a fucking word, and then suddenly he gets into some damn twelve-step program, and he says he wants to make amends."

"That's kind of a dick move," Peter remarked.

"No shit. Who is he making amends to?"

Peter stumbled forward through the snow a few more feet. The ground had leveled off, and in front of him he saw a long, narrow clearing in the trees. It must be the river. He could see no water moving but knew the ice had to be thin in such a swift current.

Martin's plan became clear. He didn't mean to shoot Peter at all. He would force him out onto the ice until it broke beneath him. Peter slowed, falling down a few more times until Martin yanked him up by his collar. He prayed, to no particular deity, that Nick would be his old vigilant self and come outside to see what had happened to him.

Please.

"Keep moving."

"Just out of curiosity, what did Rick owe you money for?"

"We'd gone in on a deal with some guys—big-time biker guys—to get a brick of weed and sell it. I sold my half, but Rick just gave his away to his friends. He didn't seem to be able to understand that these other guys would cut our balls off, you know? Asshole. When he finally got it, he panicked. Said he was going to go to Canada and hide." Martin gave a short, cynical laugh. "Like bikers can't find you in Vancouver. Bikers own that town."

"So you paid his half for him?"

"Yeah, I did." Martin paused, and Peter could hear liquid sloshing in a bottle. Vodka, probably. "And Rick said that since I'd saved his life, he'd save mine."

"Seems like a fair trade." Peter barely moved forward now, inching along, trying to feel where the solid ground gave way to ice.

"I thought it was, but then he decided to go back on it and tell the truth. What good would that do? I have an engineering degree now. It's all in the past." Martin's voice slurred slightly. Maybe he didn't need Nick after all. Maybe if Martin were drunk enough, he could take him.

Or maybe alcohol would lubricate his trigger finger.

"Plus it would come out that you deal," Peter added.

Martin shoved him forward again. "If you don't keep fucking moving, I'm going to shoot you right here, and that's going to really hurt. Once you're in the water, you won't feel anything. It will be easy."

"You want me to just walk out there?"

"It's all I can do for you." Martin seemed on the edge of tears. "If you hadn't stolen my phone, this wouldn't be happening, okay? None of this would be happening. It's your own fucking fault. Now move."

"All right, I'm going." Peter took two more steps. He knew he had to be out on the ice now, because Martin didn't follow him. He took step after careful step, knowing that Martin would try to avoid shooting him if he could—to try to make his death look like an accident.

One more step and he heard a noise like thunder. The ice shook under his feet. In an instant he lay spread out on the ice. Dark, cold water swept over his feet. The rushing current pulled at him. He scrambled forward like a sea turtle moving through sand.

"Just let it happen," Martin called. "It's better this way."

Peter struggled. Burning cold soaked his feet and legs as he pulled himself forward through the snow toward the bank, breath coming hard and fast. Swimming through the snow away from the dark water, the thunderous sound, the vibrations. At the edge of the river, he saw Martin taking aim. Then from the thicket of trees Nick appeared, taking Martin from behind in a submission hold, forcing him to the ground.

Elation leaped in his heart. He had come. He knew Nick would come.

But the ice was still cracking.

Janelle rushed from behind Nick, heading toward Peter. "Stay right there!" She unwound her scarf and threw it out to him. Kjell followed close behind her.

Peter fumbled at the scarf. His numb fingers would not close around it.

"Just stay where you are!" Janelle had lain flat on the ice just out of arm's reach. Kjell grabbed hold of her ankle. With a last desperate movement, Peter shoved his arm out to her. He knew that her fingers were around his wrist, because he could see them, but he could not feel them.

"Okay, Kjell, pull!"

Suddenly he felt himself hauled up, out, free of the frigid water—and into a deep drift of snow. His body shuddered uncontrollably as he looked up at the sky, the snowflakes, and finally Nick's face.

He said, "Okay, you were right about antagonizing the killer. I won't do it again." He closed his eyes in sheer relief.

He felt Nick's gloved hand on his cheek. "Stay awake, baby. It's too cold outside to go to sleep."

🌲🌲🌲🌲🌲🌲🌲

Two snowmobiles were parked outside the lodge when they returned. The sheriff's department had arrived, cavalry-style, homing in on the GPS in Janelle's phone.

"We took a look at the body down in the sno-park." The older of the two deputies jabbed a finger at Martin. "Now, you want to tell me why that guy's tied up?"

Nick told the story while Peter shivered, naked and wrapped in a blanket, by the fire. The sheriffs decided to take Martin back down to town with them and advised the rest of the Freezing Man crew to stop by to be interviewed on their way back home. As they loaded Martin, weeping and drunk, onto the snowmobile, the deputy said, "We'll have somebody come up and move that car that's blocking the road in the morning. You folks have a happy New Year."

Epilogue

New Year's Day

Driving back on Highway 542, Peter didn't talk much and neither did Nick. The Audi rolled along wet blacktop, snaking through the canyon of snow that had so unnerved him on the way up.

Weirdly, Peter now felt no sense of impending doom, no fear that the walls would collapse on him.

Trust a near-death experience to adjust your personal threat level.

They reached Nick's cliffside house on Wildcat Cove just after noon. Peter went to make some coffee, glancing up through the great room occasionally to observe Nick's progress in unloading their gear. He hauled the sleeping bags, camp stove, and even the pulka into the foyer. Then he sat down on the birchwood modernist boot bench and pulled off his Salomons. He looked tired.

Peter brought him a whiskey-laced coffee.

They sat together on the bench in the foyer, as if neither one of them wanted to commit to fully entering the house. Or maybe that's just how Peter read it.

Finally Nick said, "I hated that."

"It did really suck," Peter agreed.

He let Nick drape an arm across his shoulders and pull him close. Peter curled closer to Nick's shoulder, resting his cheek against the fine cable of his sweater. Nick's hand rested lightly on the back of his neck. Nick said, "I won't hold you to it."

"What are you talking about?"

"The deal we made about Kjell. If you decide to go to Austin, I'll go with you."

Peter raised his head, searching Nick's eyes for any sign of resentment. He found none there. "But what about your career?"

"I'll find a way to work it out. It's not as important to me as you are." He spoke in such an offhanded manner that Peter nearly missed the significance of his statement. When he did, he felt tears prickling at the back of his eyes. His breath felt unsteady.

Touched but embarrassed by his reaction to Nick's admission, Peter said, "You're not just saying that because I almost got killed, are you? Because that shock and fear will wear off, and you'll still be in Texas."

"I *am* saying that because you almost got killed, actually, but I don't think that makes my reaction less valid. I think it's called a moment of clarity." He pulled Peter in close again and whispered, "You don't have to say you love me back. I already know you do."

Peter gulped, his throat tightened, and he could no longer see. He sat there, breathing deeply, trying to get himself under control. Failing to keep the quaver out of his voice, all he could say was, "I don't want to leave here. And I don't want to leave you for any job. Does that make me a failure?"

"How would that make you a failure?"

"Real men follow their ambitions. Always." Peter sniffed.

"I think you're thinking of straight men. Those real men don't have to try and live with other real men. Besides, plenty of guys follow their hearts. They just don't admit it out loud," Nick said. "And in regard to ambition, you seem to do a pretty good job finding news right here." Nick rubbed his shoulder. "Though I would prefer it if you could manage to just report news stories instead of actually being a news story yourself."

"But you have to admit, it gives me a great angle when I'm writing the piece."

"You're good enough that you don't need the extra angle."

"So just out of curiosity, did Kjell ever explain about the paint?"

"He did. He said that he broke up an argument between Martin and Rick the night before we got there. Just as he was saying that, it occurred to me that I should go find out what was taking you so long."

Peter blinked, sighed, and shook his head. "Well, dammit. I wish he'd told me that earlier. That's what I would describe as a critical piece of the puzzle that could have saved me a near drowning."

"I'll mention it to him the next time I think he's holding out on me." Nick petted Peter's back and shoulder for a long moment, then said, "Not to change the subject, but is that smell me or you?"

Peter laughed. "I think it's both of us."

They managed, laughing, to get to the bathroom and get their clothes off without any further discussion of their lives or emotions, which suited Peter just fine. As he watched Nick strip off his remaining clothes, he thought, *This is mine.*

Aloud, he said, "I've made a decision."

"You're going to stay naked forever?"

"Nice try. I'm not going to the interview, but I do want something in return."

Nick watched him attentively, expression wary. "What is that?"

Peter laid a hand along Nick's jaw, scratching lightly at his whiskers. "I want you to get this thing off your face. You look like Grizzly Adams's biggest fanboy."

"How about you take it off yourself?"

"You're on." Peter found the trimmer and went to work, first carving Nick's mountain-man beard into various permutations, including the Vandyke and the seventies-cop handlebar with soul patch. Once fully shorn, Nick cranked the knobs on the steam shower. He picked up his razor and waggled it at Peter from inside the glass enclosure. "Don't start a job you're not willing to finish."

Peter smiled. Getting a smooth, clean shave was going to be a lot of fun.

BLACK CAT INK

Chapter 1

Peter Fontaine did not spend the majority of his free time in alleys. However, readers of *the Hamster*, Bellingham, Washington's most independent weekly newspaper, could be forgiven for thinking that lurking near Dumpsters was his primary hobby. His most famous piece of investigative reporting—coverage of the murder of Shelley Vine three years prior—had been an exercise in extensive alley dwelling.

And not nice alleys, either. Wet, unevenly paved downtown alleys filled with urine, drunken college students, and angry, misguided skunks.

By comparison the alleys five miles east, near scenic Whatcom Falls Park, were like country lanes. Oak and maple branches, leafed in autumn gold and red, hung over the gravel lane. Well-maintained garbage cans dotted the wayside. Here and there a rusty old engine or push lawn mower lay subsumed by rose brambles and convolvulus and dewy spider webs. The only smell of decay was the faint scent of fermentation from a dozen or so fallen apples.

And there were skunks here as well, but they seemed an altogether nicer variety of *Mephitis* happy to give Peter a brief nod and go on their way, leaving him to stalk the alley in peace.

It was six o'clock in the morning, and the sun had yet to fully illuminate the gray October fog. Faint drizzle fell, covering the foliage with a sheen of moisture. There was just enough light for Peter to see into the backyards of the houses he passed. He glanced to the left, then to the right, walking his bike crookedly, trying his best to impersonate a student returning from an epic night of drinking—all the while searching for a small granite statue.

He saw trampolines, beehives, chicken coops, tents, and swing sets—both decrepit and new—gardens and the unmistakable purple light from grow lamps seeping from one basement window. But he did not see anything that resembled the sculpture that had been stolen from the Western Washington University sculpture garden three months before.

Vexed, he headed toward Whatcom Falls Park proper. There he sat down on a curb in the parking lot to text Nick that he'd hit another dead end.

He typed. *Whatcom Falls a bust. R U home or at studio?*

Prominent local artist Nick Olson was the boyfriend that Peter'd acquired during his investigation into the Vine case. He was a big brunet ex-army intelligence officer who, after having discovered his more artistic side in the arms of an internationally renowned painter—the now six-years-deceased silver fox Walter De Kamp—had embarked on a painting career of his own.

Peter and Nick presently lived together in De Kamp's hulking modernist house that hugged a sheer cliff face above a body of water on the west coast of Washington State recently renamed the Salish Sea. On the one hand, Peter loved the house. Not only was it a better domicile than he could ever hope to afford on any salary he might earn in his lifetime; it also had a great, romantic name: the Castle on Wildcat Cove.

The only downside of the house was that it was the house Nick had lived in with another man. It was De Kamp's massive abstract paintings that decorated the walls and De Kamp's color sense that had led to what Peter felt was a strong overuse of dreadnaught gray, particularly in the master-bathroom tiling. Peter had no idea why a person would choose battleship when Payne's gray, the signature gray-blue of the Pacific Northwest sky, was so much more beautiful.

Occasionally, as he gazed at the house, a feeling very much like inadequacy would assault Peter. Look what De Kamp had given his lover, while the most Peter could hope to give Nick was a headache from his constant talking. He wished he could bring something as remarkable and original to Nick's life, but Peter wasn't an artist. He wasn't even a poet. He would look at the Castle and have no idea why Nick stayed with him, but he did. Nick was nothing if not loyal.

Now, on account of Nick's loyalty to De Kamp, Peter was shivering in the drizzle, searching backyards for a five-foot statue of... Well, Peter didn't know what it was of, exactly, since the name of the piece was *Untitled Five*. But from photographs he had decided that it looked something like a phallus.

Maybe even Nick's phallus.

There was a familiar and somewhat jaunty angle to the thing.

From deep within the pocket of his hoodie, Peter's phone vibrated.

Nick had replied. *Studio. Where R U? Want ride?*

To which Peter responded *Yes. W. Falls. By trout tank.*

5 minutes, came Nick's reply.

A chill, wet breeze moved around Peter and he pulled his hood up to keep the damp out of his ears. Skinny and wiry, Peter had always gotten cold easily. Nonetheless, when standing before the closet, he could never quite bring himself to dress in the unflattering, loose style typical of the Pacific Northwest dude. This always led to the realization that he should have worn a heavier coat. But then he'd realize he didn't own a heavier coat that wasn't a parka, and his manly pride kept him from borrowing Nick's clothes. Peter had never considered himself a slave to fashion, but occasionally he had to admit to being fashion's bitch.

As was his habit, when he was bored or uncomfortable, Peter be began to compose text in his head.

When the phone rang, early on the morning of July fifth, Nick Olson picked up on the first ring. The ability to rise quickly to alertness from a dead sleep was a holdover from Olson's army days, and his crisp-sounding voice belied the fact that he'd been snoring one second before.

Olson sat up. July sun streaming in the wide, curtainless windows dappled the dark, curly hair on his muscular chest and glinted off his small gold hoop earrings. As he spoke to the mysterious caller, this reporter felt both his curiosity and lust rising. He began to eavesdrop in earnest.

As he listened, Olson's expression darkened.

It transpired that a De Kamp sculpture, Untitled Five, *had been stolen from the Western Washington University campus.*

Somewhere close by, a cat let out a screeching wail, which triggered a chorus of early-morning barking from the resident dogs. Peter sniffed and wiped a drop of rain from his nose and glanced up the drive for Nick's Audi.

Nothing. He went back to his mental composition.

Olson, who had considered De Kamp to be his husband despite the fact that De Kamp had died before legal marriage had become a possibility, took news of the theft badly. Campus police supposed that the crime had to have been the result of Fourth of July high jinks and theorized that it would turn up eventually. It never did.

Again came the meowing of a cat, only much closer now. Peter peered through the fog toward circular gray trout hatchery tanks. A tiny black form wandered there, giving high-pitched and plaintive calls. The kitten walked with a strange stiffness. Not quite a limp, but not quite normal either.

"Here, kitty." Peter stretched his arm toward the kitten, wiggling his fingers slightly—the way he had always attracted his friend Evangeline's three-legged cat, Tripod.

The kitten picked up the pace, crossing the lawn toward him, still crying.

If it had a collar, Peter reasoned, he could take it back home. The thing was clearly lost. If not, he could take it to the shelter, where at least it could be fed.

The kitten reached him, meowing piteously and butting its head into his fingers, purring much more loudly than he would have thought such a small creature capable. He was about to scratch the kitten's back when he saw it. A circular patch of the kitten's skin had been removed from its back.

Peter pulled his hand back in horror.

Seconds later, he saw headlights approaching along the park's narrow wooded drive. The sleek silver body of Nick's Audi blended with the morning fog.

Peter scooped up the crying kitten, stood, and flagged him down. Nick smiled at him as he opened the car door. "Hey, gorgeous, need a ride?"

"We need to go to the vet right away." Peter set the injured kitten on the passenger seat before loading his bike into the back of Nick's car. Returning, he gathered the strangely docile creature in his hands and flopped down into the car. The kitten barely filled his cupped palms. In the close confines of the car, he could smell the blood from its wound.

"Where did you find that thing?" Nick leaned closer; then, catching sight of the round patch of bare flesh, he sucked in his breath sharply. "I see what you mean about a vet."

"Somebody will be at the Cat Clinic by now. We can go there."

"I don't know how to get to the Cat Clinic."

"Just head downtown. I'll give you directions." With one finger, Peter petted the kitten's nubby, rounded ear.

Nick glanced over. "What do you think happened to it?"

"I think the Halloween cat skinner came back to town."

Chapter 2

One thing Bellinghamsters love is their pets. They dote on their dogs, they dig their Indian runner ducks and backyard chickens, and adore their miniature goats. But in terms of feline-friendly municipalities, Bellingham is a little piece of heaven for Felis silvestris catus, *the common house cat. Perhaps that is why the Halloween cat skinnings of three years prior caused such collective outrage.*

Even die-hard dog lovers distributed posters and door-belled, asking people to come forward with any information that might be useful in apprehending the person responsible for removing large sections of fur from at least five black cats. Three of the animals died from their injuries, and the other two survived, but with terrible scars.

The cat skinner was never arrested, although an anonymous police officer claimed that they more or less knew the identity of the culprit but couldn't acquire enough evidence to convict him.

A piteous and deafening yowl broke Peter's concentration. Beside him, on the padded bench in the waiting room of the Cat Clinic, sat a tall, skinny man covered with tattoos and pierced in virtually every fashionable area—most likely including his nipples from the way that the fabric ruched at the man's chest. On his lap he held a cat carrier containing an angry calico. The skinny man looked vaguely embarrassed and said, "She hates to get her shots," apparently by way of apology.

Peter tapped his pen on the side of his notebook. Beside him, Nick leafed through an issue of *Cat Fancy* with a perplexed expression. They waited together while a senior veterinarian was taking a look at the kitten and advising a course of treatment for her.

The kitten, apparently, was a *her.*

Not only a *her* but a five- or six-week-old *her.*

He flipped his notebook closed and stared at the assortment of cat magazines fanned out across the coffee table in the tiny waiting room. A veterinary assistant in blue scrubs called Tattoo Guy and Angry Calico into a waiting room, leaving Nick and Peter alone with the kindly-looking receptionist and rack upon rack of special-diet cat food. When his phone vibrated, Peter jumped. Nick glanced over the glossy pages at him questioningly.

"Phone call. My editor," Peter said.

"He probably wonders why you're not at work," Nick commented.

Peter nodded wearily and stepped outside to answer. The sun had fully risen, but its light had yet to penetrate the layers of fog that blanketed the normally quiet side street, temporarily busy with morning commuters heading toward the downtown core.

"Hey, Doug," Peter said.

"Hey, did you find the big penis?"

"Penis…?" It took him a moment to understand what Doug was talking about. His alley patrol in search of the missing sculpture seemed like it had happened days ago. "Sorry. No luck on that one."

"Don't suppose you'd mind coming to work, then? I need somebody to drive the truck."

Peter winced. Long ago—well, all right, eight years ago—when he'd first started working for *the Hamster*, his duties had not only included writing articles but distributing the rag around the city. Winning a Tom Renner award had gotten him out of driving detail, but somehow every couple of months he ended up back behind the wheel of the old truck, slogging papers in the rain.

"What happened to Shawn?" Shawn was their current distro driver. A dreadlocked half-Japanese guy with a winning smile and dubious personal entertainment habits.

Doug sighed. "Shawn came in this morning and told me he had to get out of town for a while cause he owes some people some money."

"Which people? What money?"

"I didn't care to know," Doug remarked. "All I do know is I can't hump those papers anymore. Not since my hernia."

Now it was Peter's turn to sigh. It wasn't that he didn't believe in Doug's hernia—but Doug milked it an awful lot. "Isn't there anybody else?"

"Everyone else has appointments."

"Okay, I'll do it, but I'll be a little while. I'm at the vet."

This brought a politely nosy inquiry from Doug. Peter explained the circumstances, and Doug let out a low whistle.

"Are you sure it's the cat skinner? Because that would cause a real uproar in the city, and I'd want to have a veterinarian's quote or a police statement before I ran the story."

"That's what I'm waiting for." Peter glanced through the window and saw the friendly blonde vet talking to Nick. Their expressions mirrored each other. A study in seriousness.

"I've got to go. I'll be in to do the distro later."

Peter snapped his phone shut and went back in. He entered just in time to hear Nick explaining once again that *she* wasn't his cat.

Dr. Nagelschneider nodded with what could only be described as resigned understanding. She was a middle-aged woman with straw-blonde hair and tan, weathered features. Both the texture of her skin and her slight Southwestern twang revealed her to be a transplant to the area.

"Even if she isn't your cat, she certainly is a hoot," she said. Then spying Peter returning, she added, "You must be Dad."

Peter nodded, though *she* wasn't his cat either. Someone had to take responsibility—at least until she was well enough to go to the shelter.

"What was her name?"

"I haven't decided yet," Peter said. "I just found her today."

"So you don't know how she got the wound on her back?"

Peter shook his head. "It looked like the skin had been removed."

"Well, it looks to be deliberate, so I've informed the police about this," the vet said. "Just to give them a heads-up. They're on their way over here."

Dr. Nagelschneider watched his reactions carefully as she spoke, and Peter realized, with shock, that she was looking for signs of guilt. Logically, he supposed that her suspicion was only natural. Probably a fair number of injuries to animals were inflicted by the people who brought them in. Still, Peter felt a slight prickle of offense at coming under such scrutiny.

"I'd be happy to talk to the police," Peter reassured her. "But what I really want to know is if she's going to be okay."

"Oh sure, she's going to be fine. Kittens have very loose skin, so we'll be able to sew her up all right. We'd like to keep her overnight and give her some antibiotics and fluids since she's pretty dehydrated. But you're free to take her home in the morning." Her eyes flicked between Nick and Peter. "If your plans were to take her home, that is."

"I—" Nick began, but Peter cut him off like a teenager in a tricked-out Mazda.

"We sure are." He grabbed Nick's hand, lacing his fingers through Nick's thicker, browner ones. Nick seemed baffled by his sudden public display of affection but didn't pull away. "At least until we can find a good home for her."

"That's really generous of you fellas. Not a lot of people would do that." Dr. Nagelschneider glanced past Peter, out the front window. "The police are here."

Seeming to stiffen slightly at the sight of the police officer getting out of her car, Nick asked Peter, "Do you want me to stay?"

"It's not necessary. I have to go drive *the Hamster* truck this afternoon anyway." Peter released Nick's hand. "I'll see you at home."

"Right, I'll see you there," Nick paused then, cracked a sardonic smile, and added, "*Dad*."

With that, he fled the scene.

Like most other members of the Bellingham Police Department, Officers Patton and Clarkson were known to Peter. The very same officers had been first on the scene of Shelley Vine's murder. They looked very much the same. Officer Patton still sported the same dykey mullet, and Officer Clarkson's heavy moustache remained eternal, as if stamped out of some mold made in the mid seventies when *CHiPs* had still been popular.

They exchanged pleasantries. Officer Patton inquired about Nick, and Peter said he was doing great. Both police officers nodded at him as though it had been their duty to check up on the happiness level Bellingham's premier young gay couple.

Officer Clarkson said, "Dr. Nagelschneider tells us you found a cat."

Peter explained where he had found the kitten, omitting the fact that he'd been heavily engaged in skulking through the alley minutes beforehand.

"And you didn't see anyone there?" asked Officer Patton.

"Not even a jogger," Peter replied.

She nodded, jotted something down in her notebook. "What were you doing in the park that early? It's pretty far away from Wildcat Cove."

Peter thought, ah, small-city police. They *do* remember where you live.

"Riding home from a party." Peter supplied the excuse he had prepared. "Hey, do you mind if I ask a question?"

Both officers glanced up at him. Peter took this to be assent and said, "Have you seen any other instances of this kind of cat abuse recently?"

Strangely, Officer Clarkson chuckled. The receptionist, who had been silently eavesdropping on their whole conversation, shot him a glare so cold that Peter felt his testicles shrinking back up into his body.

Shaking with outrage, she stood and said, "I'm sorry, but I really don't see what's funny about that."

"I'm sorry. I just thought Mr. Fontaine was going to ask me about the statue that went missing from the university campus." The officer took off his hat, scratched his head. "I should have known you'd want the inside scoop on this. This is the third incident that veterinarians have reported to us this month, but that's not unusual for the month of October."

"Three reported incidents means there are probably more," the receptionist said. Now that she'd entered the conversation, she'd apparently decided to stay.

Officer Clarkson reapplied his hat and turned to address the receptionist directly. "I already spoke with the chief, and he told me that we'll be issuing a warning to the public later this afternoon. It should be in the *Herald* and on KGMI first thing tomorrow morning."

"Do you think it's the same sicko as before?" Peter asked.

"Hey, who's interviewing who here?" Officer Patton cut in before her partner could answer.

Peter held up his hands in mock defense. "I'm just curious. I know that the police had a suspect before."

"It's not the same one," Officer Clarkson said. Peter focused on him, since he seemed in a repentant and therefore extremely forthcoming mood after sticking his foot in his mouth.

"How can you be sure?"

"Because that individual died very shortly after the investigation began." Officer Clarkson cast a glance at the receptionist—who had finally returned to her seat—and then to Peter.

"Can you tell me who that individual was? Now that he's dead, I mean?" Peter caught himself unconsciously leaning in closer to the officer. He couldn't help it. Juicy tidbits of information drew him like… Well, like a cat to catnip.

Officer Patton stepped forward, probably to save her partner from divulging anything else. She said, "We have no new suspects at this time, but we encourage the public to come forward with any information they might have regarding this matter. You have a nice day now, Mr. Fontaine."

Chapter 3

After giving his statement to the police, Peter rode his bike the seven blocks to *the Hamster's* offices in downtown Bellingham. He picked up keys to *the Hamster's* white Toyota—the bed was already full of bundled papers—and checked the delivery route. It had been a few months since he'd delivered and even longer since he'd driven out into the county for any reason other than to go to the ski area.

His mind roved as he jiggered the old truck into gear.

Snuggled up against the largely undefended Canadian border and bounded on the west by the Strait of Juan de Fuca, Whatcom County is a place of extremes. Tie-dyed liberals from the university in Bellingham keep hope alive, facilitating the country's longest-running peace vigil—forty years old and still going strong—while out in the county the Aryan Nations holds routine meetings, complete with target practice. The one thing these disparate elements can agree upon is that the mainstream media comprise nothing but propaganda, provocation, and lies.

Enter the Hamster, *a weekly paper that, while slanting to the left at least manages to deliver the truth.*

Someone's idea of the truth, anyway.

It always amazed Peter that anyone outside of rock-throwing distance of the university would be interested in Doug's conspiracy-theory-laden editorials or his leftist views on watersheds and zoning laws.

But *the Hamster* had a strong readership in the county. Right on the outskirts of the city of Lynden—a municipality so religious that it still outlawed dancing—were vineyards producing award-winning wines and dairy farms crafting artisanal cheese. Farther into the mountains, near Glacier, survivalist militia types shared solar-shower tips with off-the-grid environmentalist homesteaders. Rifle ranges stood within sight of alternative no-kill animal-rescue organizations.

He drove from restaurant to coffee shop to corner store throughout greater western Whatcom county setting out bundles of free papers among the stacks of other free papers, the *Thrifty Nickel*, *Whatcom Watch*, and *Whatcom Independent Tribune*—the *Hamster's* rival for local news—and real-estate brochures and a paper devoted entirely to buying and selling horses. More than one person asked him about Shawn's whereabouts, some with looks of weedy desperation that gave Peter the distinct impression that Shawn had been using this route as a distro for his own sideline alternative pharmaceutical business. He wondered who exactly their delivery driver owed so much money to. Not any of these people, certainly. These were his regular customers, not his supplier.

Five hours later, with a sore back and dirty hands, Peter found himself heading west again toward Bellingham. He pulled over at Nugent's Corner to drop off a bundle of *the Hamsters* and get a coffee. When he returned, a young woman was standing by the truck, tucking a note under the windshield wiper.

Peter sidled up beside her. "Can I help you with something?"

She jumped and smoothed her straightened and streaked blonde hair, and glanced past Peter toward a black truck that sat idling close by.

Her ride, clearly.

Flame decals decorated the side panels along the truck bed, but the tinted windows didn't allow him to see the driver's face. Neither of these features was uncommon in the county, but Peter took note of the truck because it contained a large black goat. Again, animals in the backs of pickups were not unusual in this neck of the woods, but they were normally dogs.

How odd...

The girl, who had recovered herself somewhat said, "I'm sorry, I thought this was my friend's truck." She went to retrieve the note, but Peter stepped between her and the windshield.

"Is your friend Shawn?"

She smiled. "That's right. Do you know where he is? I really, really need to talk to him."

Probably really, really needed to buy some pot from him, more likely, Peter thought ungraciously. Aloud he said, "Shawn's taken a short vacation. You should try calling him."

"I did, but he's not answering."

The driver of the truck honked, and the girl jumped again. She made a second attempt to grab her note from under the windshield wiper, but Peter was quicker. He pocketed the folded square of paper, saying, "I'll make sure to give this to him, Miss...?"

"Thanks, I've got to go now." She turned and practically ran back to the truck, which started rolling away before she even got the passenger-side door closed. Peter watched them peel out along 542, heading east toward Maple Falls. Mud spattered the whole back of the truck, including the license plate.

Not that Peter had any way of looking up a license plate number, anyway. He sipped his coffee and watched the car until it rounded a bend on the two-lane blacktop.

Then he unfolded the note.

It had been scribed in big, bubbly handwriting: *Fucker. We will eat your soul.*

And there was a pentagram. Inverted, of course.

Peter pondered the note for a moment before replacing it in his pocket and heading back into town.

Unless Shawn had become engaged in some kind of live-action role-playing game, he seemed to be in some serious shit.

Peter's last stop was a Mexican restaurant directly across the street from the Vitamilk building where Nick had his studio.

Because Peter felt it was better to apologize than to ask permission, he was always in the position that he was in now—having to say he was sorry for not asking Nick about the kitten before he'd agreed that it could stay with them.

It wouldn't do any good to prolong the agony. He figured he should cross the street now and see if Nick was mad at him.

Originally a dairy distribution warehouse, the Vitamilk Building had been converted into cheap studio space sometime in the mid-eighties. Nick and seven other artists, whose prestige and talent ranged from international gallery quality to church craft fair…er, fare, produced masterpieces in the dingy interior. It was where Nick and Peter had first met, when Peter had walked in on Nick, bent over the body of Shelley Vine at what looked like the scene of a murder.

Well, in fairness, it *had* been the scene of a murder, but Nick hadn't been the culprit. Still, he'd been covered in blood.

Not exactly the best first impression, but somehow Peter had decided to ask him out anyway. The rest was history.

Walking up the wide stairs to the second-story studios, Peter always had a glimmer of a memory of that night. It had been the first time he'd ever seen a dead body, though, as it turned out, not the last.

He had no idea why Nick stayed here after that. He had enough money to rent a better space. Hell, Walter had had a better studio built into his house. It had climate control and ventilation. Nick never went into the room except to access his camping gear, which was all that he stored in that state-of-the-art facility.

Peter would have thought that Nick enjoyed the camaraderie of the Vitamilk Building, except he always kept his door closed, no matter how hot or cold it got. It was closed now, and Peter knocked, as he always did.

No matter how long they lived together, Peter didn't think he would ever be able to just walk into Nick's studio. It was Nick's sanctum, seeming almost a sacred space—if Peter had believed in sacred spaces, which, as an investigative reporter, he most certainly did not. He dearly yearned to rifle through the drawers and canvases of Nick's studio, leaf through the books, sniff the assorted solvents, and otherwise stick his nose into Nick's creative business.

But Nick liked his privacy, and Peter wanted to keep him, so he always knocked and, like a lurking vampire full of hope, waited to be invited in before crossing the threshold.

Nick answered the door and invited him in, his expression not as hostile as Peter had imagined it might be. Warm afternoon light slanted in the large, mottled windows to illuminate Nick's most recent canvas—an abstract expressionist seascape.

He wore his typical autumn studio gear: an old army T-shirt, paint stained and so threadbare that Peter could clearly see the outline of his muscular torso. Nick's only concession to the chill air had been to put on a pair of fingerless gloves, which lent him an air of starving, turn-of-the-century Paris Bohemian.

Peter perched himself on a three-legged stool that Nick had installed specifically for this purpose. He wasted no time, just got down to business.

"Are you mad about me offering to take care of the cat?"

Nick glanced over at him. "I'm not happy about it, but I'm not mad. I thought you were doing *the Hamster* delivery route."

"I just finished."

Nick nodded, taciturn as ever—but not more taciturn. That was a good sign.

After painting a few wide strokes, Nick said, "I guess as long as we don't end up keeping the cat, it'll be all right."

"Did I say anything about keeping the cat?"

"You like cats." Nick spoke as though delivering incriminating evidence at a trial.

"So what?"

"You get a cat, you're going to get attached to the cat and end up keeping the cat. And I'm just not really a cat person," Nick said. "If we got any pet, I think I'd prefer a dog."

"Yeah, a big dog, right?" Peter crossed his arms and leaned against the wall behind him. The chilly mid-October air seeped in through wide cracks in the window frames.

"I like retrievers." Nick didn't look away from his painting. Nor did Peter expect him to. After spending hours and hours in Nick's studio, he'd grown used to having conversations during which little or no eye contact was ever made.

"Regardless of the fact that you suspect me of being some kind of stray-cat sympathizer, I do not want to keep this cat forever. I just want to give her a hand until she's better, because nobody is going to want to adopt a mangled little dehydrated cat."

"She's not mangled."

"She's definitely not completely whole," Peter countered. "And I don't know why you're getting so bent out of shape about a having a cat houseguest for a couple of weeks. I live with your dead husband's furniture every day, and I don't complain."

Even as the words were leaving Peter's mouth, he knew he should not have said them. And yet, he had. More shockingly, to himself at least, he hadn't even known he was going to say them.

Normally when he was going to fire a shot across the bow of Nick Olson, he rehearsed. He carefully chose his words. He didn't just say whatever the hell he was thinking the absolute moment that it occurred to him.

Nick dropped his paintbrush into a jar of solvent, fixed Peter with his Viking blue eyes, and said, "Where the fuck did that come from?"

Peter himself did not know where the fuck that had come from. But he also intuitively knew that the words he'd spoken were nonetheless true. Peter replied, "I know I didn't pay for the Castle. My name isn't on the title, but I live there too, and I think I should get to make some sort of decision about it. That's all I meant."

"But we're not talking about the house. We're talking about a cat." Nick picked up his brush again, swished it though the solvent.

"Are you allergic to cats?"

"No, but—" Nick began, but Peter cut him off.

"Are you afraid of cats?"

"Of course I'm not."

"Then why are you fighting with me? She weighs less than a pound. She'll be there for maybe a couple of weeks. How much trouble could she be?" Again, even as he spoke, Peter knew that his argument was anything but watertight. A single kitten could cause quite a lot of trouble, and he knew it. But he stared levelly at Nick anyway, daring him to call him on it.

Nick didn't.

He daubed his brush in Naples yellow paint and said, "I'm not fighting with you at all, and I'm not bent out of shape. I already said she could stay until she's better."

Suddenly embarrassed that the fight that he'd been preparing to put up seemed now irrelevant, Peter said, "Thank you."

Nick shrugged, saying nothing. What started off as a pause stretched into silence. Peter couldn't tell if he was getting the cold shoulder or if Nick had just become absorbed in his work. Either way he'd won Battle Kitten.

Even as he savored this victory, he realized that he didn't have anything to keep a kitten in, not even a carrier to get one home. He decided that before he returned to the Castle, he should call on someone who did.

Chapter 4

Peter's best friend, Evangeline, had been his roommate during the last half of college as well as three grim post-baccalaureate years when neither of them could find a real boyfriend. During that time he'd grown very attached to her late three-legged cat, Tripod, and grown well acquainted with her family, since he was her usual date for any holiday-related event. It wasn't that Peter didn't have a family. It was simply that his own parents had moved to Austin some years back, and flying to visit them in Texas more than once a year rarely fit into his schedule.

Since then, both Evangeline and he had shacked up with men who suited them. Tripod had passed away, but Evangeline and her lover, Tommy, had recently acquired a young wiener dog from the Whatcom County Humane Society. The wiener dog had been scooped up along with seventeen other mixed-breed dogs in a raid on an animal hoarder who lived out in the county. Being a sucker for runts, Evangeline had picked the sickliest of the animals, nursed him back to health, and named him Mitch.

Peter resisted the urge to draw a correlation between the injured wiener dog and his own disastrous mental state when Evangeline had taken him in during his junior year of college. She was the first person he'd come out to, and when, drunk and bleary, at six o'clock in the morning, he'd finally managed to spit the words out, she'd said, "It's okay. I already knew that."

Shortly thereafter he'd moved into her rented house. No one had seen him through as many sad and angsty nights as she had done. Even today, when he and Nick fought, she was the first person Peter autodialed. While what had just occurred hadn't exactly been a fight, Peter dialed her anyway, out of habit. He explained the situation and asked if he she still had Tripod's old cat carrier. She did. She invited him over to pick it up.

While driving up the hill toward her house, he explained how Nick was being a jerk. Like the best of friends, Evangeline was always ready to believe the veracity of any deficit he cared to relate about Nick, including today's complaint about feeling alienated by furniture that Nick seemed attached to but Peter hated.

"So why does he care about all that stuff anyway? None of it is his," Evangeline said.

"It's all worth a lot of money," Peter said. "Everything. The chairs, the rug, the art. He could buy a whole other house if he sold just one of the paintings."

"Maybe he should," Evangeline said. "That house isn't very cozy."

"It's plenty cozy," Peter protested.

"The living room is like some kind bank foyer. I always think I'm going to get charged an overdraft fee when I'm over there. "

"Well, Walter did do a lot of foyer art, apparently. His paintings can be found in the lobby of many corporate headquarters. Anyway it's a great venue for a party. We'll be able to fit at least a hundred people in there on Halloween."

"So Nick signed off on that?" Evangeline's voice perked up. Since they'd been in college, he and she had hosted a Halloween masquerade ball. The event had steadily outgrown their and all their friends' houses as well as increasing in sophistication from a keg-and-bonfire affair to a lavish display of costumes and vintage cocktails.

"Nick says he's going to rent a limo to take people home at the end of the night."

"Smart man. He gets to kick everybody out by a certain time, plus everyone stays safe."

"He's a safety-first kind of guy." Peter rounded the corner and saw her standing on the front walk. He waved, and she returned the gesture. She pulled her big Cowichan sweater closer around her body. Because her current fashion obsession was handmade recycled clothing, she wore a voluminous knee-length skirt that had been assembled out of dismantled blue and yellow T-shirts. She wore no shoes, in spite of the October chill.

They embraced when they met. Her wavy hair smelled like patchouli and *nag champa*, which Peter normally hated but found comforting when associated with her.

"Want to come in? I just baked some pumpkin bread."

"Normal pumpkin bread?" Peter eyed her skeptically.

"Absolutely normal. No magic whatsoever. Tommy has to take a drug test to get that shipyard job, so he's detoxing."

"I can't imagine it," Peter commented. "How's he holding up?"

"Pretty well. I agreed that I'd stop with him so he didn't feel bad."

"How is that going?"

"Good." Evangeline cocked her head, thoughtfully. "Though our weekly consumption of beer has gone way, way up."

Inside the house, clutter and chaos reigned. Like Nick, Evangeline had a studio in the Vitamilk Building, but that tiny space was completely inadequate to her storage needs. Her primary artistic medium was found objects, and the house was absolutely crammed with shelves full of shiny, twisty, or unique pieces of machinery, doll parts, beads, and the like—the exact opposite of the austere beauty of the Castle on Wildcat Cove. Living here had been awkward as well, with Peter constantly in danger of knocking over some precarious tower of objects.

Peter sighed. Maybe he was just the sort of person who was perpetually unsatisfied with his environment. He cleared off a space on the sofa and sat down in it. Shortly after that Evangeline appeared with a slice of pumpkin bread wrapped in a paper towel. She handed it to him, cleared off an armchair, and sat down. "So why are you driving *the Hamster* truck?"

"Shawn had to skip town. I theorize that he owed his dealer money."

Evangeline shook her head sadly. Shawn was her younger cousin. She'd gotten him the job at *the Hamster* in the hopes that it would provide some stability in his life. "I saw him about a week ago. He is really taking the wrong drugs. I don't know which ones they are, but they are definitely not right for him."

Mitch jumped up on the armchair next to her and looked hopefully at her snack. Like the seasoned pet owner that she was, Evangeline ignored him.

Peter resisted the urge to ask whether any drugs could really be said to be right for someone. It felt fairly hypocritical to make that remark, being the great connoisseur of martinis that he was. Instead, he said, "You don't happen to know who his dealer was?"

Evangeline rolled her eyes. "Even if I did I wouldn't tell you, Mr. Nosy. You'd try to find them to find out about Shawn to satisfy your curiosity, write an article, and go for another award. I don't want to be in trouble with Nick."

"Why would you be in trouble with Nick?" Peter scowled. That was the problem with best friends. Too perceptive.

"Because you'd go out there by yourself, in the dark, and end up getting sacrificed to Satan, and it would be my fault. That's why I'd be in trouble with Nick."

Peter paused, midchew, regarding Evangeline. "So you do know who the dealer is."

"I didn't say that." Evangeline's expression became aloof, almost prim, but Peter wasn't fooled. She'd never been a good liar, nor even a good omitter of information.

Pondering the note in his pocket, he said, "Why would you bring up something so bizarre and specific as getting sacrificed to Satan unless you knew something about Shawn's dealer?"

"You know what I know? I know you've got something much more important to think about than Shawn's creepy dealer. I'm sure the cops are already worrying about him for you. Who is going to find the asshole who hurt your cat? Nobody but you."

"She's not my cat. I'm just keeping her until we can find a home." Peter finished off his pumpkin bread. "And I've already talked to the police. They're taking it really seriously."

"But you're really good at snooping around," Evangeline said. "And you have more time than they do."

"Has it occurred to you that it might actually be more dangerous to go poking around the property of an animal mutilator than a cracked-out Satanist?"

"Why? You're not a cat."

"Because cruelty to animals is one of the hallmarks of a budding serial killer."

"A budding serial killer hasn't killed yet, right? So he can't be that good at it. That's way safer than provoking a Satanist on crack. If you're going to do one or the other, the serial killer seems safer. And you only have a ten percent chance that he's gay, so you have a ninety percent chance that he wouldn't want to kill you anyway."

Peter sighed. "Your strange logic is inescapable."

Evangeline smiled. "I know. I'll go get the cat carrier."

Peter left the carrier on this desk at *the Hamster*, traded in the pickup for his bike, and started his commute home.

Chuckanut Drive wound south from Bellingham along the coastal cliffs where cedar-covered limestone plunged straight into the emerald sea. The blacktop was narrow, dark, and sometimes shoulderless, but the cars whizzing by didn't trouble him like they had when he'd first moved in with Nick.

He arrived home around six that evening, bicycling up the hill just as the sun was setting over the Salish Sea.

The ride from Bellingham wasn't long for a seasoned cyclist such as himself, but he'd already had a long day.

He dropped his bike in the garage and went through the kitchen door. He thought he'd take a shower, maybe do some Internet research on Satanism or cat care, and go to bed.

He hadn't expected Nick to be home when he arrived, but there he was, standing in the open kitchen among the slabs of granite and rough wooden beams chopping lettuce. A beer sat next to his cutting board. On the adjacent counter, Peter spied two steaks sitting in a shallow dish of marinade.

Nick glanced up at him, said hello, and went back to chopping.

Peter seated himself at the massive yet utilitarian dining room table and said, "Have you got a date?"

"I don't know. I haven't asked yet. I was hoping to lure him with meat and raspberry cheesecake."

"You bought cheesecake?"

"And vermouth. Noilly Prat. Want a martini?"

"I've never been known to resist the Noilly Prat." Peter watched in wonderment as Nick wiped his hands, fetched a shaker, and began to build a martini. Finally, as Nick was dropping a fat, round Castelvetrano olive into the glass, Peter had to ask, "What did I do to deserve this?"

Nick shook his head as if to imply that there was no reason at all, handed him the martini, and went back to work. After consigning a tomato to the salad netherworld, he said, "I'm sorry I was insensitive about you wanting to take care of the kitten."

"It's okay." Peter spoke automatically. "I know having an animal around is an inconvenience."

"It's not that big of one, really. And the vet's right. Taking care of her is a really nice thing to do," Nick said. "But I was already feeling, as you said, *bent out of shape* about responsibility when you came over."

"What about?"

"Stephano, from the university, called me again just before you got to the studio this afternoon. They're just about to give up on finding the sculpture."

"What will happen if they do?"

"They'll file an insurance claim and get reimbursed for their loss. Probably they'll use the money to commission a new work for the garden. I'm fairly certain Stephano expects to sell them one of his own pieces." Nick held a hand over his cast-iron skillet and, after chucking a handful of rock salt into it, laid two steaks inside. Hissing smoke rose immediately from the hot iron. The air filled with the aroma of grade-A grass-fed beef.

Peter sighed. "I'm close to finding it. I know I am."

"Maybe it's best if we both just let it go." Nick fetched a bottle of olive oil, a jar of Dijon mustard, and a cruet of vinegar, and he set about making vinaigrette.

"Good newshounds never let go," Peter intoned, taking a sip of the martini. Excellent, as usual. "Besides, I like that sculpture."

"Yeah, you would. The trouble is, I really don't."

"You don't?" Peter raised an eyebrow. "How could you not like it?"

"It was one of the last sculptures Walter did, and…I just never liked it, that's all. And maybe it's better if another piece of art can be commissioned from an actual living artist instead of enshrining the work of a dead man."

"A paycheck for an artist is never bad." Peter swirled his martini, watching how the liquor distorted the light. "But I still want to find *Untitled Five* if I can—if only to arrest the vandalizing assholes who swiped it in the first place. There should be repercussions for stealing from a sculpture garden. No matter how you look at it, it's a dick move."

Nick smirked at the double entendre and allowed a small laugh to escape as he flipped the steaks. "You've sure got a way with words."

"That's what they pay me for." Peter got out plates and silverware and bread from the bread box.

He should have known that a matter less trivial than petsitting was at the root of Nick's unease. And considering that, he had to admit that he too had something on his mind.

"While I was doing Shawn's route today, some girl put a note on *the Hamster* truck."

Nick raised a brow. "Do I have competition?"

"The note was for Shawn."

"Well, I suppose that there must be some contingent of the opposite sex who are into bad dreads."

"It wasn't a love note." Peter related the single sentence, eliciting a low whistle from his lover.

"Either somebody's caught the spirit of the ghosting season, or Shawn really has worn out his welcome."

"Doug thinks he skipped town to avoid his dealer."

"I thought Shawn *was* a dealer."

"I'm guessing the guy in the truck is a little higher up the food chain," Peter said.

Nick moved the steaks to the plates. "I suppose this means you're going to have to keep doing the distro until Doug gets around to hiring someone else."

"God, I hope not."

Rather than sitting at the massive dinner table, like some cartoon rich family, they sat at the counter. Dinner entertainment consisted of watching streaming video of *Lois & Clark* on Peter's laptop. It was cozy.

Neither of them mentioned Shawn, or Walter's art, or the kitten again.

Peter offered a second episode, but Nick declined, suggesting instead a shower. For both of them.

Never one to say no to an offer of a mutual shower, particularly when fueled by a martini and *Lois & Clark*, Peter agreed. Three minutes later he stood in the Castle's amazing four-head shower, soaping Nick's broad, muscular back.

Peter took his time, because Nick required time. Time and love. Simply dropping to his knees and sucking would not do with this man. Peter suspected that he'd had enough of lurid, faceless encounters in the army and now wanted it to feel personal. So Peter made it personal, slowly soaping him, treating him right. Admiring him.

And there was a lot of him to admire. His heavy thighs, his bulky calves, his soft brown hair.

Nick returned his affection, stroking, murmuring about Peter's beauty, his dark hair, his blue eyes.

Peter finished his ministrations, toweled Nick off, and led him to the bedroom.

This one room, in all the Castle, Peter had managed to make theirs. Gone were the gray sheets, the austere bedside lamps. He'd spent a month's pay to transform the dull, almost clinical room into cool blue oasis. Nick looked good against the sheets. The color accented his pale irises, his tan skin.

Peter had a choice to make—whether to make it dirty or sweet. Normally he chose to go slightly dirty, being a general fan of putting an edge of exhibitionistic glamour into their sex life. But today Nick seemed... Not fragile, but certainly not having sex for the sake of it. He wanted to be with Peter to have a connection with him.

So Peter pulled up the sheets and curled his arms around Nick. He kissed slowly, taking his time, tasting Nick's mouth, showing he cared. He moved slowly downward, finally taking Nick into his mouth, sucking slowly, then hard, tasting him, making it last.

Nick moaned, arched into his mouth. Peter took him deeply, intent on making it last as long as he could, hard himself from the taste of flesh. He loved sucking cock in general and sucking Nick in particular. He reveled in the way that at some point Nick's gentleness and restraint would break and he would push hard into Peter's mouth and shoot. He loved how Nick would pull him up beside him after that, his strong hand palming Peter's ass as Peter thrust his swollen prick against Nick's thigh.

And he loved how Nick's fingers would rest against his opening, claiming that intimacy so naturally and casually that it took Peter's breath away.

So he worked Nick with his tongue, knowing the inevitable series of events that ended, as he had predicted, with Nick's fingers deep in his ass as he rocked and moaned his way to a blinding climax.

Afterward, Peter lay panting on Nick's arm. Suddenly feeling the chill of the October night on his sweat-drenched skin, he shivered. Automatically, Nick pulled the duvet over him.

Then, just like that, Nick was asleep.

Chapter 5

During their morning toast and eggs, Peter finally asked Nick to explain why the call from Stephano, an art professor at the university, had bothered him so much. At first Nick just shook his head, focusing on his plate, using his toast and fork in tandem to subdue his egg over easy. Peter preferred his egg over hard and folded in one piece of light toast. A one-handed affair that he could not only eat while riding a bike, but which required no plate or silverware. When Nick was gone, he ate standing over the sink. This morning he sat alongside Nick at the counter. Determined not to be discouraged in his line of questioning, Peter tried again. "I know talking about it won't help you feel better, but it would make me feel better to know why you're so moody, so why not have some mercy on me?"

Nick sighed and gave him a resigned, sidelong glance. "Since I'm the executor of Walter's artistic estate, they want me to sign some paperwork stating that it was an original. I told them I'd go down there this morning."

Peter did not immediately know why this should cause Nick any great distress, but clearly it did.

"I still don't understand why that would upset you, though." Peter was trying to augment his understanding of his lover without prying, but it was hard. Prying was what he did; it was his art form, even.

"It's just bringing up a lot of memories for me; that's all. Walter completed that piece about six months before he died. It was a hard time for me."

Peter nodded. Obviously it would have been a hard time for anyone, but especially for a guy like Nick, who didn't talk much but thought a lot. From his expression, Peter could tell he was thinking right this second. Deep, brooding thoughts churned through the mind of Nick Olson, sending flickering microexpressions across his furrowed brow, his heavy-lidded eyes.

It killed Peter to see him this way—made so unhappy by a phone call and a hunk of rock that had been fashioned to look like his penis. Finally inspiration struck. "Do you want me to come with you to the university?"

"Nah." Nick mopped up flecks of yellow yolk with intense precision, as if he were manipulating paint.

"Can I come anyway? I need to write a piece on the theft, and it would give some closure."

"I feel no closure whatsoever."

"I mean to the article." Peter munched at his sandwich, eyeing Nick, noting that he wasn't putting his elbows on the table as he usually did. Best manners at breakfast indicated that Nick had gone far within. He was probably dining with the ghost of Walter, who, being from an older generation, had had higher standards at table. Peter's desire to interrupt that inner conversation could not be denied. "So, can I come?"

"What?" Nick popped up for air, looking around as though he'd forgotten Peter was there. "Come where?"

"To the university with you."

"Sure, but you won't enjoy it." Nick pushed his plate away, caught hold of his coffee cup, and finally leaned forward on his elbows.

"So long as I'm being paid, I fear no boredom," Peter said airily.

"Oh, it won't be boring. I'm going to meet with Stephano. He's handling the whole thing." Nick had a certain meaningful tone—a tone that assumed Peter knew and already disliked this Stephano person as much as Nick apparently did.

Peter tried to picture this individual and pulled a blank. "I don't think I've ever met him."

Nick smirked and said, "Then get your mental notebook ready. I'll be very interested to hear what you think."

An hour later, Peter entered a small office in the basement of the Fine Arts building and was introduced to a man who he could not, in any way, believe had been named Stephano by one or more of his parents.

Doughy and pale, with thinning brown ponytail, Stephano—just Stephano, no last name—had the face of a man who had reared entirely on cream cheese and white bread. Even his clothes were the standard white-man uniform of khaki shorts plus polo shirt. His socked and Birkenstocked feet gave a hint that he might have been a campus rebel back in the time of the Doobie Brothers but had since firmly joined the administration. On his desk sat a stack of *Artforum* magazines, along with a dish of candy corn and a small, thin aluminum can containing some sort of arcane energy drink.

But was only when he shook Stephano's warm, soft hand that Peter began, internally, to compose text about him.

In terms of generic characters that one is likely to find teaching at the average four-year collegiate institution, Failed Professional is definitely one of the most common and commonly derided. This is not entirely fair. Most university professors choose to teach—excel at teaching—consider it their calling above all else. But there are always others who are simply looking for a hot meal and regular access to impressionable eighteen- to twenty-five-year-olds—particularly in the creative arts fields.

For this reporter, placing Stephano on the continuum of competence was a cinch.

"You've probably seen my work around town." Stephano spoke mainly to Peter.

"The sculptures on Cornwall Street," Nick supplied helpfully.

"Oh, those," Peter did a little mental scramble while he searched for anything positive to say about them. Finally he managed, "Very colorful."

Even if he hadn't had his aesthetic horizons expanded by an artist boyfriend, he would have been able to see that Stefano's sculptures had very little artistic merit. They were all powder-coated steel things approximately eight feet tall and two feet in diameter. They looked, to Peter, like folded and crumpled ductwork, like the sort of product that might occur if one told a high school freshman to go to the Occupational Studies center and weld a piece of modern art. Lacking both grace and meaningful substance, the eight Stephano sculptures dotted the sidewalk on Cornwall Street at random intervals and went largely unappreciated by the general populace, who mainly used them for ashtrays.

Peter recalled that upon first seeing that the sculptures had been installed on Cornwall Street, Nick had nearly crashed his car in baffled horror at the city art commission's decision. He had wondered aloud to Peter if the artist was sleeping with someone influential. Peter had thoughtlessly quipped that artists were always sleeping with someone influential, which had struck too close to the bone and therefore had ended the conversation.

Observing Stephano now, Peter had to wonder who that person might be, because Stephano was not much to look at.

Aloud, Peter said, "The city must have your work insured for a lot, being out near the bars like they are."

"Oh the city doesn't own them. I just loaned them to the planning commission," Stephano said.

"But aren't you worried they'll be damaged?" Peter asked.

"Powder-coated steel can take a lot of wear and tear." Stephano smiled at him. It was a somewhat condescending smile.

Apparently impatient, Nick broke in. "You said you had some papers for me to sign?"

"I thought I did," Stephano said. "But it turns out that there's a snag."

"What snag?"

"It's ironic that I should have just been talking about loans, since it turns out that *Untitled Five* didn't belong to the university at all. It was on loan as well. I guess there was a handshake agreement that De Kamp was going to bequeath it to the sculpture garden upon his death, but he never got around to sending us the actual paperwork." Stephano's brows drew into an irritated furrow.

"And you want to know if I have it?" Nick leaned back in his chair and took that deep, slow breath that he always took when he was annoyed.

"Do you?"

"No, I don't."

"Do you think that you could—I know this is asking a lot, but do you think as executor, you could say that it was ours?" Stephano asked. "It really was what De Kamp intended."

"Even if Walter had meant for the university to have the statue, which I do believe is probably the case, how would that make any difference?"

"The sculpture garden is insured as a whole. If we could come up with some sort of dated letter or—"

"You want him to forge a letter?" Automatically, Peter reached for his notepad and mechanical pencil, whose abrupt appearance Stephano regarded with an expression of shock and dread.

"What are you writing?"

"Notes about what you're saying," Peter said.

"He's a reporter. He works for *the Hamster*," Nick explained.

"You said he was your significant other." Stephano cast an affronted and accusatory eye on Nick.

"It's not as though they can't be simultaneously true." Peter clicked the lead in his pencil up. "So you were just asking Nick to fabricate a letter to say that *Untitled Five* had in fact been given to the university when it had not so that the university could claim monies it has no legal right to? I think that might very well be considered fraud."

To Peter's surprise, Nick chuckled and laid a staying hand on his arm. "Down, newshound. I'm sure the man has a good reason."

Flushed and sputtering, Stephano continued, "I wasn't asking Mr. Olson to commit fraud."

"It sure sounded like that to me." Peter raised a skeptical brow.

"Look, you don't understand. The university has cut funding for the arts department dramatically. We need that money for the art department to remain competitive on the national scale. I am convinced that if De Kamp could understand our position, he would gladly have made good on his promise to sign over the piece." Sweat beaded Stephano's brow, but conviction rang through his voice.

"You know, I do believe that Walter intended for the university to have that piece." Nick's tone remained reasonable. "But you have to understand that transferring a highly valuable piece of art is not as simple as my backdating a letter."

"Which would undeniably be fraud." Peter had to point it out. "As well as forgery, since he would have to sign De Kamp's name."

"If the sculpture could be located, then I would certainly be able to donate it myself, and I would be happy to, but since it's gone missing, my hands are really tied," Nick said.

"That wouldn't solve the art department's funding crisis, though, since someone would have to steal it again in order for the insurance to be paid out." Peter glanced up from his notebook. The gears in his mind had begun to turn. What he had previously assumed to be a drunken prank suddenly had become a way for someone to make some relatively quick cash.

"What we all want more than anything is for that sculpture to be returned," Stephano solemnly assured him.

"Let's hope whoever stole it grows a conscience, then." Peter snapped his notebook shut.

Nick rose to leave, and Peter followed suit. Stephano caught them at the door.

"There's no reason for this conversation to leave this room, is there?" He searched Nick's eyes. "You understand I never meant to imply that you should do anything illegal. I was just trying to think of a way for some good to come out of this."

Nick waved Stephano's sweaty concern aside. "I understand how desperate you must feel. No one needs to know what we talked about today."

Chapter 6

"Are you serious?" Peter scowled as he sank into the bucket seat of Nick's car. "You know Stephano might very well be the guy who stole it in the first place."

"He did seem to know a lot about the insurance arrangements, didn't he?" Nick agreed.

"It seems like a phone call to our friendly city police department might be in order."

Nick shook his head. "If he did steal that ugly thing, I suspect it will be cemented back onto its podium within the week so that I can donate it. If it's stolen again, we'll know for sure he did it."

"*Untitled Five* is not ugly," Peter protested. "I happen to like it very much."

His comment drew a faint, lewd smirk from Nick. "You would."

Western Washington University was situated on a hill that seemed to rise straight up from Bellingham Bay. Below and to the south lay Fairhaven, the historic district, and beyond that, Chuckanut Drive led outside the city limits to their home. Just a few blocks to the northwest lay the city's downtown core, a collection of federal and county government buildings, college bars, and breakfast joints. And of course Peter's office—really more of a desk—at *the Hamster* was there, as well as Nick's studio in the Vitamilk Building...and the Cat Clinic. Peter glanced at the plastic pet carrier in the backseat. Nick hadn't said a word when he'd loaded it in the car.

"Where to now?" Nick asked.

"I think we have to go pick up the kitten."

Nick acquiesced with a single nod and headed downtown.

The Hamster's offices were on the way, on the second floor of the Railroad Feed & Seed Building. As they passed by, Peter caught a glimpse of Shawn, their missing delivery driver, getting into the cab of *the Hamster* truck.

He wondered if anyone knew Shawn was driving away in it. He took out his notepad and jotted down the time. Nick glanced over and must have seen him writing, but he didn't ask what.

When they got to the Cat Clinic, Nick presented his own credit card before Peter could even fumble in his wallet for cash. The bill wasn't expensive, but the kitten came with two kinds of ointment and a bottle of tiny pills.

The kitten appeared to remember Peter, or if she didn't specifically know him, she remembered that she liked someone exactly like him and began to purr immediately.

As they settled back into the car, Nick said, "I need to get some things from my studio on the way back home."

Peter said that was fine, and Nick continued explaining. "Sketchbooks. Black cat ink. Probably some watercolors."

Again Peter nodded. When the car started moving, the kitten commenced to wailing. Pathetically at first, but eventually her tiny lungs demonstrated the stamina for a sustained and operatic protest.

Peter smiled nervously at Nick, whose face showed no emotion whatsoever, as if he had a distressed animal in the backseat every day. Peter had a sudden flash of insight into what Nick must have been like when he was in the army.

Before he opened up and started expressing his emotions.

Nick parked on the street in front of his studio. He left Peter and the kitten in the idling car with the heat and radio running. Exhausted by yowling continuously since they'd left the vet's office, the kitten fell into a comalike sleep.

Freed of the anxiety-inducing noise, Peter's mind worked on two separate problems. The first was the sudden surfacing of

Stephano as a suspect in the art theft. Assuming that he was the culprit, had he known all of the particulars of the insurance conundrum at the outset? Or had he merely hoped to profit from the absence of one piece of statuary in the university sculpture garden by insinuating his own work?

And what about Shawn? Had he solved his monetary crisis and returned to ask for his job back? Or had Peter just quietly witnessed a case of grand theft auto?

He wished he'd been able to get the license plate number of the black truck, just in case Shawn was found floating face down in the Nooksack River.

Nick returned and settled his bag of gear in the backseat, next to the cat carrier. Peter blinked at it. Seeing the oversized sketchbooks, the partially crumpled tubes of paint, a peculiar sense of unrightness overcame him, as if he'd skipped a chapter in a film and missed some vital piece of information.

"Wait, you're bringing this stuff home?"

"That's what I said." Nick fastened his seat belt.

"What for?"

"Because I'm going to forge a letter to the university saying that *Untitled Five* is theirs. I need the paint to age the paper. It has to be subtle, but I think I can do it."

Peter's eyes went wide with alarm. He blinked and spluttered, "Wha-what?"

Nick broke into a wide grin. "Gotcha."

Peter sank sourly into the seat. "What are you really doing?"

"Just getting some stuff to do at home. I figure someone should stay with the kitten. Make sure she doesn't destroy the place." Nick eased the car onto the narrow street and pointed it toward *the Hamster*.

Though feeling slightly guilty about shirking his duties and sticking Nick with an unwanted petsitting job, Peter was too keen to find out the story behind Shawn's unscheduled day off to protest that he should be the one doing it.

When Nick pulled alongside the curb to let him out, Peter plopped a thankful peck on Nick's cheek and speedily quit the vehicle.

Once in the office, he ambled casually up to Doug and inquired offhandedly where Shawn was going with the truck.

The look of alarm on his editor's face concretized Peter's previous theory. The man let out a string of complex and partially unintelligible profanity that brought what little work was being done in *the Hamster* office to a halt. The other reporters stared, Peter imagined in awe at both Doug's exquisite and complex swearing abilities and Peter's apparent ability to withstand being the direct object of such cursing while maintaining a slightly bored countenance.

Doug yanked open his top desk drawer, took out a skinny bag of weed and a pack of rolling papers, and started rolling a joint.

"If he doesn't bring it back by tomorrow, I'm calling the cops."

Peter said, "Why don't I try texting Shawn?"

"If you get hold of him, tell him to bring my fucking truck back." Doug fired up his Zippo and sucked so hard on his rollie that he killed nearly half in the first drag. He took the joint from his lips, paused thoughtfully, then exhaled slowly. As he did so he sank back into his chair, as if deflating.

Peter, who'd been thumbing his phone's keypad, transcribing Doug's message, glanced back up. "Anything else?"

"Yeah." Doug picked up the nearly empty baggie and rolled it between his fingers. "Tell him I'm just about dry."

Ah, there's the rub. Any reasonable employer would have fired Shawn already, but the fact was that according to Doug, he still scored the kindest weed in town.

And really, if Peter were to be honest with himself, he'd enjoyed his editor's largesse on numerous occasions. Not because of his numerous avenues for obtaining marijuana, but for his ability to win journalism awards that made *the Hamster* editor walk so much taller than his rival at the town's other free weekly paper the *Bellingham Independent Tribune.*

Not that he was in danger of winning an award today. He would have to have written an actual article for that. As if able to read Peter's mind, Doug said, "So what do you have on the cat skinner? Anything?"

Peter flipped out his notebook. "I talked to the police yesterday. They said—"

Doug held up a silencing hand. "Write it up and send it over. How many words do you think you can get out of it?"

"Maybe a couple hundred if I stretch it. Why?"

"Hell House bounced its check, so I won't be running an ad this week. I've got a three-by-three-inch space to fill." He tossed the remainder of his joint out the window, opened his desk drawer again, and pulled out a bag full of miniature candy bars in festive black and orange wrappers.

Peter said, "I'm glad. Advertising antigay religious haunted house experiences was not something I'd like to be part of."

"I know, I know, but I advertise whoever pays me. It's part of my journalistic commitment. Candy?"

Peter took a chocolate bar, unhappy *the Hamster* was losing money, but still glad the ad had been yanked. But every October some church or other out in the county set one up. It saddened him because as a kid he'd loved going to haunted houses and psyching himself out amid the fake cobwebs, plastic masks, and strobe lights. He hated to think that this sacred venue, too, had become a battleground in the culture wars.

"I guess it's hard to overcome my objection to indoctrinating a bunch of young kids with the idea that all homosexuals will die of AIDS," Peter remarked. "Advertising it seems wrong to me."

"Have you ever gone to one?"

Peter shook his head no. "Have you?"

"I went last year just to see what it was about," Doug replied. "Substandard tableaus with bad moralistic scripts that a bunch of teenagers giggled their way through. The crowd was interesting, though. About a third of the people were true believers who really bought it. Then there was this contingent of hipster kids who were going ironically, just to be able to say they had gone and hated it, and then there was this group of people who were just curious."

"Still doesn't sound like my cup of tea."

Doug shrugged and turned away murmuring, "Could've used that money, though."

Chapter 7

The ride home was cold and damp. Slivers of light mist hung over the winding, narrow road, obscuring the tops of the cedars flanking either side of Chuckanut Drive. The asphalt glistened with a sheen of treacherous moisture. Outside of town an eerie quiet settled in.

As Peter made his way through the fog, he thought more on the idea of Hell House and of Shawn's dealer. The thing about Satanists is that they do not just spring forth from the earth out of nowhere. Satanists believed, by definition, in the Christian universe and therefore might easily be former or lapsed Christians. It then followed that if anyone were likely to know the identity of Whatcom County's Satanists—either genuine or simply poseurs trying to be provocative—it would probably be the regular churchgoers.

Peter deliberately stopped himself from following this line of reasoning. He already had two articles he needed to write, and neither of them included Satanists.

He pedaled onward into the gloaming, thoughts growing darker and returning, in spite of all his efforts not to allow it, to Satanists. He didn't believe in Satan, but what if a person did? What might they do? Would they, for example, skin a cat?

Peter's musings, like the evening, grew so dark and the shadows so deep that the supernatural seemed easily within grasp. Peter would not have been surprised to see the Headless Horseman rounding the next bend.

Instead, he saw a red Miata turning out of his own driveway. The car darted onto the open road directly into his path. Peter squeezed his brakes, skidded, and ditched his bike on the roadside, just a yard away from the Miata's back wheel. The driver of the car, a gray-haired man in late middle age, never even looked at him as he sped away.

Peter picked himself up, knocked the damp pine needles off his pants, and checked his bike for damage. Nothing seemed broken. He walked his bike the rest of the way up the hill.

The moment he stepped through the door into the foyer, he called, "Do you know who was driving that Miata?"

"His name is Bradley. He was here about the insurance claim for *Untitled Five*," Nick responded from the living room.

Like the rest of the house, the living room was a tall, airy space comprised of birch and stone. The vast expanse of an eight-by-twelve-foot De Kamp abstract dominated the far wall. Two-story windows lined the wall facing out toward the ocean. Peter had always thought this must give passing boats a nice view of their Spartan interior design.

Not that anyone on a boat could see through this fog.

Being an artist, De Kamp had understood scale. So since there was a huge painting and expansive windows, there was also a leather couch large enough to be a minor geological structure and a silk rug large enough to conceal at least two Cleopatras.

Other, smaller pieces—sculptures and small paintings—lined the birch ledge that was the room's only shelf.

Nick lounged on the gigantic sofa with a sketchbook in his lap and an open bottle of ink on the side table next to him. Also beside Nick on the sofa was a chewed and mangled shoelace of mysterious origin.

"He almost ran over me."

Nick looked up, gave him the once-over. "Are you okay?"

"I had to ditch, but the shoulder was soft." Peter shrugged. "You'd think a guy in the insurance industry would try harder to avoid hitting cyclists."

Nick went back to sketching. "Speaking of insurance, you might want to know that the cat clawed a hole in the corner of a three-hundred-thousand-dollar painting."

Peter looked down at the kitten, who sat innocently licking her front paw as if she could taste the money on it. Then she blinked and mewed and stalked over toward Nick with a bouncy lack of guile that triggered Peter's protective instincts. He swooped her up in his hand just as she was extending her needlelike claws toward Nick's pant leg.

Nick gave him a brief glance. "How long did the vet say it would be until she's recovered?"

"She said that it would depend on the next couple of days." Peter shoved her inside his jacket, as if removing her from Nick's field of vision could make him forget about both the damaged painting and the kitten's existence.

Nick drew in a deep breath and laid his dip pen aside. "I guess we should take some steps to make sure she doesn't destroy anything else. Want to give me a hand?"

"With what?" Deep inside his jacket, the kitten let out a tiny, frustrated mew and then sank her claws into his right nipple, causing him to crumple forward and lose his grip.

The kitten was away, boinging down across the great room clearly intent on some new misadventure. Peter rubbed his chest and tried to ignore the fact that Nick was smirking at him.

"I'm going to move this painting to the studio. And I should probably get most of this other stuff out of here too." Nick indicated the objects that lined the shallow shelves with a wave. "I think the more fragile pieces will be safer there."

He helped Nick maneuver De Kamp's canvas into the guest room, understanding for the first time why De Kamp had designed the house with ten-foot doorways. Then they collected the small fortune of art objects, paintings, and miniatures and secured them as well. When they returned to the great room, Peter saw that the kitten had found a way to get up on the ledge and was stalking along, attacking the dust bunnies that had been accumulating behind one of the larger paintings.

Nick regarded her levelly and remarked, "I somehow knew she'd find a way up there."

Peter repatriated the kitten to the floor. "What about this carpet?"

"I figure since she's already thrown up on it a couple of times, it might as well stay where it is," Nick said.

"She—" Peter stopped himself from arguing their tiny houseguest's case, opting for a simpler approach. "I'm really sorry."

Nick shrugged, his expression softening for the first time. "It's all right. She's just a baby. And it's just a carpet. I also decided to give her an interim name so that I'd have something to yell apart from *No*."

"What are you calling her?" Peter picked up the shoelace and attempted to engage the kitten's attention.

"Guerilla Girl."

"That's not a very ladylike name."

"She's not a very ladylike cat. And anyway, I call her Gigi for short."

"Why are you calling her Gorilla Girl? 'Cause she's a little monkey?" Peter pulled the shoelace again, but not fast enough. Gigi had it in her maw and was viciously assaulting it with all four limbs.

"It's guerilla, like the Central American freedom fighter. The Guerilla Girls are a feminist pop-artist collective. This is one of their T-shirts." Nick straightened so that Peter could read his shirt.

In large letters it read DO WOMEN HAVE TO BE NAKED TO GET INTO THE MET. MUSEUM?

It featured a recumbent woman wearing a gorilla mask, and noted, in smaller text, that although less than 5 percent of the artists in the Modern Art section were women, they accounted for 85 percent of the nudes.

While Peter didn't know if the kitten had any strong political feelings, feminist or otherwise, he couldn't deny that Gigi was a pretty cute name.

Plus it had the advantage of giving him an excuse to perform his Maurice Chevalier impression. He picked up the kitten and began to croon, "Thank heaven for lee-ttle girls, for lee-ttle girls get bigger every day."

Nick raised an eyebrow. "That's the gayest, most old-man move I've ever seen you make."

"Singing?"

"Singing a song from *Gigi*."

"I'd have gone for Lady Gaga, but this cat doesn't really have that much of a 'Poker Face.'" Peter let the squirming creature go, and she moved immediately to reengage her mortal enemy, the shoelace.

Nick nodded. "She knows what she wants and goes to any length to get it. Kind of like you."

Peter couldn't tell if that had been meant to be a compliment. Then again, he also couldn't tell if Nick liked the cat, so he said, "Thanks… I think."

"It's not like I haven't benefited from the frank and open single-mindedness of your pursuit."

"Don't make me laugh."

"It's true. I would have never had the guts to walk up to you and ask you out cold," Nick said. "I would have overthought it and choked."

"Was it because you were covered in blood when we met? Because I would have overlooked that, given the circumstances."

"You think I'm being condescending, but you don't know. I've never asked a guy out on a date."

Peter blinked. How was that even possible? Granted, Nick was handsome enough that he'd probably had customers lined up all his life, but still…

"Never?"

"Never."

"You haven't, even once, asked anyone out ever?" Peter could not conceal the incredulity in his voice.

"That's not what I said. I've never asked a guy out. I've asked out plenty of girls just fine. It's easy to ask someone out when you don't really care if they say no." As if too embarrassed to look him in the eye, Nick grabbed the shoelace and tugged gently at it. Gigi went into a sharklike killing frenzy.

Peter considered Nick's words. "I guess I forget that you weren't out for a long time."

"No, I wasn't."

"Not till you met Walter, I guess."

"Not even then." Nick caught Gigi just as she was about to fall off the sofa, plunking her back on her tiny feet. She hopped down and went to stare fixedly at a spot on the carpet.

"I don't get it. I thought everybody knew about you two, and that's why you were involved in the investigation into Walter's death." It was a subject Peter hated to bring up but couldn't make himself give up on either.

De Kamp had been nearly forty years Nick's senior. After he had developed pancreatic cancer, Nick had allegedly assisted in his suicide, an act of compassion that had made him, for a time, a suspect in a murder investigation.

"I guess it depends on what you mean by the word 'everyone.' Everyone didn't include Walter's family or anyone outside of his inner circle in Manhattan."

"But you lived with him. Didn't his wife know?"

"His wife lived in the Hamptons because she felt the city was unsafe. His sons are both older than me, so they were living their own lives elsewhere. Walter stayed at his studio in the city to work. I'm sure Walter's wife knew he had a lover, but not that it was me," Nick said. "I'm fairly certain she thought it was his agent, Felicity."

"And his wife didn't wonder why he was building a huge, expensive house out on the west coast?"

Nick smiled ruefully. "I think it's fair to assume that she didn't know he was building the Castle."

"How is that even possible? Didn't she look at the bank account and think to herself, 'Now, that's odd…'"

"Well, first, not everyone in the world is as nosy as you are."

"I prefer to think of myself as inveterately curious," Peter interrupted primly. "Especially about what other people are doing and why."

Nick cracked a wide smile at that, but the smile soon became tinged with a sort of sadness that Peter didn't comprehend. More than that, it hurt him to see Nick smile that way. He focused on Gigi, who had decided to lie down in order to stare at the carpet spot in a more relaxed, long-term manner. When he looked back to Nick, his lover seemed far away. Probably lost in some melancholy, sepia-tinged memory of the good times. And seeing Nick look like that, Peter found that his curiosity suddenly left him. He didn't want to hear about those good times when he hadn't needed to think about money or the damage incurred by somebody else's highly destructive cat.

Peter's internal monologue became morbid.

Years after the death of Walter De Kamp, Nick Olson was forced once more to confront the deep and everlasting internal pain of being cruelly separated from his one true love. Shacking up with broke reporter Peter Fontaine was not enough to ease him. No amount of consistent sex and reliable light dinner conversation could match the true communication one artist could have with another.

Blinking, Peter forced himself to stop this morose internal typing. Maybe he should just find a reason to get out, get some space. Maybe go to Evangeline's house and drink a bottle of pinot grigio. He was about to propose this very action when Nick said, "I was going to leave him, you know."

Peter blinked again, as if by doing so he could replay what he thought Nick had just said to make sure he'd heard correctly. Because that's not how conversations work, he was forced to ask, "Come again?"

"I was going to leave Walter. I'd gone to an artist's retreat to work and just to try and get some perspective on my life. While I was there I made up my mind to break it off. I realized that even though he loved me, he was never going to see me as his equal, and I needed that."

"Everyone needs that."

Nick cracked a crooked smile. "Not really. But I did, and so I had made my decision. Then when I came back, he told me that he had been diagnosed and had about a year to live." Nick stared at the blank wall in front of him. "He was afraid. I think he knew that I wasn't happy and that if I left, he'd die alone. He told me he'd changed his will to leave me his artistic estate. Essentially, he bought me."

"I don't want to seem insensitive here, but again I'd like to point out that he could have gone home to his wife. You know, the one who signed on for *till death us do part*." Peter tried not to sound callous, but journalistic training took over, as it often did when he was confronted by blatant illogic. "And what about the sons? Didn't they want to spend time with him?"

"No, they didn't want to see him. Especially not after the family lawyer leaked the information about the change in the will." Nick kept his eyes fixed on the wall, as if he were revealing his darkest secret. And Peter supposed that for a person like Nick, admitting that he had been bought qualified as his darkest secret. Or if not actually darkest, certainly the one he was most ashamed of.

"So the wife and kids didn't get anything?"

"Not from Walter. After he died there was a lawsuit. We eventually came to the agreement that I would remain the executor but all monies coming from the sale of Walter's art had to be split evenly between me, Bradley, and Troy. Those are Walter's sons."

Understanding dawned across Peter's foggy and shifting thoughts. "So the Bradley who almost ran over me was Walter's son?"

"That's right."

"He must be fifty, at least." Peter knew he sounded slightly stupid stating the obvious as he was doing, but couldn't help himself.

"Walter was in his seventies when he died." Nick finally looked at him, as if perplexed by Peter's inability to draw the conclusion that a septuagenarian could have children half a century old. "But yeah, you can see how Bradley and Troy would have reacted to meeting me. He called me a gold-digging little faggot on more than one occasion. Today he wanted to make sure he and Troy get their share of the insurance money from *Untitled Five*."

"Asshole," Peter murmured.

Nick shrugged. "It's not like he was wrong. I did fit all the criteria to be considered a gold digger...and a faggot."

Fury welled up in Peter. "You know, Nick, I think he was wrong. I don't think you stayed for the money."

"Don't you?" Nick asked drily. "Were you there?"

"No, but I've lived with you for three fucking years now, and you've never done anything even slightly underhanded, let alone outright dishonorable. I think you would have stayed with him that last year even if he didn't give you a dime, because that's just the kind of man you are." Peter paused for a breath and made another next logical leap. "Although I can see how if the whole thing ended with assisted suicide, that would have looked suspicious to everybody."

Nick smiled grimly. "Can you also see how this business with the statue is dredging up a lot of things I don't really want to think or talk about?"

"I can, but...I'm probably going to keep asking." Peter held up his hands helplessly. "It's just how I am."

"Could you not ask me anything more about it today at least?"

"Sure." Peter laid his hand on Nick's knee. "I can give you at least a twenty-four-hour reprieve from my relentless curiosity."

He slid his hand farther up Nick's thigh. "I could even put my mouth to a more therapeutic use."

Nick firmly moved his hand back down. "I'm not feeling all that sexy right now, baby."

Peter withdrew, rejected, only to be pulled back. Nick rested one heavy, hairy arm across his bony shoulders. Peter moved to rest against him, perplexed. "I thought you said you didn't feel sexy."

"I don't." Nick gave him a quick squeeze. "Can we just be together for a while? Would that be all right?"

"It's all right." Peter leaned against his chest, listening to the steady thump of his heart for a few seconds, then said, "Is she finally asleep?"

"Gigi?"

"Yeah." Peter had momentarily forgotten that she'd acquired a name since he'd been gone. "The cat."

"I think the motionless face-plant into the carpet tells us that she is."

After another moment Peter said, "I really think she's cute."

Nick sighed, ruffled Peter's hair, and replied, "I know."

They sat together for a space, not speaking. Peter would have thought that Nick had fallen asleep except for the tension in his muscles and the occasional distracted squeeze of Nick's hand on his shoulder. Evangeline had told him that oftentimes people would bring cats and dogs into hospitals and nursing homes because the patients found it soothing to pet them. Therapy animals, they were called. He thought he might be acting as a therapy animal right now.

A casual change of subject was definitely in order.

"What's your Halloween costume going to be this year?"

"I haven't thought about it." Again, Nick rubbed his hand along Peter's shoulder. "I'll probably just get some unryu paper and acrylic polymer medium. Make a mask, like usual."

Peter nodded against his shoulder. Nick did make really beautiful, surreal masks. For his part, Peter had been waiting for the excuse of Halloween to break out the cowboy boots he'd bought last time he'd visited his parents in Austin. But feeling Nick's tension and sadness, he changed his mind about mentioning it.

"I was thinking of being a slutty nurse," Peter said.

After a lengthy pause, Nick said, "A slutty *male* nurse?"

"Exactly. I don't see why women get to have the corner on the slutty nurse costume." Peter sighed and snuggled closer to Nick. "Yeah, I think I'll find myself some tight white pants and one of those hats with a red cross on it. I think Evangeline might have a pair of white vinyl boots I could borrow."

"That sounds like something she would have, but would they fit?" Nick's voice sounded more normal now. His body had relaxed slightly.

"Actually she and I wear the same shoe size."

"I guess me dressing up as a doctor would be the next logical step," Nick said. "That or a hapless, innocent patient."

"Whichever you decide. I can take orders or I can give them." Peter slid his hand under Nick's shirt and gently scratched the fur on his chest.

"You've never taken an order in your life."

"That's just because they weren't sexy enough. I could definitely take a sexy order."

Nick's chest shook with a silent chuckle. "All right, then. Doctor it is."

Chapter 8

During the following week of recovery, Gigi slept, ran, clawed, and blinked her way directly into Peter's heart. Once her stitches had been removed, he'd thought Nick would demand that she be deposited at the Humane Society. Strangely, he did not, claiming that they refused to adopt out black cats around Halloween anyway, so she might as well stay with them for a little while longer.

In the meantime, toys appeared. First, a furry mouse. Then some sort of jingle bell and feather contraption mounted on a cheap toy bamboo fishing pole. Nick never acknowledged himself as the procurer of said items. They would simply be present when Peter arrived home, as if they'd sprung up from the carpet like mushrooms bursting from a fallen log.

Gigi began sleeping on their bed. First on the pillow on Nick's side, as common cat perversity drew her toward the man who showed the least interest in her, then atop the duvet in the gully between their bodies.

One week after her arrival, Peter opened his eyes to see her struggling from beneath the covers on Nick's side while Nick snored lightly into his pillow. When Peter rose, she followed him to the bathroom, clambered up on the side of the tub, and watched as Peter showered and shaved. Within him a sense of triumph began to grow, like a hazy image of land must seem to a sailor crossing a vast and hostile ocean. Nick was not made of stone. He would never let a kitten sleep under the covers with him and then kick her out to face the windy, wet autumn on her own. Or even with the help of whatever well-meaning cat lady would adopt her.

Gigi would be theirs.

Heart brimming with love, he turned to pet her. She attacked his hand with vicious, unrestrained joy before running back to the bedroom.

Peter left her there, gently swatting a sandy brown curl that lay across Nick's unconscious forehead, and headed to the office.

When he arrived there he found the delivery truck parked out front, and the sight gave him a shudder of premonition. As he climbed the stairs to the second floor, the feeling deepened into a sense of dreadful foreknowledge. He opened the door and was greeted by the sight of Doug shaking a set of keys at him.

"Shawn dropped these in the mail slot," Doug told him.

Peter glanced furtively around the office. No one. Not a single soul inhabited the normally busy space. All conveniently late.

Clever bastards.

Doug jingled the keys again.

Peter sighed and held out his hand to receive them.

Any tourist finding themselves lost on the twisting roads in western Whatcom county might wonder if the entire economy of Whatcom County is derived from U-pick blueberry farms. This is understandable, but untrue. At least half of these U-pick farms sell raspberries. And at Halloween there's always a pumpkin patch.

U-pick, of course.

Before Peter had been a reporter, he'd had Shawn's job—driving the truck, that is, not procuring delicious kind bud for Doug. As he made his way along the route through Lynden and Everson, Peter found himself almost transported back to his student days. Before he had any such thing as a steady boyfriend. Certainly before he had a Tom Renner award. Before he even had a reliable bike light.

Those days, when he needed companionship, he went to Vancouver and found some stranger. Now his life was so simple but also infinitely more complex. Instead of finding physical release with unknown men in bars, he made love with Nick. But Nick came with all kinds of history that he was only just now beginning to know.

And with the inclusion of a pet in their small family, Peter felt a strange sense of domesticity that he would have thought would frighten him. Instead, he felt…pleased.

Pleased that he had a boyfriend and a cat. Pleased that he had a job in a town where people knew his name. Pleased when he stopped at the U-pick pumpkin patch to procure a dozen gourds for his annual Halloween Party.

Even pleased by the knowledge that he and Nick and Evangeline would, for the first time, pay for the entire gathering themselves rather than hitting up their friends for BYOB. He felt grown up. Established.

He felt like an adult, and that itself felt good.

Filled with paternalistic largesse, Peter forked over one hundred and fifty dollars for an orange and white monstrosity the size of a beanbag chair.

He drove through Maple Falls, navigating carefully to avoid jostling the pumpkin in the back. And there he caught sight of the black truck he'd seen the previous week. It was parked in front of the Cedarwood Casino. He didn't need to wonder if it was the same one, since it was not only still festooned with flames, but the same girl lounged against it, smoking a cigarette and staring out at the highway. The truck bed was, as far as Peter could tell, goat free.

Peter decided to pull over and have a chat. As he drew near he saw that the back of the truck held what looked like a bloodstained hospital gurney.

His reporter senses tingled, but observing the brightness and also the texture of the red spattering the gurney sheets, he realized he must be looking at a prop. Maybe for a house party or haunted house.

Perhaps even for Hell House. As he recalled, it had a couple of tableaus that included medical personnel and settings.

The girl caught sight of *the Hamster* truck and went from lassitude to alertness.

As Peter pulled alongside her, she straightened as if preparing to flee.

"Hi," he said. "Nice gurney."

"It isn't mine." She buried her hands in the pockets of her vest. The man working the door at the casino took note of him and began speaking into a handheld radio.

The owner of the flame truck obviously had friends inside. Peter had no illusions as to how he would fare against even one casino doorman, let alone a doorman and his friend at the other end of the radio.

"How's it going?"

In response, the girl narrowed her eyes at him until they became mere slits made of mascara and sparkly green eyeliner. She appeared to be concentrating very hard. Peter wondered if she was trying to put a curse on him. The door of the casino opened, and a young man emerged from the low gloomy interior.

From his first impression, Peter's inclination was to dismiss him completely. To Peter this kid could have won any award inscribed with any combination of the words "World's Biggest Pussy." He was thin and short, and he wore a black concert T-shirt that was way too tight. His pants left nothing to Peter's imagination, and not in a good way. The boy's product-intensive hairstyle resembled that of an anime character who has been unexpectedly doused by a rogue wave made entirely of flavored vodka. He wore much black eyeliner.

In short, he was Goth. Peter would have dismissed him immediately as a threat except that Shawn clearly feared him enough to leave the city.

And having been shot at before, Peter did not like the way the kid kept his right hand in his jacket pocket as he approached.

Peter went on, as though he hadn't seen the kid. "I just wanted to let you know I haven't seen Shawn yet, but I'll give him your note when I do."

"Yeah, you do that," the girl said. By then the eyeliner boy had come up beside her. He said nothing, just smiled at Peter in an arrogant, youthful way that could be the result of just turning twenty-one or having a .45 in his pocket.

In this case it was probably both.

Peter said, "Hi, I'm Peter Fontaine. I work for *the Hamster*."

The boy smirked, pulled out his left hand, and made a waving motion at Peter, treating him as though he were a Railroad Avenue panhandler or a mariachi roving through a Mexican restaurant. He said, "Go back to Bellingham, paper boy."

Peter didn't know whether to be insulted or amused by this high-handed dismissal. He chose amusement, since being in a truck would only get him so far if the eyeliner boy had more friends inside the casino.

As he drove away, Peter saluted the boy, who returned the salute, but with only one finger.

Chapter 9

When he returned home that evening, he related the story of his Maple Falls encounter to Nick and Evangeline. The three of them sat at the massive dining room table. An assortment of knives and gouging devices was spread before them as well as an assortment of doomed gourds. The setup for their assembly line was simple, having been honed over the years. Peter made the first cuts, removing the stem and top intact. Then, because he lacked artistic skills, it was his job to scoop the stringy, slimy, seed-laden netting from the inside of the pumpkins before sending them down the line to somebody who could do more than carve a couple of triangle eyes and a square-toothed smile.

When Nick had first started participating in Peter and Evangeline's Halloween ritual, there had been a slight tension. An edge of competition between them emerged as lover and best friend figured out their relative positions to each other. That first year, the pumpkins had been masterpieces of gourd flesh. As the two of them grew more comfortable, the need to impress each other faded, but the pumpkins kept evolving so that now carving them and preparing for the party was a two-day affair. They'd carve jack-o-lanterns tonight, then take *the Hamster* truck over to Fountain Rental in the morning to pick up tables and chairs and a punch fountain. Nick had splashed out and reserved two kerosene heaters for their patio, so that their guests could smoke without freezing to death.

This year Gigi joined them in their preparations, doing her part by walking on the table and knocking expensive and delicate carving tools down to be chipped and dented against the slate floor.

Peter was shoulder-deep in his ottoman-sized gourd when the front bell rang.

"That's probably Tommy," Evangeline said. "He said he might come by after work."

Neither she nor Nick looked up from their work or made any move toward the door. Peter knew from experience that while both of them had the best intentions of actually getting the door once they came to a stopping point in their creative process, that stopping point could take up to fifteen minutes to reach, and by then the person on the doorstep would have given up and gone away.

He toweled off his arm and went to answer the door.

It was not Tommy.

Bradley De Kamp stood on the stair, resplendent in his Burberry overcoat and generalized sense of haughty disapproval. Peter didn't wait for him to introduce himself, seizing the upper hand. He didn't generally feel the need to instantly dominate another man, but Bradley had insulted Nick, and Peter's defense came intuitively.

"You're Bradley, right? I'm Peter Fontaine." He held out his hand, which Bradley reluctantly shook. "Just to let you know, you almost ran over me the other night."

"I—"

Peter gave him a hard, bright smile. "No hard feelings, man. It's hard to see in the fog sometimes. Just letting you know, there's a lot of cyclists on this road."

"Thank you for that information." Bradley stood stiffly, without leaving the foyer, without removing his coat. "I'd like to speak with Nick Olson if he's here."

Nick saved him the trouble of yelling his name by sidling up beside him. He held a squirming Gigi in one palm.

"What's up, Bradley?" Nick's attempt at casual language was undone by his flat tone. Bradley didn't seem to notice, though.

"I want to know what's going on with the insurance payment." He stood eye to eye with Nick, though with a slightly thinner frame. He had silver hair and a lot of it.

"You could have called," Nick said. "I have company right now."

"I did call. You didn't answer," Bradley said. "If you had, I could have been spared a drive."

"Look, there isn't a payment yet. The investigators haven't even come up here." Nick lost his hold on Gigi, and she bounded away to freedom.

"Whereabouts did you drive from? Do you live in Seattle?" Peter inquired.

"I fly in every couple of weeks on business," Bradley said.

"Bradley works in the software industry, Borealis Microsystems." Nick explained. Then to Bradley, "I told you that I would forward all communications that I had with them. There just hasn't been any."

"You should be keeping in better contact than you do. It's a lot of money we're talking about." Bradley straightened imperiously and took on the air of a parent admonishing a child.

"I don't know what I can do. I can't make the insurance investigators work faster," Nick said.

"Maybe it would save us all time and aggravation if you just cut a check for the amount owed to Troy and me now."

Nick's eyes narrowed in frustration. "I don't have that kind of money."

"Oh come on. Surely you get that much on print royalties alone." Bradley brushed a raindrop off his sleeve.

Peter's patience for this pompous jackass came to an abrupt end. "So I guess you must be hurting pretty badly for cash, huh, Bradley?"

At this comment, both Nick and Bradley turned to stare at him, but for different reasons. Nick seemed genuinely surprised, with just the beginning of amusement lighting his face. Bradley looked like he'd been given a cold jelly enema.

"I beg your pardon?" Bradley actually spluttered, an action that Peter had previously never seen anyone reduced to.

"Anybody who knows anything about insurance companies would know that Nick wouldn't have the money yet. You don't look like a guy who knows nothing of insurance, so you clearly knew when you were driving up here that Nick wouldn't have the payment yet. You would have known it starting out. So why come up here?"

"To make sure—" Bradley began, but Peter cut him off.

"That was a rhetorical question. I already know why you came up here. To squeeze some money out of a guy who's young enough to be your son."

"I'm well aware of Mr. Olson's age," Bradley replied frostily.

"So why are you so strapped for cash? Software business in the toilet again, or did you just spend all your savings on hookers and blow?" Peter didn't really think that Bradley was a hookers-and-blow sort of guy, but he'd learned through countless hostile and semihostile interviews that throwing out a fatuous accusation often reaped rewards.

"I don't need cash. But as long as we're all being offensively honest, I am looking out for my and my brother's financial interests because I don't trust Mr. Olson at all." Bradley stated this coldly, as if Nick had forced Walter into homosexuality by trickery.

Peter regarded him narrowly. "I don't buy it. You came here to pressure Nick into cutting you a check. You hate him, so you must need money bad."

"It doesn't matter why or if Bradley needs money. The fact is I don't have it," Nick said, finally relaxed enough to lean against the wall, hands in pockets, scruffy as a model in a cologne ad. "Bradley, I don't know why you think that your father's art is earning millions in print rights, but you are truly mistaken. I promise that I will send you what is due you just as soon as I have it. In the meantime, I'd like to get back to my guest."

Nick gestured toward the door.

Bradley went without another word, too mortified or too angered by Peter's provocations to speak. At first, Peter thought

Nick angry with him as well, but as the door closed, he pulled Peter to him and pressed a whiskery kiss into Peter's cheek.

"You're really something," he whispered. "You just go for the jugular right away, every time."

"I can't help it," Peter said. "Mom says I was born without tact. Are you mad?"

Nick laughed softly. "Not at all. Just amazed, that's all."

From the kitchen came Evangeline's voice calling, "If you guys are done with your big family scene out there, I was wondering if you could come back and tell me all the details. I couldn't hear anything from here."

Chapter 10

The morning of the big party, Peter woke early, too excited to sleep. As usual, Nick had already risen and doubtless was somewhere in the house creating some sort of art. That or lifting weights. On the way to the bathroom, Peter peeked into the guest room, hoping to see the spectacle of reps and curls, but Nick had already been and gone elsewhere.

Peter found his lover sitting cross-legged on the silk rug in the living room, a long, scroll-like piece of Japanese mulberry paper unrolled in front of him. Nick held a sumi brush in one hand and a bottle of ink in the other, painting wide expressive strokes on the porous paper. Gigi slept beside him on the rug.

After kissing Nick good morning, Peter went to engage the shower. While he enjoyed the exquisite four-head spray, a curious thought occurred: what about Bradley? What if he had stolen the sculpture himself? He plainly needed money. He wondered if Borealis Microsystems kept a log of which of their salespeople had been in the Pacific Northwest on, say, the Fourth of July. Invigorated, he lunged from the shower and, wrapped only in a towel, first visited the Internet and then made a few calls.

Afterward, puffed up with pride, he went to crow his triumph to Nick.

"Borealis Microsystems says that Bradley De Kamp hasn't worked for them since June."

"That doesn't surprise me at all." As usual, Nick didn't look up from his work. The brush strokes began to assemble themselves into the shape of a cat. "He's always been better at selling himself than actual products."

"I don't follow."

"He keeps getting jobs but also keeps getting let go after a few years." Nick dipped his brush in the ink again. "The business world is rough for those of mediocre ability."

"So I'm thinking that we have another option in terms of people who could have benefited from theft of the statue."

Nick let out a snort of laughter. "I cannot imagine Bradley figuring out a way to move something that heavy. You saw his problem-solving skills in action last night."

"I suppose so, but what if he and Stephano worked together?"

"Not possible. They'd be working at cross-purposes. Either the university can get the money or Bradley can, but not both." Nick drew a long, sinuous stroke to represent Gigi's tail. As if sensing the complete drawing, she woke, stretched, and immediately went for the sumi brush. Nick removed the brush, saving it from a mauling. In her zeal, Gigi had darted onto the paper, walked across the wet drawing before coming to rest at the upper end of the paper, printing a trail of black cat paws behind her. Nick cocked his head slightly. "Nice background there, cat."

"Come on, admit it. You like her," Peter said.

"I like her best when she's asleep."

"So we're going to keep her?" Peter asked.

For the first time, Nick met his gaze. "Only if you admit that I was right."

"About what?"

"Wanting to keep this cat from the very beginning."

Peter hung his head. "Okay, I wanted to keep the cat from the very beginning."

Nick reached out to stroke his bare shoulders. "Me too. Now get dressed. We've got a lot of work to do."

Before Bellingham was amalgamated into the City of Subdued Excitement, *it was made up of four separate towns: Fairhaven, Whatcom, Fountain, and Bellingham. During the time of its founding, Bellingham was the least of the four start-up towns but was lucky enough to have the Bellingham Bay and British Columbia Railroad Depot. Once the canneries and sawmills of Fairhaven imploded, the railroad-endowed municipality of Bellingham subsumed the others. The names of the original nineteenth-century towns linger as designated neighborhoods with distinct characters. The original fountain that gave the neighborhood its name has long since gone, but Fountain Rental remains the place to acquire not only everything one needs to throw an average wedding or wake, but also a truck to move it all with.*

Peter had no need of any of the trucks available, though some of the big dualies appealed strongly to the four-year-old within him. He and Nick loaded the beat-up *Hamster* truck with tables and chairs and kerosene heaters. Last he carefully nestled a three-tier punch fountain between two stacks of chairs while Nick signed the rental agreement. They made good time, arriving back at their house just as Evangeline pulled up to help them unload and start decorating.

"Can you give me a hand with this heater?" she asked. "I don't want to scuff the truck."

"This truck couldn't get any more scuffed than it already is," Peter said. "You'll see when we get the stuff out of it. It's in serious need of gator liner."

As they progressed Nick knelt to run his fingers along a deep gouge in the truck bed. "I see what you mean about being scuffed." He suddenly lifted his fingers and peered at them.

"Did you cut yourself?" Peter moved to check, as did Evangeline. Nick's skin was unbroken. A splinter of rock stuck to his index finger.

"This is Italian yellow granite." Nick bent to search the crevices and crenulations of the truck bed, finding several small shards of the same stone. A couple of them were as big as a fingernail. "This is the same stone *Untitled Five* is made from. Look at how polished this side is. These are fragments from the sculpture, and this—"

"So…" Peter drew the word out as he came up to speed with Nick's discovery. "*Untitled Five* was in this truck at some point?"

"Not just at some point. Recently. And I don't even know what to make of this." Nick held up a small wad of black fur. It looked like a tuft of hair from a black cat.

"Is that from Gigi?" Peter asked. Nick shook his head.

"That doesn't make any sense at all," Evangeline said. "The only people who drive this truck are you and Shawn."

"And Doug," Nick added.

"Doug's hernia doesn't even let him lift twenty pounds," Peter said. "But what the hell would Shawn want with a statue? More than that, why is there a chunk of hair from our cat in here as well?"

"Maybe we should ask him." Nick pocketed the shards of stone. Both he and Peter turned their gaze on Evangeline, who immediately threw up her hands in protest.

"I swear I don't know anything about this."

"But you know where Shawn is, don't you?" Peter leaned in close.

"Of course I do. He's my cousin."

"Would you please, please tell us where to find him?" Nick said. "I don't want to get him in trouble. I just want to talk to him."

"He'll probably be coming to the party tonight. Why not just wait for him?" Evangeline crossed her arms, pulling her sweater closer against her bountiful breasts.

"Because I'd like answers to my questions now," Peter replied. "And because if he had anything to do with hurting my cat, I don't *want* him at my party."

Evangeline flushed, immediately ready to defend her kin. "What makes you think he'd harm any animal?"

"You were the one who said he was hanging out with Satanists and taking the wrong drugs," Peter reminded her.

"That doesn't make him a cat skinner. And a couple of marble chips doesn't prove anything!"

"I didn't say they did," Nick cut in smoothly. "I just want to find out what he knows. You saw how Bradley was acting last night. This whole thing has gone on too long, and if I can find

Untitled Five and avoid giving that dick a cent, I'd really like to. Please help me."

Nick pulled into the dirt lot behind Boundary Bay Brewery just past noon. Because of the adjacent farmer's market, the lot was crammed with both cars and people. Peter scanned the bunched-up lines of vehicles for beige Westphalias. There were three.

Typical hippie town.

He searched for signs of a tall Asian guy with dreads.

Again, not as easy to single out as one might have imagined. Then, behind a clot of cross-looking Russian women, he spied the dreads he sought. They were covered by a large cotton head wrap printed with multicolored shooting stars.

"Stop."

Nick applied the brake, and the car came to rest with a crunch of gravel. Peter launched himself out of the car, heading toward his quarry.

Shawn looked about to flee in the face of Peter's purposeful approach. Then, as if overcome with a sudden wave of calm, he seemed to steady himself and relax.

"Hey man, how have you been?" he asked mildly. "I didn't think I'd see you until tonight."

"I've been good. Listen, I need to talk to you."

Shawn glanced over Peter's shoulder and said, "Hey Nick."

Nick also seemed taken aback by Shawn's lack of guilty response. He brought himself up alongside Peter and said, "Shawn."

"So what did you need?" He leaned against the side of his van.

"I found a chunk of Gigi's fur on the back of *the Hamster* delivery truck," Peter said. "I was just wondering if you had any idea what happened to her."

"You found…" Shawn's eyes narrowed in confusion. "What did you find?"

"A chunk of fur that I strongly theorize came off the back of my cat." Peter crossed his arms, glad Nick was there in case Shawn freaked out and attacked him. From inside the beige Westphalia came a strange, high-pitched sound.

Shawn glanced over his shoulder, forehead suddenly sweaty, fingers flexing and straightening. "I don't know anything about your cat."

"Do you know anything about granite fragments?" Nick pulled his hand out of his pocket to display the almost powderlike granite that had been left there.

Shawn's eyes went wide, but he said, "No, I don't know about gravel either."

"This isn't gravel. It's a few fragments of Italian yellow granite, which is what the missing De Kamp statue happens to be made of."

Again, the animal sound emitted from the back of Shawn's vehicle. Sick fear churned through Peter's gut. He couldn't imagine Shawn ever hurting an animal, but then he hadn't predicted him having to leave town for three days to avoid his dealer either. He could picture in his mind's eye another little kitten back there, bleeding, waiting until someone had time to finish it off. He could stop it, he realized. He had that chance now.

"What the fuck do you have in your van?" Peter demanded.

"It's nothing." Shawn stepped in front of the door.

"It's not nothing. There's an animal in there." Peter reached for the door handle, and Shawn shoved him away. Nick moved in immediately, pinning Shawn against the Westphalia's side panels. Peter jerked the sliding door open, expecting to see a little ball of fur come shooting out. Instead, sitting quite calmly on the floor of the van, was a black goat. She—he could tell it was a she from the udder—chewed a mouthful of some haylike substance and regarded him with calm detachment. Then, catching sight of Shawn, she bleated. Unless Peter was mistaken, this was the very same goat he'd seen in the back of a black truck one week before.

"Let me go, you fucker!" Shawn struggled against Nick.

"Why do you have a *goat* in your van?" Nick's emphasis on the word *goat* clearly indicated that he, too, had expected to find an injured feline.

The goat stood, took a couple of steps toward Shawn, then stuffed her muzzle into the deep pocket of his North Face jacket. From this she pulled a small sandwich bag of Fritos, which she started munching, plastic and all.

"Don't let her eat the bag!" Shawn struggled again, and this time Nick let him go to disengage the goat from her plastic treat.

"Shawn," Peter said. "I'm going to have to ask you again why you have this goat in your van."

"I saved her," Shawn said. "And then she saved me. I've been clean for a week now. It's because of her."

Watching Shawn stare lovingly at the goat, a horrifying thought crept into Peter's mind. Clearly the same thought had formed in Nick's mind because he said, in the dry, unflappable tone he used when he expected to be repulsed, "How did she do that?"

"She made me understand that I'm a hero." Shawn nodded, both to the goat and to himself. He flipped his uneven, waxy dreads out of his face. "All right, I'll cop to moving that penis statue, but I didn't steal anything except this goat."

"You moved the statue, but you did not steal it?" Peter raised an eyebrow. "I think you have to explain."

Shawn didn't begin immediately. Instead he stared fixedly at the goat for a few seconds as though she were psychically coaching him. Then he nodded at her and took a deep breath. "I was in *the Hamster* office alone a couple of Fridays back answering the phones because Doug wanted to go check out the grand opening of that new vegan raw-foods place on Cornwall Avenue."

"He knows the owner somehow," Peter explained to Nick.

"She's his cousin's daughter," Shawn said. "Anyway I was there answering the phone, and somebody called about the statue. She said that she'd seen it at a house party near Whatcom Falls Park. I asked her if she knew who owned the house, and she said she didn't remember, but that it was there in the shed."

"So how did you find the house it was at?" Peter asked.

"Oh, I recognized the caller's voice. Plus there's caller ID in *the Hamster* office, so I knew for sure it was Jessica Mehrton on the phone. She's going out with my friend Billy, so I called Billy and asked him where the house party had been and he told me. Ironically, I'd been there too, but I didn't go in the shed." Shawn paused briefly to scratch the goat. "Plus I don't remember being there at all. I was really wasted."

"Just out of curiosity, why did your friends go into the shed?" Peter flipped out his notebook.

"Jessica saw Billy flirting with this other chick and got mad so he pulled her into the shed to talk about it so they didn't make a big scene," Shawn said. "Anyway, I thought it would be cool if I just went and got it instead of calling the cops."

"Why wouldn't you do that?"

"I had just been to a party there. I didn't want to be a bad guest. Plus there was no reason to involve the police since I could just claim I couldn't reveal my source for where I found it. You know, because we're a newspaper. Plus I'm an ordained minister through the Church of the Divine Man."

"I don't think the cops would have bought either of those reasons for withholding information, but I can see how you were thinking. Okay, go on," Peter said.

"So I went out to the house and found the statue right where Jessica had said it would be. I put it into the truck—"

"How?" Nick broke in.

"Well, I've been reading a lot about pyramids and how the ancient Egyptians built them—"

"You brought a bunch of Jewish slaves along to help you?" Peter could not help this interjection.

Shawn gave him a withering look. "No, I used my long board, some two-by-fours, and the winch on the truck."

"That would explain how the statue got chipped," Nick remarked.

"And how the bed of the truck got so scuffed," Peter added.

The goat, apparently growing bored with their story, stood, stepped out of the Westphalia, and ambled toward the a dirt embankment, which had been planted with ornamental native shrubbery. She sampled this and, finding it pleasing, started eating in earnest.

"So," Peter prompted, "how did you not manage to bring the statue back to *the Hamster* office after removing it from this unnamed person's garage?"

"As I was driving back here, I got a call from a guy I do some business with. He wanted to see me, so I went over there, and he started hassling me about some money that I guess I owed him."

"Does this guy, by any chance, worship Satan?"

Shawn looked up in surprise. "You know him too?"

Peter gave a noncommittal shrug.

Shawn continued, "Then you know what a prick this guy is. He said he'd forget about the money if I consecrated my life to Satan, sucked his dick, and drank the blood of a black cat. He had a cage of cats. Some of them had collars. They were people's pets. And there were skins."

"Did you do it?" Nick's eyes flicked to the goat, then back to Shawn.

Affronted horror played across Shawn's face. "*No*, man, I believe in the light. Plus I'm a vegetarian. I told him I'd pay him back in three days. I figured that since he was worshipping Satan, I might be able to trade them this big cock statue for an extra weekend." Shawn shrugged. "I told him that he could probably sell it on the black market if he wanted to, but I think he just liked it cause it looked like a dick. I gave them the statue to keep as collateral. Once I got the money and paid them off, I went back to get the penis, and it was sitting in the middle of this pentagram made of red stones. The cats weren't there anymore, but there was this sad little goat tethered to the sculpture, and I just kind of...I snapped I guess. It was like I was her...or something. I started crying, and then I just took her. Oh, Melinda..."

Peter was about to ask who Melinda was when he realized that there was only one female in the parking lot with them. Shawn sat half-inside the van and gazed at the goat. Seeming to sense Shawn's distress, she returned to the van, climbed back inside, and sat primly alongside him. She didn't seem to mind it when he draped his arm across her neck. In fact, she didn't seem to mind anything about her current living situation, which Peter found remarkably copasetic behavior for a goat.

He said, "Well, she seems to like you."

"Yeah, she's wise. She knows I mean her no harm," Shawn said.

"That or she has Stockholm syndrome," Nick muttered.

Peter went on before Shawn could comment or ask him what Stockholm syndrome was. "If this is true, then you know who owns the property where you originally picked up the sculpture. Even if we don't report it to the cops, I think Nick has some things to say to her. She owes him an apology if nothing else."

"I guess that's fair. It was at Anne Gerholt's place."

"Professor Gerholt?" Peter couldn't imagine the prim, tidy math instructor pumping her own gas, let alone masterminding the theft of a massive chunk of granite. "Are you sure?"

"Sure I'm sure. Her creep boyfriend, Stephano, was there hitting on anything with tits and telling everybody that he was going to have a piece in the Western sculpture garden soon," Shawn said.

At this Peter glanced to Nick, whose expression darkened. "Then as far as you know, the sculpture is still where you left it?"

"Unless they took it someplace." Shawn shrugged. "I didn't really think about it, since I was stealing a goat right then."

"Okay, Shawn. I'm sorry, but you really have to tell us where this Satanist lives," Peter said.

241

Shawn said, "If I tell you where to find the statue, will you keep the cops out of it?"

"Why would we want to keep the cops out of it?" Nick asked.

"Because they'll know I was the one who tipped the cops off about it, and they'll kill me and consecrate my soul to Satan against my will," Shawn said.

"Could that really happen? I mean, I know they can kill you, but I'm pretty sure the light will protect your immortal soul." Peter's mind chased after his own words as he spoke. They almost made sense in an Evangeline-logic kind of way. He went with it. "The most they could do is send you into the light faster."

"And if they do that, who is going to take care of Melinda? Technically they own her." Shawn looked miserable.

"Even if we went there by ourselves to get it, they're still going to know you told us where to find it," Peter reasoned. "Maybe the cops can protect you if—"

"What if I just gave you a couple grand and twenty-four hours to get out of town?" Nick interrupted.

Shawn stared at Nick, an almost vulnerable expression in his eyes. "You would do that for me?"

"Just promise me your love for Melinda is purely platonic, and I'll go to that cash machine right there and get you your money."

"What does platonic mean?"

"It means you're not a goat fucker," Peter explained.

"I am *not* a goat fucker," Shawn said emphatically. "I can't believe you would think something like that about me. That's why I stole Melinda in the first place. I couldn't take the idea that they might—"

"Enough said." Nick held up a silencing hand. "I'll get the cash. You give Peter directions."

Shawn described the location of the property where *Untitled Five* had last been spotted, and Peter took careful notes.

When Nick returned with the money, Shawn took it reverently. "I will use this to do good in the world. Maybe in Northern Cali."

"Just use it to save your neck," Nick replied.

They said their good-byes, Shawn even going so far as to embrace them each in his gratitude before collecting Melinda and firing up his van.

Peter and Nick watched him drive into the cool afternoon. Finally, Peter said, "I guess you probably want to get home and help Evangeline decorate."

Nick surprised him by saying. "Since I'm already in town, I think I'd like to have a word with Professor Gerholt first."

Chapter 11

Dr. Gerholt's home near Whatcom Falls Park was typical of the area. One level of unimaginative brick bungalow was surrounded by a nondescript fenced yard. Looking at the facade, Peter could easily imagine how Stephano could be appealing to the person who inhabited it. He'd never seen such severe corners on a lawn outside of a golf course.

Peter knocked, and after listening to the sound of many deadbolts and chains being undone, Dr. Gerholt answered. She looked just as Peter remembered her from his undergrad days. Slim, attractive, and neat in a way that always reminded Peter of a figurine that been freshly popped out of a blister pack in mint condition. She had dark, glossy hair done in a bob cut and the same heavy, square-framed glasses that nerds who wanted to convey some sense of style always seemed to wear.

"Dr. Gerholt? I don't know if you remember me."

"Fontaine, Peter," she said.

He smiled. "That's me. This is Nick Olson, my boyfriend."

"Oh, yes. I recognize you from gallery walk," she said pleasantly. She made no effort to move away from the door or to let them in. Her reticence aroused his suspicion but also seemed natural for a person who clearly had more than one deadbolt in a town as sleepy as Bellingham. "Did you come about the kitten?"

Peter opened his mouth to say no. Then his brain caught up to the conversation. "A little black one?"

All at once her demeanor brightened. "You found her? Is she all right?"

"Peter found her in Whatcom Falls Park." Nick had apparently come up to speed with the sudden left turn their conversation had taken. "Is she yours?"

"Not exactly, but I was still worried about her. That's why I put up the posters," she said. Then seeming to remember her manners all at once, she invited them in. Inside her home was as sterile as the outside. Lots of cream-colored carpeting that Peter couldn't see jibing with ownership of a black feline.

Dr. Gerholt started for her refrigerator. "Can I get you something to drink? I'm having some milk."

"I'm all right," Peter said. "I was just wondering if you knew how she got the injury."

"Oh, no. I don't know what happened to her back."

"How did you know it was on her back?" Nick asked.

Dr. Gerholt stopped midpour, face aghast. "I saw it, of course."

Peter moved in for the kill. "Why didn't you take her to a vet?"

"I couldn't catch her." She finished pouring her milk. "Kittens move fast."

"Especially after you've cut a chunk of their skin off," Peter said.

"I beg your pardon!" Dr. Gerholt's face went white. "That is the most insulting—"

"Then you didn't do it?" Peter stepped slightly closer to Nick. Although he had turned out to be in no danger from Shawn, he had the sinking suspicion that Anne Gerholt might chuck a glass of milk at him.

"I most certainly did not!"

"Good, then I'll send the police around here to take a statement about it. They're looking for leads in the case. They're worried that there's another cat skinner at work in town." Peter started toward the door. "Cruelty to animals is one of the hallmarks of a budding serial killer, you know. I think they'll probably want to canvass this neighborhood."

"Wait!" Dr. Gerholt rushed ahead of them, losing her grip on the milk. The plastic carton bounced to the floor, splashing milk all over the kitchen. She placed herself between them and the exit. "You don't need to send the police. I cut the kitten, but it isn't what you think."

"I truly don't know what to think," Nick commented, drawing an acid stare from Dr. Gerholt.

Peter fell back slightly, kicking himself for not locating a second exit before starting his accusatory speech. "So tell us what happened."

"I was trying to snip off a piece of her fur, and I got the skin. That's all." The professor's eyes brimmed with tears. "There's no need to inform the police."

"Why were you cutting her fur?" Peter resisted the urge to flip out his notebook.

"I was—" Dr. Gerholt broke off, stared at the milk on the floor, took off her glasses, and rubbed her eyes. "I was trying to cast a love spell on my boyfriend."

Of all the explanations Peter had expected to hear, this was the least plausible. And yet somehow, seeing this sterile environment he could almost believe it in a sick, stupid kind of way.

He said, "Go on."

"The only scissors I could find were those little curved ones you use for nails, and I guess I just didn't realize how close I was to its skin."

"So what you're saying is that while you were using nail scissors to get some fur off this kitten in order to complete a potion to put a spell on your boyfriend, you accidentally cut its skin off?" Peter could hardly believe was he was recounting. How stupid. How pointless.

"That's right. And then the kitten got away, and I couldn't find it again to take it to the vet."

"Who does the kitten belong to?" Nick asked.

"I'm pretty sure it originally belonged to the kids across the alley, but when they moved out, I think they left it," Dr. Gerholt replied. "It seemed so lonely. I was thinking of adopting it."

"She's already got a place to live." Nick's words had a ring of finality that warmed the cockles of Peter's heart.

"That's good."

If Peter had not been so upset by the idea that Gigi had been harmed to complete something as stupid and pointless and completely imaginary as a *magical spell*, he might have sent Nick a sideways glance at this statement. As it was, he focused on getting more of the facts.

"So, did the spell work?"

"What?" Professor Gerholt seemed confused.

"The spell you were trying to put on Stephano. He's your boyfriend, right? Did it work?" Peter asked.

"How should I know?" she said. "And it's not like I believe in that stuff. I was just really really…"

"Drunk?" Peter supplied the word.

"Upset." She gave him an angry glare. "I was upset that he had disrespected me."

"Did his disrespect have anything to do with a stolen statue?" Nick took over the questioning.

Dr. Gerholt's eyes popped open wide. Nick continued, "We know you had it on your property. But I don't think you were the one who stole it, were you?"

She shook her head. "He stored it in my shed without even asking me. How was I supposed to move something that heavy?"

"Why did he store it here?" Peter asked.

"Because his condo doesn't have a garage." Professor Gerholt looked miserable. "He never respects anybody's boundaries. I guess I know that, but I really thought he was making progress once we started couples counseling."

"Wait a minute," Peter said. "You two are in couples counseling? I didn't realize that you were married."

"We're not, but we were thinking of it. I thought it would help his career if he got married. You know, everyone thinks that he's gay."

"Not me," Nick remarked.

"Of course not you, but other people who aren't so familiar with the LGBT community as you are. It's because of his name," she said.

Peter marveled at the fact that she could be so clueless as to describe Nick, an actual homosexual, as "familiar with the

247

GLBT community," but swallowed the emerging comment and went on. "How could being perceived to be gay possibly hurt Stephano's art career in this day and age?"

It was Nick who answered. "You'd be surprised."

Peter nodded, taking Nick's word for it, though perplexed by why he wouldn't have mentioned something like that before now. Hadn't Nick and Walter lived together openly for years to the detriment of no one's career?

Dr. Gerholt sighed and found a towel, which she threw down on the spilled milk. "He always says that that was why no one has ever bought his work—homophobia. He feels real sympathy for the gay community because of that. He was one of the organizers of the Join Hands Against Hate project."

"But he's not gay. He's just bad. I don't think not buying bad art from a bad artist qualifies as a hate crime, unless it's been made a crime to hate bad art." The words were out before Peter could remember that diplomacy existed or that bridges work better if they aren't burned.

Dr. Gerholt turned bright red, and her lips pressed together so tightly that they became practically nonexistent. Nick, who had until this point been maintaining a grim posture of stolid Scandinavian disapproval, bent with unexpected laughter.

"Mr. Fontaine, I think it is really unprofessional for a reporter to make commentary like that about a person's significant other. I'd like you to leave now," she said.

"I'd argue that it's equally unprofessional for a professor at a university to participate in the theft of a valuable sculpture from the university grounds," Peter pointed out. "And unless you want to be charged for that, I think I get to choose when I leave."

For one moment, Peter thought Dr. Gerholt would finally strike him. She had her hand slightly raised in that way that Gigi did when she was thinking of swatting something. The professor's face went white, then red, then white again, then a kind of purplish blue.

Then she burst out in an ear-flattening wail.

"It's not my fault!" she sobbed. "It's not even here anymore. It was stolen again."

"We know. I'll be in touch about that." With that, Nick tromped through the puddle of milk toward the door.

Peter took this as his cue to leave. Converses sodden with two percent, he quit the premises and threw himself down into the passenger seat of the Audi. "For fuck's sake, is anyone in Bellingham not worshiping Satan these days?"

"I think technically Professor Gerholt was practicing witchcraft. 'Tis the season." Nick shrugged as though it was not only academic but inevitable. The autumn sun had already begun to slip below the horizon. At this time tomorrow this street would be thick with trick-or-treaters.

"Not so fast, Olson. 'Tis not just the season for Internet spells and blood sacrifices. 'Tis also the season for bite-size candy bars. 'Tis the season for little kids dressed up as tigers holding plastic jack-o-lanterns. For—"

"For dressing up like a slutty nurse?"

Peter nodded sagely. "For dressing up like a slutty nurse, indeed."

"We should be going home and getting into our costumes and greeting our guests."

"No, I want to drive out to the county and find that damn sculpture."

"Out of the question. We said we'd give Shawn a day to split town. Tonight there's nothing for you to do but drink and dance." Nick glanced at his watch. "Evangeline will be wondering why we haven't come back."

"She's got a key; she'll be fine. But what if Shawn warns those guys that we're coming. What if they move the sculpture? I've been chasing this penis for weeks now. I don't want it to slip out of my grasp."

"Baby, I wouldn't worry about any penis slipping out of your grasp," Nick said chuckling.

"Please, can we at least drive out there and look to see if it's there? It'll only take twenty minutes."

"Yes, but our guests could start arriving in twenty minutes as well."

"It's like curiosity doesn't kill you," Peter remarked sourly.

"It's like you don't remember that curiosity has nearly killed you at least twice," Nick growled.

"If you don't drive me out there, I'll just sneak away in the middle of the party and go by myself in the dark dressed as a slutty nurse," Peter said.

"What kind of ultimatum is that?"

"It's not an ultimatum at all. It's just a statement of fact. I know myself. I know what I'll do." Peter shrugged helplessly. "Some people are junkies; some people are gamblers. I'm nosy and I can't help following my gut. My gut says something creepy is going on out there with *Untitled Five*, and so I need to know. Otherwise it will just drive me crazy all night. End of story."

"If you see that it's there, do you promise that we can go back and manage to be present at our own Halloween party?"

"I promise." Peter solemnly raised his hand. "Slutty nurse's honor."

Following Shawn's directions, they got on 542 heading east, past Nugent's Corner, where Peter had intercepted the death threat, and on toward Everson, where orchards and granges dotted the country roads.

The drive was easy to find. Partly because it was well marked and partly because there was a black truck decorated with flame decals turning out of it.

This time, poking over the edge of the truck bed, rendered in beautiful Italian yellow granite, was the slightly bulbous head of *Untitled Five*.

Peter gaped, and his arm shot out like as if he were a character in a wacky seventies chase film. "Follow that cock!"

"That is the most ridiculous thing you've ever said." Nick put the car into gear and started down Everson-Goshen Road.

"I can't believe that Shawn screwed us," Peter said. "I went to that guy's birthday party."

"We don't know that he screwed us," Nick countered.

"Why would they be moving the sculpture, then?"

"Maybe they're moving it for their own reasons. People seem to be independently deciding to cart it around for reasons of their own."

"Or are they?" Peter said ominously.

"Or are they what?" Nick glanced askance at him.

"Are all these people truly deciding to move *Untitled Five* by themselves, or is the sculpture making them do it? Maybe it's got a hex on it." Peter did not believe in hexes, but the giddiness of actually being within sight of his quarry suffused him. They were going to recover the piece after all. Hours spent searching the city, following false lead after false lead would finally pay off. He could finally finish his article. "Or maybe the statue itself is haunted."

"The spirit of the season is strong with you isn't it," Nick said drily.

"I just can't help myself."

They passed U-pick blueberries and U-pick raspberries until the truck turned onto a long dirt drive lined with cars. A brand new sign at the top of the drive read WHATCOM COUNTY CHURCH OF CHRIST.

Tacked to the bottom of this, written in marker on a piece of orange poster board, were the words HELL HOUSE—NEXT RIGHT.

Chapter 12

Though the sun had just set, Hell House, being a family event, was already busy. A thick line of people wound through the field. To the casual observer they looked just like any other group of revelers. Maybe there were a few more angels than would normally be represented at a Halloween party, but everyone seemed in good spirits—no pun intended. Peter was very, very glad that he hadn't already donned his costume. This crowd was not the accepting and loving community that he'd grown used to in the sheltered little bubble of what was downtown Bellingham's art community.

Nick paused on the road, blinker on but not turning. Then he pulled onto the property, following the pickup in front of him down the loose lines of cars parked on the south side of the property. He parked, but left the keys in the ignition. "I sincerely hope you're planning to call the police."

"I am, but what do you think they're bringing the sculpture here for?"

"I have no idea." Nick turned to face him fully. "Baby, I know that you think you're impervious, but this is not a good place for us to be."

"I just want to see inside," Peter said.

"You can look it up online when we get home, I'm sure," Nick commented. "They're obviously going to put it in some display."

"But the question is which one? I'd like to get a picture for the article. I'll just be a few minutes."

"Who the fuck cares where they put it? Now that these assholes have moved it, this entire thing is over. We can report that we've seen it without endangering Shawn—"

"Assuming that Shawn didn't tip them off," Peter put in.

"That is my working theory at the moment. So, like I said, now we can call the cops to come recover the piece before it gets more damaged."

"I know I've gotten into some scrapes—" Peter had his hand on the door latch.

Nick autolocked the door. "Scrapes? You've tried to get yourself killed at least once a year for as long as I've know you. What I'm saying is this is different."

Peter rolled his eyes. "I'll be in public the whole time. No one here seriously wants to do anything to me. Especially not in front of so many people."

"You don't know that. I think I can see at least ten candidates for people who would try and do any number of things to you anywhere that was convenient for them. And you know what? No one here is going to stand up for you if that happens." Nick's gaze was intense. "I love you, Peter, and if you go in there, I'll go with you, but you should know that I can't protect you from this many people. So please don't go into that building. A photograph just isn't worth it."

"I honestly do not think I'm going to be killed in there, Nick," Peter began.

"I'm not thinking you'll be killed, really," Nick said. "I just don't want you to be hurt by what you see. Don't think you won't be. No one can stand in the face of such naked hatred and not feel it."

Nick unlocked his door, sat back, and stared forward, waiting.

Peter could see from the resigned set of Nick's jaw that he fully expected Peter to go, and he expected to have to follow—that he would follow even if Peter didn't want him to.

And what if something did happen? What if Nick was hurt? He already had the story.

He gazed out at the shifting shadows the bonfire cast across the crowd. Despite their costumes, they weren't monsters. They were just people.

People who very likely feared and hated him.

People who very well might turn on him if they suspected that he was merely gay, let alone a gay reporter hostile to their event.

Well, that's what reporters did, didn't they? Go into situations where other people wouldn't go? How could he respect himself if he didn't go in there now?

And yet the knowledge that Nick would follow him inside was unbearable.

So, was getting the photograph really worth it?

Not this time.

He took his hand off the door handle, pulled out his phone, and started to dial. He glanced at Nick, still sitting rigid in the driver's seat. "We should start heading back before our guests think we've abandoned them."

Nick's stiff shoulders relaxed.

The police answered and immediately put Peter on hold. Halloween was a busy night for them. Glancing across to Nick, Peter caught Nick pulling a strange smile that he couldn't quite fathom. "What are you grinning for?"

Nick's eyes flicked over to him. "I guess slutty nurses do have honor after all."

He cranked the ignition, put the car into reverse. Peter gazed at the black truck, watching as the blonde girl got out and walked around the back of the truck. She lowered the tailgate to reveal a slim, dark body lying in the back.

"Oh my God," Peter breathed. "They've got Melinda."

Nick's foot came down hard on the brake. "You mean the *goat*?"

"Look, she's right there."

Nick shook his head. "It has to be a different goat."

"She's got Shawn's head wrap around her neck."

"Do you see him there?"

"No." Peter craned his neck around, trying to get a clearer look. The girl was pulling Melinda by a rope tied around her neck. Eyeliner boy got out on the driver's side. Initially, Peter thought he would assist her. Instead, he lifted a video camera and started filming. From the back door of the church, a collection of costumed people emerged and gathered around. One had a heavy-duty hand truck.

Melinda balked and seemed to be bleating, though he couldn't hear her over the noise of the crowd.

"Why are they filming this?" Peter wondered aloud.

"Kids film everything these days."

Peter squinted harder at eyeliner boy's form. He definitely seemed to be giving directions. "What if these guys aren't really Satanists?"

"You think they're not?"

"They could be making a movie about Satanists."

"There's no reason they can't be doing both simultaneously," Nick pointed out. "We know for a fact that they're dealing to Shawn, so they're not innocent little kids."

"True, but the old guy standing behind eyeliner boy looks enough like him to be his father. Do you really think that teen Satanists perform rituals in front of their parents?"

"Good point."

"Holy crap. Here comes Shawn." Nick pointed to the beige Westphalia barreling down the dirt drive. "When did the cops say they'd be here?"

"As soon as possible. They have a lot of calls," Peter repeated dutifully. "Maybe half an hour or longer?"

"Goddamnit." Nick sighed and parked the car again. "I guess we have to back him up."

Peter suppressed a whoop of joy as Nick reparked the car. He got out and flagged Shawn down. He bounded out of his van, wild-eyed. "They took Melinda!"

"We saw," Peter said. "How did they get her?"

"I went back to my place to pick up some of my stuff, and they were there." Shawn hung his head miserably. "They grabbed her and took off while I was inside. They're going to kill her, I know."

The blonde girl had managed to get a rope around Melinda's neck and had her out of the truck bed. In half a minute she disappeared through the back door. Once the goat was out, the others hopped up and tilted *Untitled Five* onto its side. The rolled it down a pair of two-by-fours down into the dirt and then onto the hand truck.

They appeared to be moving it toward the same door Melinda had disappeared into.

Peter looked at the long line of revelers waiting to get in the front and said, "I'm thinking that we go in the back."

"That's exactly what I'm thinking, but what are we going to do once we get in there?" Nick asked.

"I don't—" Peter stopped short because Shawn was away, weaving through the lines of parked cars toward the back door. "Oh, hell."

The pair took off running.

If Hell House had been a dance club in LA, none of them would have gotten in. But it wasn't. No bouncers with giant forearms blocked their way.

Armed with only a polite *Excuse me*, Peter and Nick pushed their way through the back door and into a small meeting room. Two rectangular tables draped with orange paper tablecloths filled most of the room. A cooler stocked with soda and spiked with dry ice sat at the end of one table, leaking spooky mist over various trays containing cookies and sandwiches. Assorted teenagers in gory outfits lounged on folding chairs, munching. Melinda stood in a clot of three girls who had an aura of 4-H about them. One girl was feeding her a wilted piece of lettuce. At the far end of the room was another open doorway draped with black cloth, around which strobe lights flashed and through which stilted dialogue could be heard.

All that stood between them and the goat were partially demolished party trays and a short kid wearing way too much eyeliner and holding a video camera. Not an intimidating figure at all. Still he managed to stop Shawn in his tracks. "I don't want any trouble, Rory."

Rory's eyes flashed wide and darted toward the older man who resembled him.

Peter could imagine this introduction: *Hey, Dad, this is the guy I sell drugs to and whose life I threaten every now and then...*

Shawn didn't seem to make the connection between them and pulled out a wad of cash—the same cash Nick had given him. He peeled off three hundreds. "Here, this is it."

The older man, plainly curious, stepped up. "What's going on here?"

Rory lowered his video camera and said, "This is Shawn. He was doing some fundraising for the haunted house for us."

Instantly, Dad's face brightened. "We sure do appreciate it. We didn't know if we'd have enough cash to finish off the week."

A thunderous crash shook the room. Rory's dad said, "That's my cue. It was nice to meet you, Shawn." He fitted a latex "face of death" mask over his head and went to make his entrance.

As he disappeared Peter heard the unmistakable sound of cop voices asking who was in charge. Two deputies stood in the doorway. Beyond them, Peter could see *Untitled Five* lying on its side in the damp earth, abandoned.

"How about this, Rory?" Peter spoke in an undertoned rush, eyes fixed on the approaching deputies. "You give me that goat, and I don't tell them how that sculpture outside got here."

Rory smirked at him. "What do I care? Shawn gave it to me as a present."

"Do you really want to reveal your relationship with Shawn?" Peter asked.

"He's helping me with a fundraising project." Rory's expression was all defiance.

At the end of his patience, Nick leaned close. "Listen, you little fuck, that statue is stolen and worth half a million dollars.

Unless you want to be charged with receiving stolen property, just give us that animal."

Rory recoiled slightly, not sure whether to believe them. From the next room came the sound of Rory's dad's voice, reading some sort of scripture. Real loud.

He said, "Why do you want that goat so bad?"

"Why do you care?" Peter countered. "The cops're coming right now. Make a decision."

Shadows of anger and panic crossed Rory's face. He grabbed the rope around Melinda's neck and yanked her toward Peter, thrusting the rope into his hands. "Here, take it, you sick goat fucker."

"Thank you very much." Peter inclined his head cordially.

Nick said, "Now get the fuck out of my sight, you little twerp."

Rory sneered and gave them one final single finger salute before he slid behind the black curtain and vanished.

Peter handed Melinda's lead to Shawn, but there was no need. She lunged for him, yanking Peter's arm nearly out of the socket with the force of her enthusiasm. Shawn embraced her, nuzzled her. With teary eyes he whispered, "Thank you."

Peter said, "You're welcome." Then, to Nick, "I think I hear a martini and a slutty nurse costume calling my name."

Nick gave a curt nod. "After we call your cop friends and tell them about the cage of cats."

"Agreed."

As Peter saw the last of their drunken guests into the waiting limo at three o'clock in the morning, he reflected that the hard part about throwing an epic Halloween party was not the decor, the drinks, or the costumes. It wasn't attracting the bespangled and bewigged guests or choosing just the right music that allowed people both to dance and not dance whenever the mood struck them.

No, the hard thing was not drinking so many martinis that his slutty nurse costume would go to waste.

But this, he managed. He had imbibed only two of the magic elixirs and declined to drink any of the holiday-themed shots in favor of this moment, when he, tired but not too drunk, would turn to Nick and utter the words, "Well, Doctor, do you need me for anything else?"

Nick, also relatively sober and wearing a set of blue scrubs that were too tight for his shoulders, looked him up and down. Sometime during the night, Peter had abandoned his shirt and wore now only tight white pants and the white latex platform boots. His cheesy nurse's hat with a red cross on it had been lost on the dance floor. He shuddered as the chill October fog rolled off the bay and moved across his chest.

Immediately Nick looped an arm around his waist.

"I do need some assistance turning down a bed."

Peter rolled his eyes. "That's candy-striper work. Call me when you've got a real medical emergency."

Nick leaned close. "I've got a great big case of priapism that no candy striper within five miles has the credentials to help me with. I need a professional slutty nurse, *stat*."

Peter snickered, trailing his hand down Nick's abdomen, past his drawstring waist. "Dealing with problems like this is my specialty. Let's get you into a bed right away, and I'll see what I can do."

Taking Nick by the hand, Peter led him back inside the house, picking his way through the carnage of the party and tiptoeing past the sleeping Gigi to their room. Peter quietly closed the door.

"So just get out of those things and lie down right over there." Peter indicated the bed with a gesture reminiscent of Vanna White revealing the location of the letter E on *Wheel of Fortune*. Not exactly nurselike, but Nick didn't seem to mind. He stripped off his scrubs, crawled onto the bed, and lay down on his stomach.

He said, "I hope I don't have to get some sort of injection. I'm afraid of them, you know."

Peter paused. This was new.

"Don't worry, it will only hurt for a second." He ran his hand along the curve of Nick's shoulders, following it from the dip in his lower back and back up the rise of his buttocks. A shiver went over Nick's skin. "Are my hands too cold?"

"Not too cold."

"I just need to prepare my instrument, and I'll be right there." He almost managed to say this without laughing, and Nick laughed too, slightly nervously. Peter wished he'd thought ahead enough to have a pair of latex gloves on with him, but alas, he had not. Instead he made a production of fetching lube and warming it in his hands. "Now if you'll just ease your legs apart, I can examine you."

Nick shifted, allowed him access. Peter made a slow and careful assessment of Nick's anatomy, murmuring reassuring phrases he'd heard on medical dramas. Finally holding Nick's rigid flesh in his hand, he said, "This seems to be the problem right here."

"Is there anything you can do?"

"There is an experimental treatment, but I'm afraid you will need an injection. Shall I call a specialist, or do you trust me to give it to you?"

"I trust you," Nick glanced over his shoulder. "You come highly recommended by the International Sisterhood of Slutty Nurses."

Peter smiled, stripped off his boots and pants, freeing his own cock from the confines of the now very tight pants. He settled himself between Nick's legs. "Now I'll just start with a couple of fingers. You tell me if this is getting uncomfortable."

Peter took his time working first one and then two fingers inside Nick. The construct of his role allowed him to be careful and ask questions that would seem timid or amateur out of context. When he finally pushed his own stiff cock inside that tight, hot entrance, Nick stilled against that blanching shock of pain Peter knew so well.

"Just take your time," Peter breathed into Nick's ear. "This injection could take a little while. Relax."

"It's been a long time since I've gotten a treatment like this," Nick said.

"I know." Peter wrapped his hand around Nick's erection, running his thumb gently across the glans. "I'll monitor your progress by this. You'll be just fine."

Nick began to move, at first almost shy. Then, thought processes consumed with making friction, Peter's character broke. He moaned against Nick's back. Then they weren't a nurse and doctor turned patient, just two men fucking.

Nick bucked back against him, and Peter responded pumping faster and harder, chasing release inside this mass of hot muscle beneath him. Nick came first, ejaculating into Peter's hand while Peter kept pushing into his clenching body until he broke through that barrier of effort into ecstasy.

He collapsed onto Nick, breathing hard, his own heartbeat hammering through his ears. Peter rolled off him to lie flat on his back. Then he regained himself enough to ask, "Are you feeling a little better now?"

Nick moved to kiss him—a grateful, appreciative kiss. "I am. Thank you, nurse."

He pulled the covers up around them both. Hovering on the edge of sleep, Peter heard a quiet scratching and meowing at the door. He was about to rouse himself when Nick gently disentangled himself, rose, and went to open the door.

Gigi was scaling the side of the bed in half a second. Upon reaching the summit of Mt. Bed, she trundled across the plateau of twisted covers until she reached the head. She gave Peter one vexed meow and settled in the hollow between two pillows. Nick followed, slipping back into bed, gathering Peter against him, breathing softly into his neck.

Peter asked, "So, how does it feel for the doctor to become the patient?"

"I'm feeling some relief, but I'm not sure I'm completely cured. You'll probably have to repeat your treatment a few times for me to be sure it's working."

"Anything you say, Doctor."

About the Author

Nicole Kimberling lives in Bellingham, Washington with her wife, Dawn Kimberling, two bad cats as well as a wide and diverse variety of invasive and noxious weeds. Her first novel, *Turnskin*, won the Lambda Literary Award for Science Fiction, Fantasy and Horror.